praise for psychics of oracle bay

<u>Not in the Cards</u>

An Exciting Introduction: Amy's books immediately go to the top of my queue when they are released and they never disappoint. This was an exciting introduction to Oracle Bay and I'm looking forward to getting to know the rest of the inhabitants in future books.

Found Another Great Author!: I didn't know what to expect when I went into this book. The premise of the book sounded like something I would enjoy. At first, as I started reading the book, I wasn't sure I was going to like it. However, after a few pages, I was drawn into the book and it never let me go. In fact, by the end of the book, I was so ready to find out what was going to happen next from all the hints that were given, I wanted the next book right then. This book was well-written, had a great plot (both romance and intrigue), and I loved the characters, even the villain who I loved to hate. Can't wait to read more and I highly recommend!

Fantastic: A well written story with great characters and the location of Oracle Bay was inspired. The heroine in this story is a tribute to enduring heartache and finding a new life and love.

First Hand Knowledge

The author does a bang up job of making this mythical place not only enchanting, but a place I'd want to go. To live, even if I were the only mundane in the lot. She also expands characters from her previous book 'Not in the Cards' and keeps the story arc alive and moving forward. There's something to be said for a series that continues with the lives of all the characters, even when the focus is on only two at a time.

Wing and a Prayer

I have this terrible problem with Amy Cissell's books. I get hooked within the first few sentences, and want to read the whole thing in one sitting. They're addictive, fun, clever stories about people you wish you knew.

Belle of the Ball

This is the third book in the series, and I think this series is getting better each book. I love how silly, fun, and interesting this book is. Drew and Bill's romance was great, touching, and romantic. And, the mystery was great, too. Add to that, there were some revelations that were hilarious. There was a also point at the very end of the book that made me laugh out loud because when Drew couldn't see Bill, I thought he'd been turned into a toad. What really happened and why? You'll have to read this and find out. If you love a fun, cozy, romantic mystery, give this book and series a try; you'll love it! Highly recommend! I was provided a copy which I voluntarily reviewed.

· · · ★ ★ ★ ★ ★ · · ·

<u>Hell and High Water</u>

I throughly enjoyed this book. It touches on so many possibilities of paranormal people. It has a good lead in, full rich characters with quirks and an unexpected ending.

· · · ★ ★ ★ ★ ★ · · ·

<u>Tempest in a Teapot</u>

The ending got me! I have really enjoyed this series, and I was so darn excited to see another one in the series.I was extremely happy with this book as I couldn't figure out who the villain was. I had ideas, but the author was skillful at red herrings. Then the end hit...I was so darn angry! LOL! Highly recommend.

There are curses and bonds, mystery and mild romance, friends and family-both related and found. I do love Oracle Bay. I'm excited for the next story for Morgana

Psychics of Oracle Bay

Not in the Cards
First Hand Knowledge
Wing and a Prayer
Belle of the Ball
Hell and High Water
Tempest in a Teapot
Elements of Surprise
Dead Giveaway*
Bad to the Bones*
Shoot for the Stars*
Fun and Prophet*

Box Sets (ebook only)
Seeing is Believing in Oracle Bay (Books 1-4)

* forthcoming

tempest in a teapot

PSYCHICS OF ORACLE BAY
BOOK 6

AMY CISSELL

BROKEN WORLD PUBLISHING

TEMPEST IN A TEAPOT
Amy Cissell

A Broken World Publication
13820 NE Airport Way, Suite K395495
Portland, OR 97251-1158
Tempest in a Teapot

Cover Design: Cissell Ink
Edited by: Suzanne Lahna at The Quick Fox
Proofread by: Christopher Barnes

*For all the members of my various covens -
whether magic or murder, I couldn't do without you.*

prologue

Today was Morgana Bellflower's last chance to snare the witch responsible for the ritualistic murders of nine women in Vancouver, British Columbia.

She sat on a bench near the steam clock in downtown Vancouver and let the spring breeze ruffle her shoulder-length brown bob. She pulled a romantic suspense book out of her Coach purse, tucked a strand of hair behind her left ear, and started reading.

After an hour, the wind turned cold, and the khaki trousers and mint-green sweater set were no longer enough to keep her warm. Morgana glanced at her watch. It was just after one p.m. on Thursday, March twenty-eighth.

She tucked her book back into her purse, stood, and walked into the wine bar across the street. The Silver Eye had sent her to Vancouver after the third murder four weeks ago, and since then, she'd spent more time in the Canadian city than at home. And she still had nothing to show for it. Once she had her glass of wine and was tucked into the darkest corner in the bar with her back to the wall, she pulled out her iPad, ensured it wasn't connected to any Wi-

Fi or cellular system, then pulled up the documents and photos she'd downloaded yesterday before leaving Oracle Bay.

Every victim had disappeared from the Gastown district between ten a.m. and one p.m. on a Tuesday, Wednesday, or Thursday. And each of them had been found the next day in Stanley Park, nude, drained of blood, and covered in bloody symbols.

The most recent body that'd been discovered looked like all the others and was being investigated by the police as the ninth in a series of murders by a newly active serial killer with Satanic leanings and a vampire fetish. But Morgana knew the truth. The characters that were carved on every surface of the body weren't Satanic. Rather, they were a mixture of elemental and runic symbols that, when combined, signified the victim had been killed by ritual black magic designed to draw the power out of a person via their blood.

She pored over the photos, looking for a clue that she may have missed. Hopefully, the witch responsible had left something behind that would help identify the murderer. Morgana pulled all nine photos up, arranged them in three rows of three, and let her eyes glaze over, looking for the small differences that would jump out when she wasn't so intent.

The symbols were the same, but they weren't in identical locations on the bodies, except for the three Ogham runes right below the collarbone.

Quert — Straif — Gort
Madness, Division, and Harvest — Dark Magic, Transformation, and
Death — Transformation and Scarcity

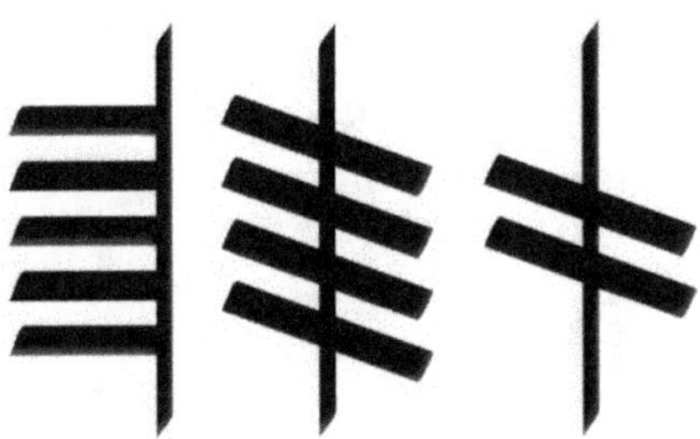

THE ONLY THING THE NINE MURDERED WOMEN HAD IN COMMON WAS HOW absolutely ordinary they appeared. They were all women in their thirties and forties with plain hair, quietly attractive faces, average lives—and deep wells of powerful magic that'd never been woken.

one

Morgana crossed her ankles, smoothed down the slim pencil skirt she was wearing, and steadfastly avoided her reflection in the window of Gate D6 in the Portland International Airport. There was no way in hell she wanted to spend any more time than was necessary looking at the stupid brown bob, pearl necklace, and salmon-colored sweater set she'd been hiding in for the last year.

"It's necessary," she muttered to herself with clenched teeth. She couldn't risk blowing her cover now, no matter how far away she was from Vancouver and the string of murders that had stopped a month ago as abruptly as they'd started. The killer had struck three times in Seattle, but with none of the precision and rigidity they'd shown in Vancouver. And now they'd dropped off the map again.

Morgana was tired of working for the Silver Eye—had been for a couple decades—but this would be her last job. She'd spent too much time hiding who she was over the centuries, and a year of dressing like a PTA president at their behest, regardless of the reasons, was too much. She'd saved five witches in the last year, one from a rogue warlock, two from vampires, and the last two from mundane cis men who used a different kind of power to subjugate the innocent. But she hadn't saved anyone from the blood witch who'd gone on a rampage in the Pacific Northwest in the last couple months. As soon as either she or another of their operatives found the blood witch, Morgana would cut ties with the organization that'd been set up centuries ago to protect witches and other magic users.

Her stomach clenched, and she forced a breath out through her nose and tried to concentrate on the fierce joy she took from putting abusive men in their places and not her overwhelming nervousness. Her hands twisted in her lap until her knuckles turned white, and she had to force herself to relax her fingers before they cramped.

"Afraid of flying?" a man asked, dropping into the seat next to her.

Morgana stiffened. She hated talking to strangers, and when she wasn't dressed up like a PTA president, strangers never talked to her. "No."

"It's a pretty common fear." His voice was deep and husky, everything Morgana liked in a voice.

The seats creaked a bit as he shifted his weight. Morgana glanced over to her left to see long, blue-jean-clad legs finished with black Dr. Martens stretched out next to her. The man's presence and invasion of her personal space might irritate her, but that would not stop her from admiring the strength evident in his thighs.

"I'm not afraid of flying," Morgana said, although this time a lot less forcefully. She looked back down at her hands. She wanted to see this man's face even less than her own at this point. If he was as attractive as his voice and legs hinted, she'd risk blowing her cover. And if he wasn't, Morgana would be disappointed, and she'd had enough of that lately.

"My name's Donovan Davies," he continued in his slow, easy voice, completely oblivious to—or perhaps ignoring—her dismissive tone. "Are you heading out or heading home?"

"A little of both," Morgana admitted. And before she could stop herself, she tilted her head up and towards him. Oh my goddess, he was even more beautiful than he'd sounded. Long, black hair with streaks of grey spilled over his shoulders, and light, honey-brown eyes glowed against his russet skin.

The man chuckled, and Morgana realized she'd been staring. She felt a flush start at the base of her neck and held it back with a force of will she'd been honing for centuries.

"Are you going to tell me your name?" Donovan asked.

"No." Morgana pulled her phone out of the ridiculous handbag she carried to match her prim librarian persona and tapped the e-reader app. She wished she had a physical book with her. Those were a better deterrent.

"Have it your way." He didn't get up to leave.

Morgana glared at her phone, then back to Donovan to give him a piece of her mind. His eyes were closed, and the lines on his face that marked him in his mid-fifties had smoothed out. There was an energy emanating from him, and it raised goosebumps on Morgana's skin. She recognized it, of course.

Power. The kind that drew people to Oracle Bay. But his was somehow different, and Morgana couldn't put a finger on it. A smirk quirked up the corner of her mouth when she considered all the things she could put a finger on.

She shut down that line of thought immediately. Now was not the time to appreciate attractive magical men. Although she—and the Eye—believed it more likely that the blood witch was a woman based on the type of magic used, she couldn't discount anyone. This man had power, but he didn't feel like a warlock, nor did he feel like a person who'd bound themself to the goddess. At least, not quite. There was something earthy about him, though.

"Like what you see?" Donovan asked without opening his eyes.

Morgana gritted her teeth. She should've known better than to assume someone with that much raw power emanating off them would be unaware of scrutiny no matter how tightly their eyes were closed.

"No." She left it at that and turned back to her book after a quick glance around the gate area. There were a few empty seats for the flight that was due to leave in less than an hour, but all of those were next to other people as well, and she would not give him the satisfaction of moving seats.

"Hmmm... Are you always such a liar?"

She gasped at the audacity of his question and forgot her resolution not to look him in the eye again. She met his gaze, ready to kill him with a look. She'd done it before, although it'd been a long time since men were so intimidated by her reputation that she could induce heart failure with a glance.

The dancing amusement in his light brown eyes did nothing to quell her anger; in fact, it ratcheted it up a few notches. "How dare you?" she growled under her breath. "You don't know me, and you accuse me of dishonesty?"

His gaze unfocused, and for a second, it felt like he was looking through her instead of at her. "From where I'm looking, the entire package, from your sensible coral pumps to your bland brown bob, is nothing but a lie wrapped in beige. You can't tell me this is who you really are. The fire in your voice doesn't match the country club couture, sweetheart."

Morgana's jaw dropped. Calling her dishonest was one thing—he was a stranger, and she'd forget that handsome face soon enough—but calling her sweetheart? Anger rose in her chest with a force she'd not experienced in more years than she could count.

It was all she could do to hold the power back. There were a lot of reasons not to lose her temper in an airport. The most pressing one right now was the need to arrive at her destination before sunset to begin the Beltane festival with the coven she'd founded six hundred years ago. She seldom traveled back for the holidays, but they'd requested her presence to ascertain the innocence or guilt of a junior member of the grove in a crime serious enough to summon her for but not so serious—she assumed—that they needed her in anything more than her capacity as a witch rather than an agent of the Silver Eye.

Turning this impertinent disrespectful man into a toad, or better yet, a cockroach that would make Kafka jealous, would likely disrupt her journey and result in a lot of unwanted attention and uncomfortable questions.

She clamped her mouth shut so hard her teeth clacked together, the shock reverberating through her head. She turned back to her book and swiped through to the next page.

A low chuckle beside her had her grinding her teeth. Morgana checked the time. Boarding wasn't due to start for another thirty minutes, and there was a bar just a couple gates down. She stood, grabbed her cheerful pink and black polka-dotted carryon, and stalked towards the bar. She seldom drank when traveling in case there was an emergency landing and no one else could fly the plane —that man had been right when he'd guessed she was afraid of flying—but today would have to be the exception to the rule.

She sat on a stool at the bar, and as soon as the bartender appeared, Morgana ordered without looking at the menu she held out. "I'll take a shot of your best Irish whiskey and a glass of your house red."

The bartender, a nice-looking white woman in her mid-twenties with a blond undercut and a plethora of facial piercings, titled her head at Morgana. "Whiskey and...wine? Most people do beer."

"I don't like beer very much, and if I'm going to drink in an airport, I'm going to enjoy myself," Morgana said.

"Okay, ma'am! They're your drinks. Do you want to make them doubles?" The woman smiled cheerfully as she pulled a large wine glass and a small tumbler out from under the stainless-steel bar.

"Both of them?" Morgana asked, glossing over the "ma'am" in her mind. "I didn't know you could make wine a double."

"Sure, it's just a double pour for only fifty percent more. It's cheaper than buying two glasses." The woman paused, waiting for Morgana's answer.

"I will have a double of the wine, but only a single shot of whiskey," Morgana decided.

"You got it!" A couple minutes later, the bartender placed a wine glass, delightfully full, next to a couple fingers of Redbreast 25.

Morgana tipped the whiskey back and drank it one swallow, grimaced slightly at the burn, then took a sip of the water the bartender had discretely placed next to her elbow. Then, she turned her attention to the wine. Twenty minutes to drink the equivalent of two very generous glasses of wine wasn't a lot, but she was up for the challenge.

She was halfway through her glass, and her shoulders had relaxed enough to be below ear-level, when her phone pinged with an incoming text. She glanced down at it and wrinkled her nose.

A notification of a group text greeted her, and since she was part of only one group text, it was the group of psychics she'd aligned herself with in Oracle Bay. It was an unusual community. They were all quite different and, in another place and time, wouldn't have become the tight-knit group they were. But a small town has ways of bringing people together, especially a town like Oracle Bay, with the highest per capita number of genuine psychics in the United States.

The town was full of tarot readers, astrologers, palm readers, and scryers. They even had a prophet, a fallen angel, and a necromancer. And whatever she and Paska were—witches are what the modern age called them, but neither of them were modern, and they were much, much more than "witches."

She opened the text, unsurprised to see it was from Misty. Mystic Greene was one of the youngest in the group, but she was the only one who'd grown up in Oracle Bay, and that gave her access to a deeper well of power than most of the others. She was also the owner of most of Main Street, the president of the Chamber of Commerce, head of the informal city council, and chair of the fall bazaar, Halloween party committee, and the Yule Ball.

In other words, she was in charge of a lot of things, and she very much liked to add to the list.

Morgana sighed, took another drink of wine to brace herself against whatever committee Misty was forming and recruiting her fellow psychics onto, and opened her text messages.

Misty: *I can't believe Morgana left town without saying goodbye!*

Drew: *I can. She's wily like that and has been doing it every week for months. She definitely has a double life that doesn't include us. Probably a secret husband and some secret babies. And a few skeletons in her closet.*

Paska: *We all have skeletons in our closets.*

Ceri: *Not all of our skeletons are literal, Paska.*

Paska: *I don't keep skeletons in my closet.*

Ceri: *No, you keep them in a leather pouch made of human skin that you wear on your belt.*

Paska: *And in my garage.*

Jezebel: *Is there a point this text is coming to, or am I cool just muting y'all and scrolling through the inanity later?*

Drew: *Wow. Morgana's been gone less than a day, and already, Jez is gunning hard to be her replacement. Too soon, Jez, too soon.*

Morgana rolled her eyes and thumb typed. *I didn't say goodbye because I will only be gone a few days. I told the old man and the fallen angel I was leaving. It did not seem necessary to announce my departure as though I was nothing more than a dirty bus leaving the station. However, since you all seem so concerned with my absence, you may expect me to return a week from tomorrow. Now, I hear my flight being called. I am going to turn off my phone. Please restrain yourselves on this message thread.*

She closed the text app and went back to her wine. She ignored the first seven text notifications, then sighed and opened it up with the eighth.

Ceri: *I can't believe you told Andy & he didn't tell me.*

Andy: *The witch told me this morning, and I haven't seen you since.*

Sandy: *Airport? Where are you going? Why didn't you ask someone for a ride? Are you at PDX or SeaTac?*

Russell: *Are you sure I need to be included in this group chat? If I sic ghosts after every one of you, will you delete my number?*

Andy: *If I have to be on the list, so do you. I'm not even an oracle.*

Drew: *Sandy had good questions, Morgana. Where are you going and why didn't you ask for a ride?*

Paska: *Why do you think she'll volunteer her business over text when she didn't tell any of you in person? It's like you don't know who you're talking about.*

Jezebel: *Why would we, though? It's hard enough getting to know regular people.*

Morgana shoved her phone in her purse, finished her wine, and dropped three twenties on the bar. She made a quick detour into one of the ubiquitous stores selling books and magazines, before walking to her gate.

First class seating was being called when she got back, so she pulled out her boarding pass and strode forward to join the queue.

She stowed her bag with the help of a flight attendant, ordered a glass of sparkling wine, accepted the hot towel, pillow, and blanket, then settled into her seat with the three paperback thrillers she'd purchased.

Movement next to her pulled her attention away from the book so she could accept the wine. Instead of the flight attendant she expected, her wine was being passed to her by the man sitting down next to her. None other than Donovan Davies.

"We're seat mates," he grinned. "Isn't this fortuitous?"

two

The change in pressure as the plane descended into Amsterdam popped Morgana's ears and jolted her out of the half sleep she'd finally settled into.

Donovan hadn't said another word to her after sitting down. Instead, he'd drank two vodka cranberry cocktails, then opened his laptop and queued up a movie. Morgana wasn't certain as she'd never seen either, but it looked like he'd watched "When Harry Met Sally" and "French Kiss" back-to-back. Morgana was old enough to know gender stereotypes were as mutable as gender, but it still amused her.

She'd had one more glass of sparkling wine before burying herself in her book. The nice thing about being this old was that alcohol had very little effect on her anymore. She wasn't sure why—the only one who might understand was Paska, but he'd never admitted to knowing—but she didn't want to give the impression she was over drinking. And there was still the possibility of needing to land the plane, after all.

The wine and the book had the effect she'd hoped, and she'd drifted off somewhere over the eastern seaboard, trusting in the crowds and her personal wards to protect her from anything short of a plane crash.

As soon as the doors opened, she stood, brushed past Donovan, retrieved her carry-on from the overhead bin, and walked as fast as she could without breaking into a jog in the airport. She had a long enough layover before boarding the plane to Dublin that she didn't need to rush to get through customs, but she was hoping to leave Donovan behind.

After passing through customs, Morgana settled in at a coffee shop and started the process of acclimating to the huge shift in time zones. Her process involved taking in more caffeine in one morning than she usually did in a week and trying to convince her body it was noon and not four o'clock in the morning.

Her phone vibrated, and she pulled it out of her pocket, a grin already threatening to form on her face at the thought of catching up with the dozens of messages that had likely been exchanged by her friends after she'd boarded. Then she grimaced. Friends. That was a word she seldom used anymore, and she wasn't sure when it'd become true for this group.

The notification wasn't from her text messages, though. Instead, it was the airline app she'd installed. Her flight to Dublin was delayed by three hours. Seconds later, the same announcement went out over the loudspeaker.

Morgana bit back a curse. It was only ninety minutes to Dublin, but the delay would mean she wouldn't be landing until almost five in the afternoon, and even though the sun wouldn't set until nine, that didn't give her much time to find her rental car and drive to her destination.

She marched up to the desk, nearly vibrating with stress, and joined the queue of irritated, angry, or frantic people. She tuned them out and concentrated on calming her energy. She found she often had a better chance of getting what she wanted when her energy soothed instead of incited. It was a technique she'd honed and perfected during the centuries she'd spent with Paska, who, better than anyone, could infuriate her with ease.

The woman at the desk looked frazzled and exhausted by the time Morgana arrived at the front of the line.

"I am sorry," the woman said in heavily accented English. "There is nothing I can tell you about the reason for the delay."

Morgana smiled sympathetically. "Do you prefer Dutch?"

Relief washed over the woman's face. "Yes. Thank you. I am running out of English."

"I know you can't tell me anything, but I was hoping you could help me find another flight. I'll gladly pay the cost; there is no reason to transfer my fare," Morgana continued in Dutch.

"I wish I could help you, but there is nothing. All flights to the UK and Ireland are delayed. There is an unexpected weather event."

Morgana bit back her anxious sigh. "Thank you."

"You are welcome. I appreciate you being so kind." The flight agent smiled softly, then looked up and behind Morgana, pasting a bright, false smile back on her face. "I am sorry," she said in English as Morgana walked away. "There is nothing I can do."

MORGANA DRUMMED HER FINGERS ON THE ARM OF THE CHAIR AT THE GATE. She'd long since finished the last book she'd purchased at the Portland Airport and was too full of nervous energy to read on her phone. It was approaching four hours after their scheduled departure, and they still weren't boarding.

Finally, just as Morgana was contemplating how long it would take to swim to Dublin, the plane pulled up to the gate and, a few moments later, started boarding. She sat in her window seat, trying not to imagine the ramifications of not arriving in time.

It would delay the ceremony, or they'd be forced to start without her. Either way, it would disrupt the evening and make the proceedings less smooth than they should be. Perhaps the only thing she hated more than being late was being late and creating waves for other people. If she was going to make waves, it would be through purposeful action and not because of the incompetence of an airline.

She wasn't going to be late. She took a deep breath and willed herself to let go of the tension caused by the worry she was borrowing. She didn't have to go through customs again, so all she needed to do was hit baggage claim and dash to the rental car agency.

She pulled up the map app on her phone as the plane taxied and lifted off. From the airport to her destination, it was a two-hour drive. If they landed at six, she wouldn't be out of the airport with her car until six-thirty at the earliest. If she was in Portland, she knew she'd be able to drive faster than Google maps thought she could, but it'd been a long time since she'd driven on the left side of those now unfamiliar roads, and she couldn't guarantee she'd be able to speed around the shoulderless curves with the same speed she could at home.

"What are the chances we'd end up seat mates again?" Donovan's smooth voice interrupted her frantic mental math as she tried various route scenarios.

"It seems a highly unlikely coincidence," Morgana muttered, looking up at him. She hadn't noticed how tall he was earlier, but he towered over her as he stowed his bag. In a moment of angry indulgence, she let her gaze travel his body from his long, muscular legs encased in tight denim, past the tight, skin-hugging t-shirt that showed off his muscular chest and shoulders—Morgana's Achilles heel—to the face that she couldn't get out of her head.

"There are a couple other people on this flight from Portland," he said, dropping into the seat next to her. "I chatted with them during the layover. So, maybe not as much of a coincidence as you believe."

Morgana licked her lips before she could catch herself and flushed slightly at his knowing grin. She'd have to be quick to lose him in the Dublin airport if she was going to get changed. If she didn't need what was in her checked baggage, she'd leave it behind and come back for it tomorrow. Alas, airport security frowned on carrying on marble and obsidian knives, or knives of any kind, no matter how ceremonial they were.

"You still haven't told me your name," he said. "We could be friends, you know. We're from the same place and heading to the same destination. I wouldn't mind getting to know you better, and from the way you looked at me, I don't think you'd be averse, either."

Morgana's temper snapped. "Leave me alone, Donovan Davies. I don't know how you're used to treating women, but continuing to push where you're not wanted is harassment. It doesn't matter how attractive I find you. If I am not interested—and I've made it clear that I am not—it would behoove you to back off."

"Behoove?" Wry amusement twisted his voice. "But you're right. I'm being unforgivably rude. I am glad you find me attractive, though." He held up a hand as if to forestall any further comment from her. "I will say nothing more. In fact, I will see if the flight attendants can help me switch seats with someone else."

Donovan stood up, flagged down a flight attendant, and a couple minutes later, a mousy blond man of no more than thirty dropped into the seat next to her, glanced at her, then quickly away. He pulled a book out of the small knapsack he was carrying and buried his nose in it.

The man didn't speak to her once during the entire flight, a fact for which Morgana was grateful.

When the plane landed, once again, she was out of her seat as soon as the fasten seatbelt light went off. She pulled her carry-on bag down and was the first one off the plane. She strode towards the baggage claim, beating the luggage there. Taking the opportunity to change, she headed into the bathroom, and after ensuring there was no one else around, commandeered one of the large, empty stalls.

She stripped out of the pencil skirt and sweater set, crumpled them up, and shoved them into her bag. Then she peeled off the pantyhose she was wearing, creating a long runner on one leg, and balled them in her hand. She hoped to never see another pair of hose again. They were quite possibly the worst sartorial invention of all time, including whalebone corsets—which she'd worn only once before deciding fashion wasn't worth it, something that hadn't changed since.

Morgana reached into her bag and pulled out a black, low-cut blouse, black leather pants, and a large comb. She dressed quickly, exchanged the awful, practical pumps for black lace-up boots with a higher heel than was probably practical for driving, but if she couldn't have her figure-hugging maxiskirt to avoid getting tangled while driving, she was at least going for the boots. Once everything, including the horrid purse, was stowed except a small toiletry bag and the comb, she grabbed her bag, shoved her phone, wallet, and passport into the side pocket of the polka dotted suitcase, and walked out to stand in front of the mirror.

Morgana stared at her reflection for a long moment, then pulled out a makeup remover cloth. After washing her face of every trace of the soft makeup she'd been wearing, she quickly reapplied her "face." But this time, it was dramatic lines, eyeliner, and dark red lipstick. Once she was satisfied, she tucked the makeup away and added a large silver necklace made of interlocking Celtic knots with a raven skull pendant winking with a ruby eye.

One thing left to do. She glanced around the room again. This was something she didn't want anyone else to witness. When she ascertained she was completely alone, she took the comb and ran it through her hair in three large pulls. As she finished each swipe, her hair followed the comb, lengthening from the smart brown bob into a midnight black curtain that fell lower than her bra strap.

Morgana sighed in relief as she washed away the last of the costume she'd been wearing for too long. The weight lifting from her straightened her shoulders and tipped her chin up. She no longer looked like a too-subservient country club member who was ready for a round of golf with her beige husband and bland friends. Now, she looked like herself again—bold, darkly attractive, and exuding enough power to make even ordinary mortals wary in her presence.

She grabbed the handle of the carry-on and grimaced. Almost

like herself. It was too bad she hadn't thought to commission a luggage comb when she procured the one she'd just used on her hair. Hopefully, she'd have her matching luggage stowed away in the rental car soon enough and wouldn't have to think about it again. Or at least until she reached her destination.

When she emerged from the restroom, the luggage was spilling out onto the baggage carousel. Her bright suitcase was one of the first ones off. She elbowed her way to the front of the line, earning a few muttered reproaches that trailed off when the irritated traveler caught sight of her. She received a couple more odd looks when people registered that the bright, ultra-feminine luggage belonged to the woman Morticia Addams only wished she could emulate.

Morgana permitted a small, enigmatic smile to break the resting witch face she usually projected. The luggage might not be to her taste, but it was fun to leave people guessing.

Suitcase secured, she made her way to the rental car office, cut in front of the small line that'd formed—tipping the rental agent two hundred dollars to not make a fuss about it—and was in her Mercedes C-class and on the M50 on her way out of town.

three

The sun was slipping quickly towards the horizon when Morgana turned off the small road onto the nearly over-grown private drive. There were three other cars parked along the edge of the grassy drive. Morgana screeched to a halt, ripped open her suitcase, and grabbed the large bag laying on top. Then she jogged towards the field, hopping over the stile, and only slowed when she saw the glow of the setting sun reflecting off the top of the dolmen she was headed for.

She paused for a moment to catch her breath, using the opportunity to take her athame out of the bag, smooth her hair, and settle a sheer veil over her face. Then she strode forward. There were twelve figures in a rough circle around the dolman and a thirteenth in the center, sitting cross-legged and leaning against the stone edifice. There was a palpable air of resignation and fear in the circle, but oddly, none of it was emanating from the figure—likely the accused—in the center.

"Sisters," Morgana called out, walking forward and taking her place in the circle.

"Morgana. You're late," the woman to Morgana's left said flatly.

"I am not, Bridget," Morgana replied smoothly. "The sun is still fifteen minutes above the horizon. And considering everything I have done to ensure I was here when I was needed, I think my timing is to be commended."

"Yes, yes. Well done, Morgana," an elderly woman said testily. "Did you bring it?"

Morgana held out the athame, balancing the black blade on both hands. "Of course, Lydia. As promised."

"Excellent," a woman across the circle from Morgana said. "Kerry, Amelia, Sorcha, and Jane, set up the altar the way I taught you."

Morgana didn't recognize the voice, although that wasn't surprising. It'd been forty years since she'd celebrated the turn of the wheel with Willow Grove—the grove she'd founded almost six hundred years ago—and the only members she recognized were Lydia and Bridget. Bridget had been as young as the women setting up the altar were, and Lydia had been in her late forties when Morgana had last seen them. Lydia was old now and had settled comfortably into her role as crone. Clouds of wispy white hair curled around her neck, her voice quavered, and the furrows and lines that marked decades of life were visible through her veil.

Bridget had aged what modern opinions would call "gracefully." Her face was unlined, and her thick, glossy black hair showed no strands of grey. She gave off an almost youthful vibrance, but nothing had changed the cheerful expression she'd had since she was a child.

The youngest women, likely new initiates into the goddess's mysteries, finished arranging the altar to the specifications barked out by the tall, commanding woman Morgana didn't know.

"Miranda," Bridget whispered in answer to Morgana's raised eyebrow. "She's the most powerful witch I've met since... Well, since you. She leads us now, although there are some who wished she didn't."

Morgana watched Miranda more closely, wishing the veils the

women had decided were traditional about fifty years ago weren't obscuring everyone's features in the deepening shadows that preceded the sunset. Bridget's assertion that Miranda was the most powerful seemed on the surface to be true, but there was something simmering underneath that raised questions. If there was a hint that Miranda was abusing her power, Morgana would have to step in, no matter how loathe she was to take more than a ceremonial role in the group.

When the candles were lit and the flames burning determinedly straight and tall despite the light breeze that rustled the dark robes of the older members, Morgana walked forward and reverently laid the athame on the altar.

The sun slipped beneath the horizon and Lydia began the call. Morgana startled when she began. She'd encouraged the group to move towards the modern interpretations of witchcraft when Wicca gained popularity, but she hadn't realized how far away they'd moved from rituals she'd practiced when she was young.

"I welcome the guardians of the East, sprits of Air and thought. The spirits of new beginnings, laughter, and adventure. The spirits of truth and rebirth. Breathe into us the joy of life.

"I welcome the guardians of the South, spirits of Fire and divine creation. The spirits of energy, will, and desire. The spirits of animation and illumination. Kindle into us the flame of spiritual awakening.

"I welcome the guardians of the West, spirits of Water and purification. The spirits of dreams, emotion, and intuition. The spirits of radiance and release. Water my deepest roots that I may find peace.

"I welcome the guardians of the North, spirits of Earth and abundance. The spirits of the body, land, and home. The spirits of healing and sanctuary. Nourish me so my hopes may grow to fruition.

"I welcome the spirits below, above, and center. The spirits of our ancestors, the shadows, and guidance. The spirits of mystery and transformation. The spirits of cosmic consciousness and the divine soul that links all life together. The spirits of balance, harmony, and beauty. The spirits of wholeness and bliss. The spirits of source, self, journey, and death. Blessed Be."

When the circle was cast, the attention of the witches shifted from the otherworld to the girl—no, she was a young woman, Morgana realized—in the center of the circle opposite the altar.

"Hazel, rise and take your place at the altar so you may account for your actions and receive the sentence of your betters," Miranda said coldly.

The young woman rose and looked defiantly at the grove members. The veil that had presumably been forced on her slipped, revealing her features.

A shock jolted Morgana at seeing her face for the first time. She was the spitting image of the daughter Morgana had lost over sixteen hundred years ago. Morgana studied her face, looking for a small difference that would break the spell the woman held over her.

She leaned forward, nearly taking a step. Bridget caught her arm before she could break the circle. "Wait. You will have a chance to question her yourself before sentencing, and time again before sentencing is carried out."

"Hazel, you stand accused of murder with the aid of blood magic," Miranda said.

Morgana had to force herself to stay still. Something about this trial wasn't right. There was a lie on the wind, maybe more than one. Hazel turned her jade-green eyes towards Morgana and smiled. It was her eyes that broke the spell. Elaine's eyes had been as brown as Morgana's.

Better able to concentrate now, Morgana turned her attention to Miranda and the proceedings.

"I killed no one," Hazel declared. Her West Coast American accent was clear, and it rang with the clear bell of truth that even the most powerless in the circle should feel and recognize.

"How do you explain the body that was found in your room, drained of blood and marked with dark symbols?" Miranda demanded.

Morgana tilted her head. Something was off about this question, but she couldn't put her finger on it yet.

A ripple of suspicion floated by Morgana, and she saw the other grove members stiffen. A dark thought took root in Morgana's mind as she looked around the circle. The gazes of the other witches had turned from wary suspicion to judgmental anger.

"I was at work," Hazel replied. "Anyone could have planted a body in my room, and any of you could've done so with the aid of black magic."

"Why would someone do that?" Miranda's voice had risen into a near shout, and it blanketed them, pushing down Morgana's awareness.

She shook her head. She couldn't be sure Hazel was innocent; but she couldn't be certain she wasn't, either. Even with the wavering of her mind, she knew that was a very stupid question.

Hazel snorted contemptuously. For a young woman who was on trial for murder by black magic—and the penalty for that if you were caught by those who traveled in the light was always death—she was poised and confident. "Are you kidding? If there was a witch using blood rites, why not frame someone else, particularly someone who'd refused to join your grove? And it'd be easy to get the victim into a locked room, wouldn't it? It'd just take the last bit of energy you got from the blood."

Miranda took half a step forward. Her shoulders were so stiff, Morgana had to roll her own to disperse the tension. "It sounds like you know a lot about blood magic. How long have you been practicing?"

Miranda's anger was palpable now, pulsing through the circle like an accelerating heartbeat. It must feel like a crushing wave to those less powerful than Morgana, who lacked personal shields of their own.

"Stop." Morgana's voice was barely audible, but it served as the perfect counterpoint to Miranda's rage.

"How dare you interrupt me," Miranda hissed. "Who do you think you are?" Her power rose and rushed against Morgana.

Morgana drew herself to her full height and let go of the shields that contained her magic. The silvery light spilled forth, washing Miranda's anger away. "I am Morgana, first in this grove for over six hundred years. You meet in the light of the moon above you because I willed it. You congregate in this sacred space where the elements meet because I allowed it. And you consecrate the earth beneath you with my athame because I created it. Do not presume to test me."

Miranda shrank back for a moment, then planted her feet. "You lie. You're nothing more than a stupid American who happens to have inherited our greatest treasure. And as head of Willow Grove, I will reclaim what is ours, and you are no longer in our circle. Now leave."

"And break the circle?" Bridget asked.

Morgana might be imagining things, but Bridget sounded a little smug. Morgana wondered if that's why Bridget had called and asked her to come. The athame was powerful, which is why Morgana kept it in the false bottom of her ornately carved tea tray. It was deeply connected to this land. She'd crafted it from materials found in Ireland, consecrated it with fire made from the branches of the willow trees that were ubiquitous in the nearby bogs, water from Lough Gowna, and her blood, and the magic in the blade resonated nowhere else but here. However, it wasn't necessary for any ritual, even a trial designed to ascertain the guilt or innocence of a witch accused of blood magic.

If putting another witch in her place was the sole reason for Morgana's presence, she would be displeased. Had Bridget asked specifically for assistance in investigating Miranda, Morgana would have been happy to comply at a full moon that summer rather than rushing to the middle of Ireland for a Beltane circle during a murder investigation. She narrowed her eyes, first at Bridget, who wasn't looking at her, then at Miranda, who was still glaring and buffeting Morgana with waves of ineffectual power.

"She has already broken it with her lies and accusations," Miranda said. Her voice was giving over to wildness as she lost control of the power she was wielding and steadily sending against Morgana's silver shield.

"The circle stands," Morgana said. "But I will take over the questioning, and you will be quiet." She put force behind her words. Miranda's magical battering ram disappeared, and she sank to the ground with a feral growl under the weight of Morgana's displeasure.

Morgana looked around the circle. No one met her eyes but Bridget, who looked delighted, and Lydia, who looked resigned, although the deepening crow's feet suggested she was biting back a smile.

She turned her attention back to Hazel, who'd witnessed the entire showdown with wide eyes. "Hazel, are you responsible for the death of the person found at your home?"

Hazel hesitated, and Morgana felt disappointment curl in her soul. "I don't know," the girl finally answered. "It is possible."

"Did you kill her?" Bridget asked.

"Certainly not," Hazel said almost before Bridget finished her question. "I would never. There are already too many innocent people who die."

"Was the victim innocent?" Lydia asked.

"I think so?" Hazel's reply turned into a question. "I mean, I didn't know her well. We'd only been dating a couple months. She seemed nice. I guess she could've had a secret dark side or something, but if she did, I didn't see it." Hazel's shoulders drooped a bit. "We'd just decided to get a flat together in Galway."

"You are using magic to disguise your features, though, aren't you?" Morgana had expected the glamour to drop when she'd dampened Miranda's power, but the girl's appearance held steady—except for the eyes.

"Is that why you're the spitting image of Selina?" Bridget asked. "Except for the eyes. Selina had cornflower blue eyes along with her blonde hair."

Hazel grimaced and closed her eyes. When she opened them again, her appearance wavered. In place of the dark-haired dark-eyed daughter Morgana had lost even longer ago than she'd founded Willow Grove was a lithe, willowy redhead with a sprinkling of freckles against her pale skin, green eyes, pointed ears, and a frightened expression on her face. "I was hoping if I looked like someone you loved, you'd be inclined to believe I was innocent. But I promise, I am."

Despite the young woman's use of magic to influence the outcome, Morgana believed she was innocent, and she had a way of verifying it. "Take the athame in your hand, slice your palm, and swear by your life and your blood that you are not a murderer nor a practitioner of blood magic. Then let three drops fall onto the earth."

Bridget gasped softly at Morgana's command, but Morgana didn't look at her. She knew as well as Bridget did that if Hazel lied, the athame with a Connemara marble handle and obsidian blade would bind the swearer's blood to the earth whence it was quarried. From the look on Hazel's face, she knew this was a serious oath, even if she didn't know the actual consequences.

But Hazel didn't hesitate. She grasped the athame with her right hand and sliced across her left palm. She hissed a bit with the pain of the cut, then squeezed her hand together. "I swear by my blood and my life that I did not kill Rowan." She let three drops of blood fall to the earth, then looked directly at Morgana. "And I swear by my blood and my life that this truth telling is the only blood ritual I have ever performed." Three more drops hit the ground.

Morgana held her breath, then released it slowly when nothing happened.

"I am satisfied with your innocence," Morgana said. "Does anyone disagree?"

No one said anything, which Morgana took as agreement. "Then let us release the circle. Tomorrow, Bridget, Lydia, Hazel, and I will decide what to do with Miranda. For tonight, she will be held in custody." Morgana did not relish spending the night watching a purported powerful witch, but there were few other options, and Lydia was too exhausted to sit in judgment tonight.

"Why Hazel?" asked one of the younger members timidly. Morgana recognized her as the one who'd lit the cardinal candles.

"She was the one accused. Since your High Priestess is the one being judged, I will stand in her stead as the founder of Willow Grove. Lydia—with all apologies—is the crone, a former high priestess, and one with the most knowledge of this circle, and Bridget, who is known in other places as Sister Mary Margaret, is the second ranking priestess after Miranda. Now, let us give thanks to the spirits and our ancestors."

The grove members reversed the calling and broke the circle. The younger members collected the materials they'd brought, folded up the altar, and scurried back towards the road. Morgana stepped towards Hazel and held out her hand.

Hazel gave Morgana the athame, and while Morgana cleaned it, Lydia bandaged Hazel's hand. When she was finished, Lydia and Bridget stood on either side of Morgana, and the three of them linked hands, then looked at the accused and accuser.

She squeezed Bridget's hand. Her friend squeezed back, then let go. Bridget pulled two linked leather bracelets out of the pouch tied around her waist, then walked forward, squatted down, and slipped them over Miranda's wrists. Morgana knew the cuffs had all the elements woven into the cuffs and had been blessed over a sacred flame on the new moon. They didn't look like much but would prevent all but the most powerful witch from performing any magic. Her hands wouldn't have needed to be bound; the cuffs could've been worn as a bracelet and been equally effective and much less obtrusive. But binding added an extra level of security.

Bridget stood, pulling Miranda up with her. "I'll take her and lock her up in one of the rooms in the basement. It's where we keep anyone accused of a crime."

"Are you going to kill me now?" Miranda asked. Her voice was smaller than Morgana had expected, and she looked at the woman curled up on the ground, arms tucked around her knees and hands now bound.

"No. I do not kill unless there is no other choice. And unless you murdered Hazel's girlfriend with blood magic and framed her, I have a choice."

"I won't swear by my blood and life unless you force me into it. Is that what you'll do?

"Not yet," Morgana said. "Not until I figure out what's going on. I hate being surprised, and right now, I don't know how that oath would turn out."

Miranda met Morgana's eyes with a mixture of defiance and fear. "Neither do I, Morgana. Neither do I."

four

Morgana sat in the back corner of the An Craoibhín public house and rubbed the knots in her neck. A tumbler of whiskey and a pint of dark liquid topped with creamy-white foam appeared in front of her.

"I don't like beer," Morgana muttered. She pushed the beer away and pulled the whiskey towards her.

"This isn't beer any more than that's just whiskey."

Morgana yanked her head up and looked at the person who'd delivered the alcohol to her table. Instead of Bridget, who she'd been expecting, Donovan Davies stared down at her.

"You!" she gasped, then grimaced. She'd looked nothing like she had when he'd seen her on the plane. Maybe this was all a terrible coincidence, and he would not recognize her, a faint hope since he'd seen through her disguise before.

He tipped an invisible hat, then pointed at her drinks. "The bartender assures me that is the best whiskey in the house, and that you can't drink it without a good Irish stout."

"What are you doing here? Are you following me?" Morgana picked up the whiskey and took a long drink, nearly emptying the glass in one go. She savored the burn, then took a drink of the Beamish. It did go well with the whiskey. The bartender was right about that.

"Not following so much as taking the same path to find the same thing. You beat me here, though. Out of curiosity, what did you do with Miranda?"

Morgana felt her jaw drop, and for the life of her, she wasn't able to clamp her mouth shut again. "How... You know, never mind. You are stalking me. Tell me who you are and why you're here."

"Donovan! You came!" Bridget slid into the seat between Donovan and Morgana. "I wasn't sure you would."

"Of course, Bridget. You were so sure I'd have a witch to take into custody, and you've never been wrong before. I have to admit, though, I had expected the renegade to be someone else." He slid a look towards Morgana, then back to Bridget. "I'm relieved I was wrong. I don't relish trying to contain this one. I've heard enough rumors about Morgana to want to tread softly."

Morgana stiffened. She hadn't told him her name. Then, she forced herself to relax. Bridget knew him. That's how he found out. He'd probably known who she was from the beginning.

"Oh, you two have met!" Bridget clapped her hands in delight. "I am pleased I don't have to introduce you."

"We met at the airport in Portland," Morgana said tightly. "You could've warned me I wouldn't be the only one making the trip."

"I didn't know. Why were you in Portland, Donovan?" Bridget asked. "I thought you were living in London at the Scales chapter house."

Morgana tensed. Of course, he was a member of the Scales. His magic didn't feel right to be a warlock, but if he was here to arrest a rogue witch, it made sense that he was an operative of the organization dedicated to hunting down witches they believed to be dangerous. Of course, he could be using his association with the Scales as a cover for his crimes.

Donovan shrugged easily. "Some of us like the element of

surprise, and some like to study our quarry first. When you told me you had a friend flying in from the Pacific Northwest, I wanted to tag along. Besides, I've been thinking of moving back. There's a lot going on near my old home, and someone has to keep an eye on things."

Morgana bit back an angry retort. He didn't need to see how much his words upset her, even though she'd been "keeping an eye on things" in the Pacific Northwest for almost as long as this man had been alive.

Bridget regarded him with narrowed eyes for a moment, then smiled and turned to Morgana. "Donovan Davies is one of my oldest friends."

"And you told him about me without returning the favor," Morgana said tightly.

"Oh no," Bridget said. "I haven't told him anything about you except that we had a grove member flying in from the Pacific Northwest. I'm not a terrible person."

The sinking feeling was back. "How did he know my name, then? And how did he recognize me?"

"I've known about you for a very long time, Morgana. Oracle Bay is replete with people of rather unusual abilities, and I have a file on every one of you. I wasn't sure which of you—" He paused and looked at her expectantly.

"What?" Morgana glared. Nothing about this trip was going according to plan, something Morgana wasn't used to and didn't enjoy. She'd engineered her entire life for centuries so she could maintain control and anticipate every variable.

"Which? Which witch? I thought you oracles loved nothing more than a good pun." He looked rather too pleased with himself.

"Why are you telling me you have files on all of us? Aren't you worried about what I'll do with that information?"

Bridget had leaned back with her beer and was watching the exchange with a small smile on her lips. Morgana briefly transferred her glare from Donovan to her friend. Bridget's smile widened.

Donovan scoffed. "You're a witch, and there is nothing you could do to me that hasn't already been tried. Stronger magic users than you have come up against me, and you'll notice I'm still standing."

He didn't know who she was after all; at least not more than what she presented on the surface. From the corner of her eye, she saw Bridget lean forward and open her mouth. Morgana kicked her lightly on the ankle. Right now, Donovan Davies was underestimating her, and she wanted it to stay that way.

This time, it was Bridget who glared. "Do either of you want another drink?"

Morgana eyed her beer. It was nearly empty. She looked towards the bar with the wall of whiskey and considered. A couple walked in —a short, curvy woman with pale skin and dark brown hair and a tall, white man with close-cropped shockingly red hair wearing a long, brown leather duster. They moved in front of the whiskey display, blocking Morgana's view. She blinked twice, but when they settled at the bar, she knew it was a sign. She could feel the jet lag pushing past the adrenaline high she'd been running on since leaving Dublin, and it was almost midnight here, which meant she hadn't had a good night of rest since she'd slept in her own bed... She gave up trying to do the math with her sleep-deprived brain. "No thank you, Bridget. I am exhausted and need to get to my room. Are you sure Miranda is secure where you have her?"

"If she's not secure in the convent's holding cell, I don't know where she would be."

Morgana shook her head. "I've known you for..." She glanced at Donovan out of the corner of her eye and amended what she was going to say; no need to give him any more information about her age than he already had. "I've known you for a very long time, and you never told me there was a convent here, much less that it had holding cells. How long has it been here?"

"Four hundred years," Donovan replied.

"I don't believe anyone was talking to you," Morgana said. "Are you the kind of man who not only stalks women but insists on interrupting and talking over them?"

Donovan clamped his mouth shut and sighed. "I will see you both tomorrow. Let me know when you're done with the witch, and I'll take her back." He rose and stalked out of the pub after dropping several euro notes on the bar.

Morgana had a lot of questions about that. Bridget was going to get an earful in the morning. "You have a lot to answer for, Sister Mary Margaret. I expect to see you bright and early for breakfast. I'll inform the innkeeper I'll have a guest."

"I hate it when you trot out the Mary Margaret," Bridget grumbled.

"And I hate it when you trot out a witch hunter without warning," Morgana retorted. "Why would you bring him here when you knew I'd be here and could manage anything that came up? Surely you did not expect him to take me, did you?"

"Oh no, of course not," Bridget hastened to reassure her. "I just wasn't one hundred percent sure you'd show up. You haven't the last few times I've asked, and none of the rest of the grove members were equipped to handle a blood witch."

Morgana pushed back the guilt that constantly bubbled under the surface when she thought of Willow Grove. She'd founded it, led them for centuries, then abandoned them.

"Don't get caught up in your head. Not tonight," Bridget said kindly. She stood and slipped an arm around Morgana's shoulders.

Morgana stiffened. It'd been a long time since anyone had touched her with casual affection. Bridget gave her a little shake, and Morgana relaxed a little.

"Get some sleep, Morgana," Bridget said. "I will see you at ten for breakfast, and tomorrow we'll sort through this mess."

Morgana dropped a few Euros on the table and walked through the door and into the dark night of the non-existent town.

five

Religious buildings always gave Morgana a deep, uncomfortable feeling that started at the base of her spine and traveled outward like cracks in a heavy sheet of ice during the spring thaw. She shuddered and looked at the stone building that had stood for four hundred years in the village Morgana had founded and hidden, and that she'd somehow never seen.

She took a hesitant step forward, then remembered who she was, and strode confidently—even if she was faking it—across the threshold. A quiet woman dressed simply and unobtrusively in a black, cotton shift dress and black head covering led her through a maze of corridors, down a flight of stairs, and left her in a large, windowless room that was empty except for five chairs in the center of the room and a small table by one wall with a sweating pitcher of water and five empty plastic cups.

"How'd you do it?" Morgana asked Bridget when she appeared with cushions to pad the hard chairs.

"Do what?" Bridget asked absently. She was wearing the same simple, black shift and head covering as the nun who'd led Morgana to this room, and the beads on the rosary she carried sparkled and shone under the overhead lights. The black garb, along with her long black hair, pale skin, and dark brown eyes paired with her slim frame and long, sharp nose, created a severe profile. All she was missing was a wart on her nose and a hairy mole to fulfill the stereotype and mark her as the witch she actually was.

"Don't do that." Morgana's voice was too sharp, revealing too much of her inner turmoil. She modulated her tone and continued. "You know very well what I meant. How did you hide this place from me for so long, and how is it that Donovan Davies knows more about it than I do?"

"I'm not sure. I wasn't here when it was founded—I don't even know the names of the sisters who did. All I know is that we're not supposed to tell you—or anyone not of the order. Last night seemed a good time to break that silence. And besides, I don't like keeping secrets like this. It feels too close to a lie for my comfort."

Morgana reached out with her senses. There wasn't anything obvious hiding this building. Of course, there wasn't anything obvious hiding the village, either. In fact, most of the town's hundred and fifty residents didn't know they were hidden. They'd come to town with another resident, or had been born here, and once they were rooted, they could always find it. And once they could find it, they could bring others. But those of ill intent, those who threatened any of the town's residents, would find themselves increasingly uncomfortable until they fled rather than go mad.

"If the convent is hidden the way Kilnamanagh is hidden, you probably shouldn't leave Miranda here too long if she is a blood witch. Although she shouldn't have been able to stay in town for very long. Unless…" A thought that had never occurred to Morgana reared its head. "Is she from here? Did she grow up here?"

Bridget nodded. "We grew up together. Her mother was Samara —do you remember her?"

Morgana cast back into her memories. It was difficult to remember the more immediate past sometimes. The older things, the things that'd happened when she was young and learning, were often clearer than the rapid progression of more recent years. "I'm not sure," Morgana said slowly. "Time moves so quickly now, especially in the outside world. Faces and events become blurs."

Bridget nodded thoughtfully. "That makes sense. It is the same for everyone, after all. The more days shorten compared to our overall lifespan, the more difficult they are to separate from each other. When I was five, every summer day lasted for a lifetime, and now... Well now, I don't remember what I did last week without looking at my calendar, and I'm not even sixty. Samara was our high priestess for almost fifty years. She was tall and intimidating and fiercely kind."

The light switched on in Morgana's memory. "I remember. She was powerful, one of the most powerful witches to be part of the grove in decades. Fiercely kind is a good way to describe her. So, she moved here and had Miranda. Miranda didn't inherit the power of her mother."

Bridget's eyebrows pulled into a V in the center of her forehead. "Are you sure? She's always seemed to carry the same weight. That's why she's the high priestess and not Lydia."

"I'm positive," Morgana said thoughtfully. "There is something about her, though. Something about the entire situation. I don't believe she is the blood witch."

"You don't?" Bridget looked mildly surprised. "She wouldn't swear to it last night."

"Refusing to confess does not equal guilt," Morgana said lightly. "I don't think she uses dark magic—or at least not as dark as we've been talking about. But I believe she had a hand in that poor girl's death, if only inadvertently."

"What will you do with her?" Bridget asked. "If it turns out she's only a little guilty."

Morgana sighed. "I don't know. I certainly can't leave her here to corrupt the circle, but I don't want to take her with me, either. I'm also not going to kill her, if that's what you wanted to know."

"And Hazel?" Bridget's question was sharp enough to cut through the air between them.

Morgana glanced over at her friend. "I will need to talk to her some more, and then I will make her an offer."

"Donovan will want them both," Bridget said, looking down at her hands, which were tearing strips off a paper napkin.

"And what will he do with them?" Morgana asked, then remembered the earlier question Bridget still hadn't answered. "And how does he know about this place when I do not?"

Bridget shrugged. "He'll ensure she's rehabilitated if possible or stripped of her magic if not. And I don't know how he found out. He just showed up at the door twenty years ago, offering his services."

"An American witch hunter appeared at the door of a hidden convent in a hidden village off an unmapped road in the middle of Ireland to offer his services, and no one thought this odd?" Morgana knew she was likely burning bridges, but she made no effort to keep the scathing notes from her voice.

"I wasn't responsible for his appearance nor the sisters' welcome," Bridget said stiffly. "Over the years, we became friends, and when I took my place in Willow Grove, we became...colleagues of a sort."

"What do you mean colleagues?"

"When he was concerned he had a particularly tricky case, he would call me in to assist. I may not ever rival you in power, but I do have a very specific gift."

"And that wonderful gift has proven to be a lifesaver more than once," Donovan said from the doorway.

Miranda was in front of him, her wrists bound with the leather cuffs.

Behind him, Hazel was barely visible, and she looked like she would bolt at the first loud word spoken to her. Her fear looked natural, but it contrasted with the cool confidence the young woman had shown last night. Bridget walked over and slipped an arm around her, murmured something in her ear, and Hazel straightened up and smiled tremulously.

"I expected Lydia, not Donovan," Morgana said, looking at Bridget. She should have expected the witch hunter to be there, but part of her had hoped she would not encounter him again.

"She didn't feel well this morning, and she isn't necessary for this piece." Bridget finally looked up at Morgana, and light blazed in her eyes. "Miranda, come and sit."

The bound witch stumbled forward and took the chair furthest away from Morgana. Donovan sat next to her, and Hazel took the empty chair next to Morgana.

"It was Hazel," Miranda said. "I swear on my life it was her."

"She swore her truth on her blood and life last night, and the earth supported her claim," Morgana said mildly. It was interesting that Miranda was taking the offensive this morning and answering questions that hadn't yet been asked.

"I don't know how she got around your spell, but she has to be guilty. Nothing else makes sense." Miranda's eyes swiveled between the four people in the room, but her determination was rapidly being displaced by fear and uncertainty. "She has to be guilty," Miranda whispered.

"How was the crime discovered?" Donovan asked.

Morgana swallowed a curse. It was a good question, and the next one she'd intended to ask.

Miranda clamped her mouth shut. Donovan glanced at Bridget, and Morgana narrowed her eyes. Was he asking her to use the special skill she had, that one that made her so valuable to the witch hunter? The one Morgana didn't know about? There were too many secrets in this valley, and she'd been away too long.

"I came home from work and unlocked the door," Hazel whispered. "Rowan's bag was on the end table, which was weird, because she shouldn't have been there. She should've been at work. I walked back towards the bedroom to see if she was there, if she was sick or asleep, and that's when I saw the symbols on the door. Death magic, a warding. I was afraid. I called Miranda. She's the most powerful witch I've ever met. I thought she'd know what to do." Hazel's voice trailed off, and tears filled her eyes.

"And then what?" Donovan prompted more gently than Morgana would've given him credit for.

Hazel wrapped her arms around herself. "She showed up, did something to make the runes disappear, and opened the door. And that's when I saw her." Hazel lost the tenuous control she'd been maintaining and sobbed, rocking back and forth in her chair.

Morgana knew she should go the girl and put a comforting arm around her—she didn't remind Morgana of Elaine anymore, but that first surge of maternal feeling hadn't dissipated with the fall of her disguise—but she couldn't. The girl might not have performed the blood rites that murdered the woman with whom she lived, but she could still be connected to her murder as an accessory. Anyone in this room could be involved. There was something off with all four of the other people, and until she knew what it was, she would display nothing but power and coolness in front of these people.

When Hazel's sobs died down, Donovan asked another question. "Did either you or Miranda touch the body—"

"Rowan!" Hazel said fiercely, looking at Donovan. "She had a name. She wasn't just a body. She was my girlfriend, my lover, and the woman I thought I'd spend the rest of my life with. And she was murdered."

"Of course, my apologies," Donovan murmured soothingly. "Did either you or Miranda touch Rowan?"

"I didn't," Hazel said. "It was too horrible, too terrifying. What had been done to her..."

"I saw the scene," Bridget said. "Miranda called Lydia and I in to contain Hazel and help dispose of the evidence before the garda got wind of anything. The bod—" Bridget glanced quickly at Hazel and amended her sentence. "Rowan was lying in the middle of the bed with her arms at her side and her eyes closed. She was nude and covered in runes that had been carved into her body. When I approached the bed, it appeared that she had been drained of her blood."

"Was the blood found?" Morgana asked.

"A vial of blood was discovered in the suitcase Hazel had packed that was by the front door," Bridget said. "But nothing else."

"We were going on a trip," Hazel said. "We were going to Galway to find a place to live. It was supposed to be the start of our lives together. And I didn't put blood in my suitcase. I would never."

Morgana leaned back in her chair and regarded Hazel. She knew the young woman was innocent; there was no doubt in her mind. She turned her attention to Miranda, who was staring straight ahead, silent and stony-faced.

"Since we have already determined Hazel to be innocent, I'm not sure we need to dwell too much on the evidence that points towards her guilt," Morgana said. "It is probable that she was framed, and the evidence was planted to incriminate her. Does anyone disagree?"

Bridget murmured her assent, but Donovan didn't say anything. He stroked his chin and looked between Morgana and Hazel.

"Are you positive Hazel is innocent?" Donovan asked. "How can you be so sure?"

"I will not reveal any of our secrets to a witch hunter," Morgana said. "It is odd that you think I might do so. Suffice it to say, I guarantee this young woman has never practiced blood magic, nor did she murder Rowan."

"Do you guarantee it with your life?" Donovan asked. The fire in his eyes bore into Morgana, and for a second, she quailed under the assault.

Then she straightened. The witch hunter had power of his own, but it would never be a match for hers. "I guarantee it with my life," she said evenly.

Donovan nodded, then looked at Miranda. "If you have any defense to offer, now is the time to do so."

"I did nothing. This girl called me to report her own crime. It was in her room, and we have only her word that she was at work until a couple minutes before she called me. The state of the body was appalling, and yet Hazel didn't run forward and throw herself on her lover as one would expect. She didn't even cry. She stood and stared as if she was seeing exactly what was expected."

"Grief and shock manifest in many different ways," Donovan said.

Morgana wasn't sure how she'd allowed this man to assert himself so thoroughly into this questioning that should've only been attended by women, by her sisters, but she couldn't let her simmering resentment pull her attention away from what Miranda was saying.

"She's guilty. I have no doubt in my mind."

"Yet, you would not swear last night that you were innocent," Morgana said. "You would not take the same oath as the woman you believe guilty. Why?"

"Because she's afraid," Donovan said slowly. "She knows who it really is, she was directed to point a finger at Hazel, and she's afraid that if she reveals what she knows, her life will be numbered in hours and not years."

Morgana knew he was right. It was the conclusion her subconscious had been moving towards since the night before. She wasn't angry that he'd gotten there before she had—much.

Miranda paled and looked around the room frantically. She stood, ran towards the door, then stopped in her tracks and dropped to the floor. Morgana was at her side in an instant. She rolled the witch over, then stared into the lifeless eyes of Miranda Kelly.

six

Morgana tapped her foot impatiently while Bridget and Donovan finished their examination of the body. She knew where her expertise lay, and it was not determining the cause of death of anyone, whether by magical or non-magical causes.

"This wasn't a natural death," Donovan finally said, rising to his feet.

"Why do you say that?" Morgana asked, walking over to him.

He pulled down Miranda's collar. Just above her right breast was Straif, the Ogham rune that sometimes meant death, carved into her skin. It was the same rune that had been on every body she'd seen in Vancouver, although this time it was alone.

"Although not conclusive, it does suggest more dark magic," Donovan said.

Morgana threw up her hands. "I thought I was coming for a simple ritual for a magical crime. Instead, there have been two murders by blood magic, a secret convent, and a shifty witch hunter who stalked me halfway across the globe."

"Where's the first victim?" Donovan asked. "Both women will need to be transferred somewhere they can be properly magically autopsied."

"Rowan was cremated as soon as we determined what killed her in order to prevent any magical contagion that might have been spelled into the body from escaping," Bridget said. "Her family was notified of her death, the appropriate papers created and filed, and the case was closed."

It had only been two days since the woman was murdered. Cremating the body so quickly was neither the correct course of action when someone had been murdered nor did it fit in with any possible religious traditions the young woman and her family would have followed. The puzzle pieces that had been presented did not fit together. Indeed, they appeared to be from different puzzles altogether.

Donovan's lips thinned, and for the first time since Morgana had met him, he lost his easy-going jocular aura. "That's not the procedure," he said, echoing Morgana's thoughts.

"It was the best we could do on short notice to protect ourselves, the grove, and this convent," Bridget protested.

Donovan looked down at Miranda. "I guess there's nothing more we can do now. I'll contact my colleagues to meet me at the village boundary to take custody of this body. In the meantime, Hazel will need to be taken into custody."

Hazel whimpered, and Morgana's temper flared. "If she wasn't responsible for the first murder, why would you accuse her of this one?"

"I'm not accusing her of anything," Donovan said. "But someone is out to get her, and until we figure out who, she needs to be protected."

"Where will you take me?" Hazel asked so softly Morgana had to strain to hear.

"We have a secure facility in London. You'll be safe there until we figure out who's responsible for all of this." Donovan's voice was soothing, but Hazel didn't look convinced.

Before she could stop herself, Morgana said, "She will come home with me. A secure facility might be safer, but Oracle Bay is nearly as secure, and not nearly so isolating."

Donovan looked at Morgana with raised eyebrows. "Are you trying to say a bunch of two-bit 'psychics' are the equal of an entire company of men like me?"

"I'm saying we are better; mostly because we are not all men," Morgana retorted. "Chance is the one thing that makes Oracle Bay not as secure as your 'secure facility.' However, that also makes it a better life in case you and your 'men' cannot find the person who may or may not be targeting Hazel. How long would you keep her cut away from the world while you look for someone you might never find?"

"If there is someone after me, they'd have a better chance of finding me if I went with Morgana," Hazel offered quietly.

Morgana spun on her. "Are you saying I cannot keep you safe?"

Hazel held up her hands. "No, I'm saying they'd be easier to catch if they knew where the bait was."

Morgana took a step back and looked more critically at the young woman whose life had been turned upside in the space of a week and was now offering to move to a new country and act as bait to lure out a powerful blood-path witch who may want her dead. "You should know this isn't the first murder like this. There have been several others in the area of North America where I live. I do not know if they were all committed by the same person, or multiple people working in concert, but you may not be safer there than in Donovan's secure facility."

"There have been similar murders in Dublin and Galway," Donovan said. "There might not be anywhere you'd be completely safe without being under constant scrutiny."

Hazel shrugged, but the fear in her eyes increased. "That makes me even better bait. And if we go to the States, I won't have to worry about my visa, right?" Her grin looked forced.

"It's a good idea," Donovan said. "Maybe Morgana can teach me a thing or two about disguises, and I can tag along, too."

Morgana shot daggers at him with her eyes. "I have no idea what you're talking about."

"I bet you some polka-dotted luggage that you do. I wouldn't mind having a second mystery to solve while I wait to snare our big, bad witch." Donovan looked at her, and the heat in his eyes drew a flush to Morgana's cheeks.

"Do you know what he's talking about?" Bridget asked.

"Not in the least," Morgana snapped. She drew in a breath, reminded herself that no man was worth losing her temper over, and turned to Hazel. "Ultimately, this decision should be yours. I agree with Donovan that you should consider leaving the area in some sort of protective custody. There will be a reason Rowan was chosen as a victim and you as the scapegoat. If it wasn't Miranda, that means the witch in question is out there and might still be hunting you. It would be safer for you."

Hazel made a small noise but didn't interrupt.

Morgana paused for a second to let her speak if she wanted to, then continued, "However, since you have committed no crimes, no one has the right to force you into anything. You can choose to live your life as you would, to go with Donovan to his all-men's-club secure facility, or to come with me to Oracle Bay. It's a coastal town in the Pacific Northwest, and there are a lot of good people there. We don't have a grove, but we have seers of almost every stripe. We even have an Irish scryer, so you can compare hair colors and talk about the Old Country." Morgana smiled at the girl, who was even less Irish than she was.

"I'm from Las Vegas," Hazel said, then glanced at Donovan. "I agree with Morgana," he said.

"A phrase you'll find yourself uttering a lot if you insist on staying close," Morgana muttered.

"Does anyone care what I think?" Bridget asked.

"Your opinion is always welcome," Morgana said.

Bridget smiled. "I support Hazel going to Oracle Bay. And with the chaos of the last few days, not to mention the death of our high priestess, I'll have my hands full here."

Hazel blinked back large tears. "Can you come with me? At least for a week or two? You're the only person I know in the entire world, really, now that Rowan's dead." The tears she'd been blinking back broke free and streamed down her face.

Morgana gritted her teeth and willed Bridget to say no. Hosting one person was already too much. A second would be overwhelming and crowd the home she considered her sanctuary.

"I'd really rather stay here. With Miranda gone, someone will need to step into her role, and if I'm not here, it might end up being someone completely inappropriate." Bridget smiled. "You'll be fine. Morgana might seem cold and unkind, but she is very kind when it counts. Besides, Oracle Bay is surrounded by water, and that much water inevitably contains fish. I hate fish." She shuddered.

Hazel bit her lip and looked at Morgana out of the corner of her eye. "Okay. I guess that'll be fine."

Morgana sighed. "Bridget, I would be honored if you'd accompany Hazel and help her get settled. It will be easier for her if there is one person she knows well. You can also aid with the defenses we will need to strengthen. And although Oracle Bay is bounded by the ocean to the west and the bay to the east, I have never encountered any land fish. If you stay out of the water, you will remain unmolested."

Bridget opened her mouth to speak, but Morgana held up a hand. "After this is over, and we have neutralized the threat, I will return with you to Willow Grove to help choose the next high priestess."

"If you're sure," Bridget said hesitantly.

"I'm sure," Morgana replied with forced cheer.

"It's settled then." Bridget stood and smoothed down her skirt with her hands. "Besides, any opportunity I have to wear something that isn't black is an occasion not to be missed."

Hazel looked around and worried at her lower lip. "Okay, I guess."

Bridget clapped. "It's settled, then. We're all going to America! I'll pack my bags."

seven

Morgana glanced around the boarding area in the Dublin airport and sighed in resignation. It was time for her to resume the costume of a 1950s-era housewife. Her contact at the Silver Eye had insisted she not break her cover until the blood witch was apprehended, and Morgana admitted it made sense if the killer had seen her in Seattle or Vancouver. Of course, if she and the earth were wrong, and it *was* Hazel—or Donovan—her cover was already compromised.

She stood and walked over to where her imminent houseguests were sitting.

"I will be changing my clothes and hair back to the style my friends and neighbors in Oracle Bay are accustomed to seeing me in. I would take it as a great kindness if neither of you mentioned the way I look and dress here. My other persona makes me appear more personable, which increases the number of people who are willing to confide in me and come to me to have their tea leaves read." Morgana waited for them to nod in acknowledgement, then grabbed her polka-dotted carryon and disappeared into the bathroom.

There had to be a way to make this all work, and work quickly so she could shed the sweater sets by the end of the summer. She looked down at herself, admiring the expanse of creamy, white skin that peeked out above the black tank top, and turned her ankle to let the light glance off the silver buckles of her knee-high 3-inch laced boots. A few minutes later, she was dressed in a mint-green sweater set, pearls, sensible heels, and capris.

Maintaining the disguise was proving more and more difficult— not least because Paska, as the only one who had an inkling why she was doing it, continued to encourage the others to mock her.

Morgana grinned a little. Maybe she'd get a sundress and see if she could make Sandy's and Misty's heads explode. The disguise chafed, so she had to find the small joys, and that lay primarily in messing with people's minds.

Morgana walked out of the bathroom, then dashed back in and pulled her comb out of her bag. She'd almost forgotten the most important part. She closed her eyes and ran the comb through her hair. When she opened them again, a pale woman with delicate features and a sensible brown bob stared back.

Ugh.

When the plane landed in Portland, Morgana rounded up her charges, led them through customs, collected their luggage from baggage claim, and went to reclaim her car. This one was a little more sedate than she preferred—a mid-range beige Lexus—but at least it would fit all three women and their bags.

"How long is the trip?" Bridget asked, settling into the front seat.

"About three hours," Morgana said. "It's a pretty drive, though."

"Will we stay with you?" Hazel asked.

Morgana wrinkled her nose. She was losing control of her carefully orchestrated life one stray person at a time.

"Yes," she said decisively, not wanting them to know how little they were welcome. "You will both stay with me until we decide what to do next. When Bridget returns to Kilnamanagh, you and I can talk about how long you'll want to stay and if you wish to find a place of your own. It'll be safer to stay with me or one of the other psychics, but again, you will not be forced to do anything you don't want to. This is not jail. You are free to come and go as you please and stay as long as you want."

"Thank you," Hazel said. "I hope I'll be welcome. How much will people know about me?"

"I will have to tell them everything I know," Morgana said. "They cannot keep their eyes open for the threats that may follow you if they don't know what they're looking for."

eight

Morgana gritted her teeth and pulled open the door to the Pour House. Zeke, a prophet of the Judeo-Christian god and head bartender, lifted his hand in a small wave. It was the friendliest gesture he'd ever made, and Morgana nodded back, hoping he didn't know something she didn't about what was happening next.

She made her way to the private alcove that was always reserved for the town's oracles. Just before she walked in, she lifted her head, straightened her spine, and let the essence that was Morgana settle over her. She might have to wear this ridiculous disguise, but she didn't have to act the way she looked.

"Morgana! You're back." Sandy smiled at her, and the girl's smile was so infectious, Morgana almost smiled back. She'd have to ensure Hazel was attached to Sandy—the two would be well-matched in friendship and experience.

"Of course I am," she said brusquely. She took an open seat near the doorway, ending up between Paska and Jezebel, then looked around. "We will need two more open seats closer to me. My guests will arrive soon."

Chairs shuffled as people moved around. If Andy or Zeke decided to join in, they'd find themselves with standing room only.

"Guests?" Misty asked, eyebrows flying up to her hairline.

Morgana pasted a tight smile on her lips. She'd anticipated a reaction like this. In the ten years she'd spent in Oracle Bay, she'd never had a houseguest. "A young woman who needs a place to stay for a while and an old acquaintance who has come to get her settled while she does so. I will tell you their story so that you can be prepared for the fallout that may come from having them as my guests and residents of this town."

"Sounds interesting," Sandy said. "Are they in danger?"

Morgana pursed her lips. "I believe the young woman, Hazel, is in danger. But I do not want to start the story there. There is some background information you may require, and I am considering how much I need to tell you."

Something touched her ankle, and she jumped. When she looked down, she saw Paska's beat-up sneaker tapping against her foot. She recognized the cadence for the shorthand language they'd developed to communicate when they couldn't be certain they weren't being spied on, although it'd been a number of years since they'd had occasion to use it.

It would take a couple minutes for the language to flood back into her mind, but she knew what he was asking, anyway. He wanted to know how far back she was going to go, and if he needed to be prepared for her to reveal any of his secrets.

Morgana shrugged slightly, then tapped back in a rough precursor to Morse Code. *You are safe.*

Paska's shoulders relaxed, although she didn't think anyone else at the table would notice how tense he'd been.

"Before you get started, can I tell everyone the news I've been holding onto for a few days?" Misty asked. "I didn't want to talk about it until I was sure, and then I didn't want to say anything until we were all together."

"Get on with it, girl," Paska growled. "You're holding up

Morgana's most fascinating tale, which I'm sure she'd like to get through before her guests arrive—and before the bar closes."

Misty wrinkled her nose at Paska. "You are the most cantankerous old fogey I've ever met."

"Flattery will get you nowhere except out of time to make your big reveal." Paska grabbed a full pint of beer and drained half of it before setting it back down on the table with a solid clunk.

Misty tossed her dark, wild curls over her shoulder. "Fine. And I'll even make it quick. As you know, Oracle Bay's police department has had a few...challenges over the last year. I'm pleased to report we've finally hired someone to serve as Chief of Police for Oracle Bay."

"I fail to see how more cops are good news," Drew said. "We already have an entire barrel of them."

"Two isn't a barrel," Misty said. "And the reason why I'm pleased is because he comes with a supernatural résumé and a list of recommendations as long as my arm. He's well-versed in dealing with magical crime—something we've had a lot of—and has zero hesitation about working with psychics and other magical creatures. He's less interested in policing and more interested in keeping the peace."

Morgana closed her eyes, pinched the bridge of her nose, and exhaled. She already knew the answer to the question she was going to ask. "What's his name?"

"Are you okay?" Misty asked.

"His name, Mystic," Morgana said, dropping her hand to the table to grab the whiskey Paska hastily slid in front of her.

"Donovan Davies."

"Isn't that just fucking great." Morgana drained her whiskey, then looked up to see six pairs of eyes staring at her in shock. Paska was shaking with silent laughter next to her.

"Do you know him?" Misty asked hesitantly.

Morgana grimaced. She'd lost the careful control she'd cultivated more times than she cared to think about in the last week. "I do. And

I'm sure he's eminently qualified. He certainly knows a lot about supernatural crime. He's a witch hunter."

Misty and Sandy stared at her blankly, but Ceri paled—no mean feat for a woman who was already giving paper a run for its money.

"Do you trust him?" Ceri asked. Her eyes were darting around as if looking for an escape route.

"No," Morgana said bluntly. "I will never trust a witch hunter. However, he won't be in town to surveil any of us. He will be here to monitor Hazel, my younger houseguest, and to serve as the trap for which she is the bait. I thought he was going to watch from afar. I had no idea he would find a way to secure a job in Oracle Bay within three days of deciding the course of action."

"He applied two months ago," Misty said. "We've only just now got through all the paperwork and formalities. I offered him the job before you left for your trip, and he accepted the day before you left after a final in-person interview."

Morgana drained her beer, stood, and walked out of the alcove to stand in the middle of the bar. She could hear the whispered conversation behind her.

"Should I apologize? Fire him? I don't know what to do," Misty said.

"No to both," Paska replied. "What's done is done. She said she knew he'd be around anyway, so she was expecting his presence. It will take some getting used to, and she hates it when she doesn't see something coming."

"We all do," Ceri said in a strained voice. "I might need to leave town for a while. I don't think I can do this."

Morgana lifted her chin. She needed to reassure Ceri she was safe. The woman, not quite four hundred years old, was still a child compared to Morgana, and had been through enough lately. Having to leave Oracle Bay, the town that could buoy and restore her as she continued to recoup her strength, would set back her recovery. Morgana liked Ceri, although she might not admit it. She even liked the scryer's fallen angel, something she definitely wouldn't admit.

"What have you said to my woman to make her panic?" Andy's voice was low and dangerous.

"Does she like it when you call her 'your woman'? Because I would wager that she would not appreciate it."

Andras Sterling, fallen angel, master brewer, and Pour House proprietor, not to mention Ceri's partner, took another step forward to stand by her side. "No need to repeat private conversations, is there, witch?"

"If you say so, demon," Morgana answered. "She is not taking well the news that Oracle Bay's new police chief is a witch hunter. This is not my doing, by the way. Misty and the town council hired him. I only revealed the news that policing wasn't his only job. Or at least policing towns. He is more used to policing people like us."

"And what does that mean?" Andy asked.

The smell of smoke and sulphur was making its way to her nostrils. "Tamp it down, demon. You might not care if people know you're a fallen angel, but you'll damage your bar if you burst into flames, and Brandy would never forgive you," Morgana murmured.

The odor disappeared almost immediately. His control really was almost total now. When he remembered, anyway.

"He and his *order*," she sneered the word, "find rogue witches, those who use blood magic or perform dark rituals, and handle them."

"And let me guess, sometimes they're a little too loose with the definition of 'black magic' and accidentally 'handle' an innocent?" Andy's voice was scathing.

"You have the right of it," Morgana said. "I do not know him well. We only met a few days ago. I will say to his credit that I believe he is more careful and cautious than many others I've met and seems to have zero desire to rush to judgment. However, I have been fooled before."

"You? I don't believe it." Andy's mocking laugh grated at her, although not as much as it usually did.

"You are correct. I should do away with false modesty. I have never been fooled and never been wrong."

Andy smiled down at her, his sea-grey eyes enforcing his sincerity. "Hopefully, this won't be the first time. Now, shall we go comfort my woman?"

Morgana shook her head at him. "I will give Ceri what reassurance I can, and perhaps finally get to tell the tale I came here to impart."

Andy bowed slightly, his silver hair glinting in the muted bar lights, and swept one arm out in front of him. "After you, witch."

"My pleasure, demon."

nine

"I promised her my protection and the protection of the town," Morgana said after finishing the mostly unabridged recounting of last week's Irish witch trials. "I don't know any of the players in Willow Grove, the coven I founded when I lived in Ireland, except Bridget and Lydia, but neither of them seemed to believe it could be a grove member who's attempting to frame Hazel for their own blood magic use."

"What are they doing?" Russell asked.

Morgana raised an eyebrow at him, and when he smirked, she glared. Just because she looked more like a librarian than a witch didn't mean she could be laughed at.

Russell had the grace to look slightly ashamed. "I mean, what is the black magic witch doing with the blood and dark rituals? What's the goal? If we know what they're doing, maybe we can figure out why and who."

Morgana nodded. The boy, or rather middle-aged man, was brighter than his tattoos and too-bushy beard had initially led her to believe. "That's an excellent question. Donovan Davies was staying behind to see if he could find any evidence of blood rites in the vicinity that had been missed by the Scales—the organization for which he works when he's not policing small towns. It is possible, probable I would even say, that if there was no immediate evidence of a witch using black magic that she, or he, is raising and storing power."

"How do you store power like that?" Sandy asked. Her eyes were wide, and Morgana couldn't tell if it was fear or fascination. Likely a bit of both.

"A focus stone or something similar," Ceri answered. "It'd have to be something strong to hold that kind of magic. There are a few crystals that would work, although crystals aren't really my area. Quartz probably, although I'm sure there's more to it than that. A witch could even have multiple stones if she was hoarding a lot of power for a great work."

"What kind of 'great work' needs death and blood?" Jezebel asked, revulsion evident in her voice.

Morgana let a wisp of satisfaction curl through her soul. The psychics here were good, strong people who would be resistant to the pull of black magic. And, if she wasn't mistaken, they'd have to be because she'd just put Oracle Bay in the crosshairs of a blood witch.

"Revenge. Murder. And the ability to continue to use the power stolen to take power from stronger and stronger magic users, either through brute force or subtle siphoning." Morgana turned when movement in the corner of her eye drew her attention. Brandy was leading two women to the alcove. "They're here. You don't have to tell them any more about your abilities than you wish to. Please behave yourselves." She looked at Paska, and he shrugged and favored her with an innocent smile.

Morgana stood and ushered Hazel and Bridget into the alcove.

Once they were seated and had drinks ordered, Morgana started introductions. "Hazel Jackson is a young witch who was living in Ireland, although she hails from Las Vegas. She is also, unfortunately, the victim and possible target in the issue I've told you about. She was framed for the dark magic murder of her girlfriend. She has been acquitted of that accusation, and I am completely satisfied that she is innocent." Morgana glared at every person at the table.

"Morgana, no one here thinks you'd bring a wicked witch to Oracle Bay," Sandy said.

Morgana nodded in satisfaction. "The other woman here is Bridget, also known as Sister Mary Margaret. She is one of the three senior members of Willow Grove and has traveled to ensure Hazel settles in."

Bridget waved and said, "If anyone here calls me 'Sister,' I will turn you into a stoat."

There was a wave of chuckles around the table.

"She's kidding," Hazel said shyly, then looked at her mentor. "Probably."

"We should do introductions and icebreakers," Misty said with a rather wicked grin.

"We are not doing icebreakers," Morgana said. "But we can do introductions. To my left is Paska Cooper. His method for seeing into the future is rune work or casting bones."

"Whatever you do, never ask if you can touch his bones," Sandy advised.

"You wound me," Paska laughed. "I am not the dirty old man you make me out to be."

Sandy snorted.

Paska shook his head and turned to Hazel. "I am pleased to make your acquaintance. There can never be too many red-headed lasses in Oracle Bay."

Russell raised his hand. "Hey. I'm Russell Black, bartender at the Sleeping Inn. Nice to meet you."

"I'm Misty Greene. Russell's my sort-of cousin, which is why he's here." Misty pursed her lips as if she wanted to say more, then apparently thought better of it. "I'm a palm reader. I'm also on the town council."

"She's being modest," Drew said. "She owns most of the town and runs all of it. Without her, Oracle Bay would go to the dogs."

Hazel's eyes were so wide, Morgana's ached in sympathy.

"And since I've already started talking, I'll introduce myself. I'm Drew Hardy."

"He tells the future by looking at balls," Paska said, completely deadpan.

Drew glared, but his lips twitched in amusement. "I tell the future by looking into my crystal ball. I also can recommend the best coffeeshop in town, if you need to move past tea and on to the good stuff. Caffeind Dreams has amazing coffee and fantastic pastries."

"Nice plug for your boyfriend's shop," Ceri said. She still looked pinched and tense but was at least loosening up enough to joke.

Morgana was positive that Andy's presence at her side was partially due the credit for that.

"I'm Ceridwen Kenny," she said, slipping into her Irish brogue. "I grew up near Knock, but have lived in the United States for…" She glanced at Morgana. They hadn't covered how much to reveal to the newcomers, and Morgana didn't want any of the permanent residents, any of her friends, to say anything they weren't comfortable with. Morgana shrugged. "…for quite a while now. I spent some time in Atlanta, then Los Angeles, where I met Drew, and he dragged me here. I'm a scryer, although I'm not doing too much of that right now, so please don't throw any mirrors at me."

"I can promise that," Hazel said, a tentative smile on her face as she regarded the woman who could've been her older sister or a close cousin. "Bad luck anyway."

Ceri's answering smile was free and easy and devoid of the last of the tension that'd been pinching her shoulders.

"I'm Andy Sterling," the fallen angel said. "This is my bar. I brew beer. I do whatever Brandy—that's the bar manager who showed you to your table—tells me to, and I try to keep Ceri as happy as possible."

Morgana grinned. "Is that because she's your woman?"

Ceri glared. "That's ridiculous, Morgana. Why would you trot out that sexist crap language?"

Morgana glanced at Andy, who was glowering at her, although not seriously enough to spark a flame. "My apologies. Since Andy called you that a couple of times when we were chatting earlier, I thought it was something of which you approved."

Ceri's jaw dropped. She elbowed Andy so hard in the side that he oofed in surprise, then she started laughing. "Morgana, it is so lovely to hear you joke. You do not do it often enough."

A warmth formed in Morgana's chest, right about where she thought her heart had shriveled to nothing.

"The softer, gentler side of Morgana is funnier, too," Russell said.

"If you don't stop with the jokes, I will ask Bridget to turn you into a stoat." Morgana smiled sweetly at Russell, who grinned and winked.

"I'm Jezebel Jones. I'm an astrologer. Let me know if you need your natal chart done. I've got horoscopes and more." Jez grinned and tossed her long, black braids over her shoulder. "You can also come see me if you need a break from the rest of these weirdos."

Hazel smiled at Jezebel. "I'll let you know. Thank you."

Sandy waved. "I'm Sandy Franklin. I'm the tarot reader and the newest in town until you."

"Zeke is newer," Ceri said, then turned to Hazel. "He's the early 40s looking guy behind the bar and is a prophet of the Judeo-Christian god."

Bridget gasped. Morgana turned toward her in time to see all the blood rush from her face.

Catholics. Morgana shook her head.

"Joanna is even newer," Russell said. "We really should invite her to one of these meetings."

Ten pairs of eyes turned towards him. "Who?" Hazel asked.

"You remember Joanna," Russell said. "She was there when Felicity stabbed you."

Ceri stiffened and Hazel gasped. "You were stabbed?" the younger woman asked.

"She's clearly fine now," Morgana said. "And she is the only one of us who has been stabbed in Oracle Bay."

"I was shot," Sandy volunteered. "But it was a hitman hired by my ex-husband. Nothing to do with being psychic."

"None of the rest of us have been injured living in Oracle Bay," Misty said. "Our crime rate is very low, and we just hired a new chief of police well-versed in supernatural crime and mundane law enforcement."

"Donovan Davies," Morgana said, hoping they'd moved far enough past Joanna, the newest witch in town, that no one would bring her up again, at least not today. Morgana hadn't had a chance to test her yet, and they wouldn't be inviting anyone new into their informal oracular grove without being vetted. Especially since the young woman could be considered an accessory to attempted murder, and she didn't want Donovan Davies to get any bright ideas about enforcing laws against people Morgana considered under her protection.

Bridget raised her eyebrows. "He moves fast."

"He set the wheels in motion before I even flew to Ireland," Morgana said.

Misty shifted at the end of the table, rattling the glassware and drawing all the attention to her. She smiled cautiously. "Now that we're all here and introduced, should we talk about what we're going to do to protect Hazel and solve the mystery of her black magic stalker?"

Morgana nodded in satisfaction. "That is exactly what we need to decide. We have a lot of powerful people here, and we are in a powerful town. If we can't keep you safe here, there are few places that could."

"That doesn't sound as reassuring as I'd like," Hazel said.

"I cannot lie to you about your safety, but you will be protected here. Keep your amulet on, and that will help." Morgana turned to the rest of the group to explain. "She's wearing an amulet of black tourmaline I made, and if any of the rest of you would like one as well, please let me know. Black tourmaline is crystal made of—in part—magnesium and iron, which are excellent protections against black magic."

Bridget had regained her composure, and she leaned forward, planting her elbows on the table, causing her crucifix to swing out of her jacket. She tucked it back in, snagging a green bead—it looked like the same Connemara marble that composed the handle on Morgana's athame—on the zipper, then asked, "Please forgive me, but none of you are witches. I don't see how seers would be any protection against a powerful witch."

"There is more power in foresight than you'd guess, Sister," Paska said. "Never underestimate what you don't understand. That's when you'll find yourself in trouble, and that is one thing I can guarantee you won't see coming."

ten

Morgana sat in her kitchen in slippers and a black, silk robe, sipping a cup of tea. It was an herbal blend she'd created with Antonia, the proprietor of the To A Tea tea shop in town, and she only drank it when she was exhausted and stressed.

Jet lag was hitting her harder this time than it had in longer than she could remember, and the meeting with the psychics hadn't been as comprehensive as she'd wanted, nor did they walk away with the hoped-for definitive plan.

"Do you mind if I join you?" Bridget asked, padding into the kitchen.

Morgana groaned inwardly. There was an excellent reason she never entertained houseguests and hadn't indulged in a sexual relationship in decades. She did not like people in her space. However, Bridget was one of her oldest living friends, and she was a guest.

"Of course not," Morgana said. "Would you like a cup of tea? I'm drinking a blend of Cinnamon, nettles, red clover, raspberry leaf, orange peel, and lemon balm. It is both soothing and balancing."

"That sounds lovely." Bridget stretched and groaned as several joints cracked. "I am not as young as I once was, and I find traveling at this age to be much more difficult than it was when I was young."

Morgana pulled a teacup out of the cupboard and hit the button on the electric kettle. She took out one of the sachets Antonia had prepared for her and dropped it into the teacup, then waited for the water to boil. "Do you find yourself traveling a lot now? Donovan Davies said you had accompanied him to use your gift to help him accost witches."

Bridget tsked. "He said nothing of the sort. He said I occasionally aided him in determining the innocence or guilt of a witch accused of wrongdoing."

"And he said you used your very special gift to do so," Morgana pressed. "A gift I'd love to talk about. I don't believe you've ever mentioned it."

"It's a much less dramatic variation of the way you determined young Hazel was innocent," Bridget said placidly, taking a seat at the table. "And less reliant on the cooperation of the accused."

"That's fascinating," Morgana said. The kettle beeped, and she lifted it to fill Bridget's cup. After a moment's consideration, she grabbed a fresh sachet and made herself another cup as well. "How long have you had this gift?"

"I spent years believing that I had little in the way of magical powers. Just enough to sense it, but not enough to do more than light a candle if I concentrated hard enough. Then, about fifteen years ago, I caught one of the sisters with her hand in the collection box. I was so angry, and when I demanded she confess to the Reverend Mother, she not only confessed to petty theft, but a number of other small crimes that had gone unsolved in the village over the previous few years." Bridget swirled her sachet around.

"It happens that way sometimes. A surge of emotion can awaken a skill a person didn't know they had." Morgana nodded. "It probably happens even more often than we're aware of. There must be so many people who awaken a gift then spend the rest of their lives pretending it didn't happen and trying to hide it."

"Or who waken gifts that have the potential to be dangerous in situations where it's not safe to do so. Imagine having road rage and accidentally blowing up your own car?" Bridget cackled.

Morgana eyed her askance. She'd lived for years and didn't have the same views of life and death as many of her acquaintances who'd lived for less than a century, but she respected life and the earth it came from too much to ever joke about the accidental death caused by a new power waking in an innocent soul. "I am surprised you would laugh at that possibility. It seems inappropriate."

"Because I'm a nun, you mean?" Bridget asked. She pulled the sachet out of her cup and set it on the small plate in the center of the table that existed for that purpose.

Morgana followed suit, then picked up her cup and held it in her hands, absorbing the warmth as she determined what she wanted to say next. "Not because you are a nun. You know my views of the church and other organized religions." She permitted herself a small smile. "I prefer my religion to be decidedly disorganized. But because you have taken in the earth's magic, you have felt the goddess's spirit stir in your soul. You have been witness to creation and destruction in ceremony and ritual. Life is all around us, and it is to be celebrated. That's why the dark magics and blood rites are so terrible. They destroy without creating and upset the balance."

"Light couldn't exist without dark," Bridget said. "That's why there's a devil to counter our angels. And we wouldn't know white magic if we didn't have black."

Morgana pursed her lips. She'd lived long enough to know there was no one true way, and for every religion that rose to prominence, there were as many interpretations of it as there were people who believed. She didn't interfere with other people's beliefs unless they threatened harm to her or someone she'd taken under her protection. But the belief that metaphorical darkness was necessary for people to walk in metaphorical light had always bothered her, in no small part because the people who typically espoused those beliefs were doing so to explain away some great and terrible thing that was happening, throw the blame squarely in the lap of the darkness, and take zero responsibility to address the problem themselves.

"It is true that day and night exist literally in our world," she said slowly. She had few enough friends and didn't want to alienate one, particularly one who was staying in her house. "But it doesn't take evil to know what good is."

"Of course it does," Bridget said. "That's why there are hells in so many religions. If God didn't believe evil was inevitable and necessary, why would He allow the Morningstar to betray him, and why would he cast Lucifer into hell to rule over those who were sent there?"

"Careful, Sister, your Catholic is showing," Morgana said more sharply than she'd intended. When she saw Bridget's wide eyes, she rubbed her face. "It is late, and I do not care to have a theological discussion with you at my kitchen table in the middle of the night. This is something to do over wine tomorrow evening when we can both maintain our good humor."

"You're right, of course," Bridget said. "I'm sorry for coming down for tea and then starting in on the God talk. After all, it's not like we can ask anyone who was there at the creation, right? We'll just have to do the best with what knowledge we have. Or maybe ask that bartender—Zeke was his name?—if he has any insights into God's mind. I'd love to know what He thinks about... Well, about everything."

Morgana opened her mouth to offer Andy's expertise, then snapped it closed again. If Andy hadn't said he was a fallen angel and recently, at least in the overall time elapsed since the Fall, risen demon, she would not out him. He was a lot more forthcoming with his nature than he'd been for decades, but she would not put him on the spot. At least not now.

"Zeke doesn't like to talk about prophecy," Morgana temporized. "I wouldn't march down to the Pour House tomorrow and demand he give you a speech about his god."

"But surely, since I'm a nun, it'd be okay for him to share."

Bridget looked hopeful. "There are so few prophets born these days, and he must need someone to prophesy to and record His words."

Morgana shook her head. "If he wants to talk to you, he'll seek you out. Don't hold your breath, though. And now, I'd love it if you headed back to bed so I can tidy up my kitchen and do the same."

"I can clean up if you want," Bridget offered. "And I promise not to call Zeke in the middle of the night to demand answers."

Morgana laughed and finished her tea. "If you want to put away the tea things, please do. I am suddenly barely able to keep my eyes open."

Bridget stood and put her hand on Morgana's shoulder. She barely flinched and congratulated herself for the control she could still exert, even when exhausted.

"Go sleep, Morgana. I'll see you in the morning."

"Thank you, Bridget." Morgana turned and walked up the stairs. Her bedroom was at the west end of the second floor, and the other two bedrooms shared the east wall. There was an entire hallway, a bathroom, a laundry room, and two closets between her and her guests, but tonight it didn't feel like enough.

She locked herself in her room, did her skin care routine—she might be eternally young as long as she didn't stray too long from magical wellsprings, but she hadn't kept her skin this flawless by being careless about moisturizing—pushed back the curtains, and opened the windows as far as she could.

It was too dark to see the ocean in the light of the waning crescent moon, but the sound of the waves crashing against the shore was enough to bring the stillness to her soul she needed to fall asleep. She put on her lavender-filled silk sleep mask, slid between the sheets, and closed her eyes. There'd be time enough tomorrow to make plans—both to protect Hazel and avoid Donovan Davies.

eleven

Morgana looked around the small shop where she conducted business. It was Saturday morning in June, and the tourist season was well and truly underway. She seldom opened her tea leaf reading business to the public during the off months, but it was fiscally unsound to not stay open a few hours a day during the summer months and holidays. She didn't need the money—a very long life, a keen mind, and a knack of seeing how to be in the right place at the right time was beneficial to creating a sustaining financial reserve—but it never hurt to have diversified income streams.

When she'd determined the interior of the shop was to her satisfaction, she flipped the sign from "Closed" to "Open," and turned on the burner of the small stove she used to boil her tea. No electric kettle here. People felt a lot more confident about her readings if they heard the tea kettle whistle, so no matter how much it irritated her to hear the sound multiple times a day, she gave the people what they wanted.

She arranged her tea service on the delicately filigreed silver tray, ensured the black tea she favored for readings was in the teapot, and waited.

It didn't take long for the first customer to hesitantly poke their head in.

"Come in," Morgana said, trying to project trustworthy calm. People occasionally seemed disappointed that she looked like a suburban housewife who routinely served tea to her husband's guests, and she missed the looks of wide-eyed surprise followed by excitement she'd gotten when she had long black hair, expansive cleavage, and wore nothing but black.

"Are you… Are you a tea leaf reader for real?" A young, curvy white woman with shoulder-length brown hair asked as she walked into Morgana's shop. She was wearing tight blue jeans and a pink tunic shirt that landed just below her hips. She looked around with wide brown eyes that were magnified by her glasses.

"I am. If you'd rather just have tea for breakfast, there is a tea shop further down the street," Morgana offered. She always offered, and only one person had admitted they were in the wrong place and exited. People often felt compelled to pay for a service even if they were somewhere they hadn't meant to go.

"No, no." The woman took three more steps into the room and bit her lower lip. "I wanted to be here. There are a lot of psychics to choose from."

Her look was almost accusatory, and Morgana had to bite back a smile.

"We have more psychics per capita, perhaps more in actual numbers, than any other west coast town," Morgana said. "And most of us are never wrong."

The woman laughed nervously and took the remaining steps necessary to stand in front of the small table with the tea service.

Morgana slid a small card across the table that had the details of what she offered as well as the price. "I will require payment in advance, but there is a money-back guarantee. If what I tell you does not come to pass within the time frame we agree on, you may return, and I will give you a full refund."

"That seems fair." The woman sat down and looked at the service list, then pulled a credit card out of a thin wallet and pushed it across to Morgana.

Morgana ran the card, then handed it back, along with the phone she used for business transactions only. "Please sign and accept."

The woman did as she was requested, and Morgana noted that her finger hovered hesitantly over the screen before decidedly pressing her finger in one place on the screen that indicated she was tipping rather well, then completed the transaction and handed the phone back.

Morgana tucked her phone away, then turned up the heat on the kettle.

It whistled within seconds, and the woman jumped.

"I should've warned you, Violet. It is a very loud whistle." Morgana grabbed the kettle and poured the boiling water into the tea pot.

"How'd you know my name?" The young woman's eyes were wide, and she blinked rapidly.

"I just ran your credit card," Morgana said gently. She pushed the button on her discreet timer, then leaned across the table. "Tell me a little about what brings you here today and what you're hoping to learn."

Violet smiled, but it faltered after a second and tears filled her eyes. "I'm in trouble."

Morgana nodded encouragingly. She kept her magic contained when she worked. She kept it contained most of the time; she wasn't interested in being a performative witch during this life she'd made for herself. But she was tempted to use it to reach out and encourage the woman to trust her enough to share what her trouble was instead of waiting for her to make up her mind.

She mentally shook herself. As brief as her time in Ireland had been, using her magic and feeling the power rise again hadn't been good for her resolution to keep it tamped down. Instead of letting the temptation of hurrying things along overtake her, she smiled patiently. As long as she kept quiet, Violet would eventually start talking. They always did. Most people weren't comfortable with long silences.

"I've been having dreams," Violet said, looking at her hands. "Scary dreams." She looked up at Morgana as if looking for validation.

"Dreams can be a path to our subconscious, but they can also be a harbinger of outside interference," Morgana said. She picked up the teapot and slowly poured out two cups of tea. "When the temperature is acceptable, drink the cup until only the barest amount of liquid remains at the bottom. Be careful not to drink the leaves.

Violet picked up her cup but didn't drink. Instead, she met Morgana's eyes. "In my dreams, I saw a dark-cloaked figure standing over me with her arms outstretched and her hands spread wide. There were pieces of string, more like tinsel, really, stretched between me and her. And it felt like she was pulling the tinsel out of me. When I woke up, I was exhausted."

Morgana tipped her head to one side. "Is that the reason you think you're in trouble?" she asked. She'd often encountered people seeking guidance after a series of weird dreams, but this didn't feel typical. "And how long have you been having them?"

"Three days." Violet took a drink of her tea, then another. "But before that, there was something else. This is going to sound weird..."

Morgana nodded at the young woman. "So much of what happens sounds weird to our own ears, but not to those who are versed in the mystic arts. I have heard and seen many strange things from the querents who come to me looking for answers. Do not hesitate to speak freely."

Violet took another sip of tea, then nodded decisively. "I was in Ireland a couple weeks ago on my honeymoon." She held up her left hand, and the diamond on her ring finger nearly blinded Morgana when it caught the light. "My partner is an absolute nut when it comes to old, mystic sites. We must have visited every stone circle, every dolmen, and every ancient graveyard that Ireland had to offer, and then some he just invented when we ran out." She laughed, and the smile that lit up her eyes brought color back to her cheeks. "But the last place we went was creepy, even for him. We got lost and made a wrong turn, then found ourselves in a little village that wasn't on any of our maps."

Morgana tensed, and she had to force herself to let go of the teacup before she shattered it with her grip. "Do you remember where you were? I've spent some in time in Ireland myself, which is why I'm interested."

"I can't remember the name of the village, but it was near Carrick-on-Shannon," Violet said. "But that wasn't even the freakiest bit. There was a bed-and-breakfast with a vacancy, and a pub with excellent food, so we decided to stop for the night. The next day, a young woman offered to take us to the nearby dolmen. She told us a wonderful tale of the immortal witch who watched over the town, although the rock itself was pretty unimpressive." Violet shrugged, and Morgana kept the smile pasted on her face.

"If everything was lovely and bland, you wouldn't be adding this to your tale," Morgana said.

Violet took another sip of her tea, then swirled the remaining liquid and tea leaves counterclockwise with her left hand. She didn't even know it, but she was completing the ritual without prompting. On the occasions that happened, the fortunes were always the most clear.

"The second morning we woke up there, I could barely move. I felt like I had the flu or something. The innkeeper urged us to stay until I felt better, but Tom—that's my husband—insisted on getting me back to Dublin in case I needed medical attention."

"And that's when the nightmares started?" Morgana prompted after the pause grew too long, even for her comfort.

Violet nodded. "They weren't bad at first, and I barely remembered them. But when we came home a few days ago, they started up again, and have been getting worse every night."

"Home?" Morgana asked. "You're not a tourist then?"

Violet blushed and shook her head. "Nope. Long Beach born and bred. I grew up working in the kite museum and lost my virginity in the Shelburne on prom night when I was supposed to be at the church after-prom party. That's how I knew about Oracle Bay."

Morgana aimed her much-practiced warm smile at the young woman. A local to the Pacific Northwest who was in Ireland right around the time of Rowan's murder, who'd stayed overnight in a town that she shouldn't have been able to find—Violet must be one half of the couple Morgana had seen in the pub in Kilnamanagh—and was now visiting psychics in the town where Hazel was staying raised alarm bells. This fortune would hopefully be illuminating. "If you've finished your tea, set the cup on the saucer."

Violet did as she was told, and after she set the cup down, Morgana pulled the saucer closer, then looked down.

Her eyes widened briefly. She'd been practicing tasseography for centuries—for as long as the western world knew that futures could be told in the random arrangements of organic materials such as birds, entrails, bones, and leaves. She was good at what she did and barely needed to tap into the wellspring of power that bound her to the earth in order to interpret the leaves. But she'd never seen anything so clear. It all but spelled out, "Danger! Run!" The only trouble was, Morgana couldn't tell if it was aimed at Violet or at her.

Morgana looked up at Violet, who was shaking slightly and fixating on a spot high on the wall behind Morgana. The message might not be clear, which was unusual, but it was likely Violet who was in danger. Morgana needed to warn the woman without scaring her. Scared people made terrible choices, and frightening a woman with supernatural bad news might turn her into a skeptic who got herself killed through lack of belief.

"You are right to interpret your dreams as nightmares," Morgana began. "I think you encountered something…dark at the dolmen in

Ireland, and because of your highly sensitive and empathetic manner, the darkness latched onto you." Telling people they were highly sensitive to the spirit world and natural empaths was a time-honored way to gain their trust and ensure they listened with less skepticism than they would usually.

"How do I get rid of it?" Violet whispered.

Morgana kept her eyes on the leaves, trying to find that answer in the teacup but coming up short. There was no other recourse but honesty. Partial honesty, at least. "I don't know. You are not the first young woman I've seen in Oracle Bay who's been bothered. That you recently came from Ireland is new information."

"What do I do?" Violet pleaded. "I can't sleep anymore; I'm too afraid."

This she could help with. "Please wait a moment." Morgana stood and walked through the back door to the small kitchen. It had little besides a sink, a mini-fridge, a two-burner stove, and a small cupboard, but it held the proprietary tea blends—those she was willing to share with a client—she'd created. She never sold any of them here. The only service she transacted was fortune-telling. But there were those people who came to see her who needed a little extra magic in their lives, and unless she was gravely mistaken, and she never was, Violet was one of them.

Morgana pulled a small tin out of the cupboard, then looked at the sachets available. She pulled out seven and placed them in a small box.

Violet was still staring at the table when Morgana walked back in. "I cannot stop your nightmares completely, but I can help keep them at bay." Morgana smiled in what she hoped was a reassuring fashion. "Your future shows nearly unbearable pain and fear, but it is also time limited. I've put together some teas that might help with your dreams. Three of the sachets in here, labeled 'Serenitea,' will serve as a high-powered chamomile tea. Drink thirty minutes before bedtime, and it should help you fall into a dreamless sleep. If you find that's not powerful enough to keep the dreams at bay, try the

'Tranquilitea.' It's more powerful but will make you feel a little hungover in the morning. And if that still isn't enough, the single tea bag in there with the red sachet tag is the last resort. 'Necessitea' is guaranteed to knock you into a dreamless state. It is fast-acting, which means it could put you to sleep anywhere between two and twenty minutes after finishing a cup and will keep you down for the count. Don't drink it if you have to be up at a set time the next morning or if you have to do anything involving brain power the next day. It might keep the dreams away, but it's a steep cost and should only be used if you haven't slept for over forty-eight hours." Morgana closed the lid of the tin and slid it towards Violet.

"This is a lot," Violet said, laughing nervously.

"It is, but I am so glad I met you. Not only because I have had the opportunity to help you sleep at night, but also because you've added another piece into a puzzle that's been forming in my mind lately. Thank you, Violet." She stood and waited for Violet to follow suit. "If you need more tea or more guidance, my door is open to you."

Violet scooped up the tin of tea and stood. "So, what's the future I'm waiting on that will guarantee me my money back if it doesn't happen?"

Morgana thought for a moment. In the intensity of the situation, she'd nearly forgotten about her money-back guarantee and wasn't prepared to throw something out there without careful consideration.

Violet clapped her hands. "I know! If I haven't died of fright or from my dreams in one month's time, I'll come back and thank you again for listening." A note of hysteria underpinned her words, and Morgana suppressed a wince.

She couldn't promise the young woman that she'd be able to collect on that. She shook her head. "I don't want to spoil your surprise, but if you promise to be patient, I'll write down your future, and then in a month, you can look at it and marvel at my brilliance."

Violet laughed. "It's a deal."

Morgana wrote a quick note with a fountain pen she'd purchased at an estate sale fifty years ago, folded the parchment, then used the heat from the hotplate to melt the sealing wax she had under the table. She dripped the hot, black wax onto the fold of the parchment, then took her seal and pressed it into the wax. The relief of a raven looked up at her, and she smiled.

Violet picked up the paper and practically ran out of the shop. She paused just before the door closed behind her. "Thank you! I'll be back."

Morgana's smile dropped off her face. Violet had spoken truth. She would be back, but there was a finality floating around her that Morgana couldn't interpret without tapping deeper into the young woman's mind and Morgana's own magic, and that was not something she wanted to do this morning. Later, though. She had the leaves from the tea Violet had drunk, and that would be enough to find her again and see what future Morgana was missing.

twelve

Morgana pushed back from her table and stretched her arms over her head. Most of the tourists she read for were easy. They wanted to know when they'd find love or money. Violet had not been easy. It took a lot to drain Morgana, but she was tired. There was no reason to stay open when it made more sense to find out more about Violet and her vacation to Kilnamanagh.

She walked towards the front door to flip the sign over, but before she could, the door opened and a tall, dark, and handsome... acquaintance walked in.

"Donovan Davies," she said flatly. "I'm closed. If you want your fortune told, you'll need to find someone else."

He chuckled and swept his glance over her. "I don't need you to tell me the future. I know exactly where I'm going to end up before this summer is over."

The leer in his voice wasn't overt, but Morgana flushed anyway, then cursed her pale skin. The last few months had disrupted everything about the life she'd settled into. She wouldn't have blushed at a suggestive comment from a man a year ago. This outfit was ruining her.

"Don't flirt with me, Donovan Davies." Her voice wasn't as firm as she'd wanted it to be, and she gritted her teeth against his knowing smile.

"My apologies. It's hard to help myself in the presence of such an attractive woman."

That's all she needed to pull her armor back down. "That's a poor accounting of your character if all it takes for you to lose control of yourself and step towards the line of impropriety is a pretty face. Did you need something, or are you just here to harass me?"

Donovan smiled but pulled back the flirtatious edge. "It's my first day on the job. I'm stopping in at as many Main Street businesses as I can to meet my fellow citizens. I want everyone to feel comfortable now that there's a new sheriff in town." He stuck his thumbs in the belt loops of his tight jeans and grinned.

"The sheriff is an elected county position. You are a hired police chief living in a time when a lot of people here have little cause to trust you. I suggest you find a better town to terrorize." Morgana let her voice drip with the disdain that'd been building up all.

Donovan's eyes glinted, and he dropped into the querent's chair without invitation. "I am not interested in harassing you or anyone else in Oracle Bay. If there's a violent crime, I will work with the appropriate people to solve it. And if there's a petty crime that doesn't hurt anyone, I'll let it go. I'm here to keep an eye on the supernatural elements. I've learned a lot more talking to the mundane citizens than I did during the interview process. Do you want to tell me about the..." He pulled a small notebook out of his back pocket and flipped a couple pages. "...theatrical production over the bay last Christmas? Or the influx of odd characters, some of whom have wings, that's been happening since Thanksgiving? Or what about the increase in murders and attempted murders that draw in the psychics?"

"No." Morgana picked up her tea service and took it to the back room. She left the door open. She had no illusion that Donovan would leave once she turned her back on him, and she wasn't about to leave him unsupervised in her space. She rinsed the teapot and cups, then packed them into the padded case she used to transport them back and forth between her house and her business.

When she could delay no longer, she returned to the front of her business, finished the job she'd started earlier of flipping over the sign, and picked up her beige purse covered in "Cs."

"If there's nothing further." Morgana fished the keys out of her purse and picked up the case with her tea service.

"Just one more question," Donovan said smoothly. "Does anyone here know you've been working for the Silver Eye, tracking down murderers for the last seventy years?"

There was no point in denying it. "No, and neither should you."

Donovan shook his head. "You already know I work for the Scales. Did you think they wouldn't know who you work for?"

Since that was exactly what Morgana had thought, she kept her mouth closed.

"Why do you think this place isn't crawling with warlocks to back me up?"

Morgana closed her eyes. "The Eye and the Scales are working together on this one, aren't they?" If he knew and she hadn't been equally well informed, that meant she was deliberately being kept in the dark. It was one more thing to cement her decision to break ties with the Eye after the murderer was neutralized. "Are you supposed to reveal yourself to me?" Morgana asked, then closed her eyes when the wording of her question replayed in her brain.

Donovan smirked but didn't take the bait. "Does it matter?"

"Of course it matters. If you're not supposed to tell me you know who I work for, that means you've been sent here to watch me as well as be the trap for whoever's targeting Hazel. It might even mean I'm a suspect. When you put things in motion with the goal of arriving in Oracle Bay, it was because this wasn't the first time you've seen a murder like that of Hazel's girlfriend." Morgana put her purse and the tea service case back down on the floor and sat down.

"As I said in Ireland, there have been other, similar murders, and until we interrogated Miranda together in Ireland, you were the prime suspect." Donovan placed his elbows on the table and rested his chin on his hands.

Morgana nodded. "You think the events in Vancouver are related to the murders you've been tracking in Ireland." It wasn't a question.

"You have to admit that they coincided perfectly with every visit you made to British Columbia," he said.

"And if you know who I am and what I'm doing, you know my visits were to investigate the murders after the fact," Morgana countered. "I might as well accuse you of Rowan's murder, since you knew about it before I did."

"I arrived after you did. How could I be responsible?"

"You could've flown to Portland after the murder, then flown back with me. Don't try to pull the wool over my eyes." Morgana crossed her arms over her chest and glared at him. "We are going around in circles now. Do you suspect me of the chain of murders in Vancouver?"

"No. You don't have the right kind of energy. Besides, Bridget says you aren't capable of murder."

Morgana's eyes blared. Satisfaction rose in her chest when she saw him flinch. "Do you know how old I am, Donovan Davies?"

His eyes widened slightly, then narrowed as he looked her over. "It's not polite to guess a woman's age, but older than a hundred if you've been working for the Silver Eye for seventy years."

Morgana debated with herself for a moment. No one but Paska knew her true age, and she wasn't sure she wanted to trust this witch hunter with any of her secrets. "I am significantly older than one hundred," she said finally. "And anyone who's lived as long as I have knows that anyone is capable of murder if the motivation is there."

"Have you ever committed a murder?" Donovan asked.

"Do you mean for personal reasons or because of the job you and I both do?" Morgana asked. "And should I be asking you the same question? You're on your first lifetime, so you might not have come against an immovable force, yet. But if you live as long as I suspect you can, you will find yourself at that line more than once. So, ask yourself, do you really want to know what I'm capable of when pushed to the limit?"

Donovan leaned back in his chair, dropping his arms to his lap. "Did you kill any of those people in Vancouver?"

"No. Did you murder Rowan in Ireland?"

Donovan shook his head, then wiped his hand on his jeans and held it out. "Truce?"

Morgana regarded his hand for a moment, then reached out and shook it. "For now."

"We should compare notes," Donovan said. "Maybe over dinner and drinks at the Sleeping Inn?"

Morgana considered. She wanted as little as possible to do with Donovan, but if they were looking for the same blood-rites witch, it made sense to work together. Besides, the sooner they figured out who was killing the Stepford wives with wells of unrealized power, the sooner she could shed this ridiculous costume and step back into black.

"I will work with you on these cases which are likely connected, but it will not be over dinner and drinks," Morgana said. "It is difficult to get much work done over dinner. Meet me at the Shelburne Hotel in Long Beach this afternoon at five."

"A hotel?" Donovan's eyebrows rose until they disappeared into his hairline. "That doesn't sound more conducive to getting work done."

Morgana smiled tightly. "Meet me at the pub in the Shelburne Hotel. There are a couple tables we could take over and spread our notes out on, and it is far enough out of the way that no one in Oracle Bay will stumble on us. Bridget and Hazel are planning on watching a movie with Sandy and her fiancé, so they'll be safe. I am free to leave town, at least for a while."

"It's a date." Donovan unfolded his long, lanky body from the chair and rose to his full height.

"It's not a date," Morgana corrected. "Now leave. I have things to do."

Donovan's chuckle followed him out of her shop.

"What have I gotten myself into?" She sighed, grabbed her things, and left, locking the door behind her.

thirteen

Morgana ordered a glass of the house red, double-checked that all her electronics were disconnected from Wi-Fi, cellular, and Bluetooth, and pulled out a spiral-bound notebook.

Donovan arrived five minutes later, did the same check with his phone and Apple watch, and ordered a beer from the server when they dropped off Morgana's wine. "What do you have?"

"Case files and photos of a dozen murders; there were nine in Vancouver, BC and three in Seattle. You?"

Donovan dropped a Manila folder and a notebook on the table. "Five in Dublin, four in Galway, and one in Carrick-on-Shannon. Timeline?"

Morgana smiled tightly at him when she saw the server approaching. They dropped off Donovan's beer with a flirty wink he didn't seem to notice.

Morgana turned her notebook to the page where she'd calendared in all the days and places the women had been killed. "One or two a week in Vancouver between February twenty-first and March twenty-sixth. Then three in Seattle on April fifth, fifteenth, and twenty-first. You?"

Donovan flipped open his notebook and turned it around so Morgana could read it while he talked. "The first Galway murders happened on February first and fourteenth, then there was a break until the end of March, and things escalated. There were two more murders in Galway on March thirty-first and April third. The first two Dublin murders happened the tenth and twelfth, the third on the eighteenth, and the last two on the twenty-fourth and twenty-sixth."

"And Rowan's was just before Beltane on April twenty-ninth?" Morgana asked, adding the Irish murders to the calendar she'd created.

Donovan nodded. "There were four murders in February, eight in March, then eleven in April in two countries and three different cities before Rowan's murder. I don't follow the same calendar you do, but even I couldn't help noticing the twenty-three murders were fairly neatly bookended between Imbolc and Beltane."

Morgana had already made that notation, but she nodded in acknowledgement. "There was a murder on Ostara, too, and one on Valentine's Day, although that isn't a pagan holiday."

"Unless you're a devotee of Cupid, I guess," Donovan said. "Which I very much am every time I look at you."

"What makes you think they're targeting Hazel and not planning on moving on to another city to continue the power harvesting?" Morgana asked. She had her private reasons but wasn't about to let go of the opportunity to get another opinion.

"Rowan's murder was the first to happen in the home of a loved one, and the body was the first not to be moved after. Hazel lived alone and had only been seeing Rowan for a short time, thus it could be inferred that the murderer might have killed first and looked for the power after. Rowan was also the only murder victim we know of that didn't have untapped power."

"But Hazel's power was already active," Morgana countered, leaning back in her chair. "She wouldn't have fit the profile, either."

"Have you looked deep into her?" Donovan asked. "She's barely skimmed the surface of her magic."

Morgana shook her head. "I haven't. I could sense power when swore she hadn't killed Rowan, but I didn't look any further once I was satisfied she hadn't murdered anyone."

"She's the second most powerful person I've met in the last few years, and almost completely untrained and unable to defend herself. That's why I think the killer will strike her again. They're escalating, they're over-confident, and my guess is they hate losing almost more than anything."

Morgana nodded slowly. "And if Hazel is not only the one who got away, but a huge power source they missed, it makes sense that they'd want to finish the job. I'm not one hundred percent convinced that they'll follow her to Oracle Bay, especially not now that you and I are both here. If you could sense my power even though it ought to be hidden, they'll be able to as well, especially with as much power as they've absorbed recently."

Donovan was shaking his head before she could finish talking. "If they're cocky enough to murder this many people in such a short amount of time, they'll be overconfident. It'd be a rush to take her under our noses. And the opportunity to take your power, too, as well as the rest of the oracles in Oracle Bay, will be a motive."

Morgana cocked her head and regarded him. "You must be joking. What interest would a power-mad blood witch have in the seers of this town? Me, I understand. I am more than a talented fortune-teller."

"Don't pretend the rest of the oracles in your town are low-level powers, no matter how much they might try to project that image. I met with every single person in Oracle Bay with even a modicum of power. Do you know how many people with unrealized potential there are? It's almost like the town draws them in." Donovan raised an eyebrow and pulled his notebook back to his side of the table.

Morgana sighed. He was right. Oracle Bay would look like a cheap Vegas buffet to someone who was harvesting power from those who didn't look like they could defend themselves. Then a thought hit her. "Can you see untapped power? Is that why you're on this mission?"

Donovan nodded. "My primary job is to find potential victims, protect them, and do everything I can to aid you when you stop the murderer."

"So, you're my assistant?" Morgana asked, taking a sip of her wine. She grimaced slightly. Adriana Covington had been a terrible person—and a murderer—but she'd always had superb wines in stock, and the lack of a bottle shop in Oracle Bay was even sadder than drinking inferior wine in bars on the Long Beach peninsula.

Donovan scoffed. "Your assistant? If anything, you're mine. I get the noble job, and you're my cleaner."

Morgana smiled at him. It was possible this working relationship would work after all. He had a sharp mind and a good sense of humor. The job would be easier if they were working together. Once they found their killer, he'd be out of her life, and she could walk away from the Silver Eye for good.

"Now that I'm not the Canadian bait, do you think I can go back to my regular aesthetic?" Morgana asked wistfully.

He shook his head. "I'd recommend against it. In fact, I wish you hadn't changed in Ireland. You never know who might've seen you. That was sloppy, Bellflower."

He was right, and she hated that he was. "I couldn't have very well show up to a full moon ritual dressed like Mary Tyler Moore," she said, wincing at the petulance in her voice.

"You very well could've. How did you explain your change in appearance to Hazel and Bridget? Surely you didn't tell them the truth." Donovan drained his beer and caught the server's eye when they passed to order another.

"I told them this costume made customers trust me and my advice more, which means I make more money, and that it was an experiment since I was tired of my old look. It's much the same story I told my friends when I altered my hair and clothing. I've told no one the truth." Morgana pursed her lips. "Paska knows I am lying, though. I've known him for ages, which means he knows me well enough to know I'd never choose this look, no matter how desperate I was for clients."

"Does he know who you really work for?" Donovan asked.

Morgana shook her head. "I don't think so, although I can't say for sure. The secrets that man knows could fill volumes. He wouldn't talk about it or betray me, though." She paused for a moment, then added, "Unless he had an excellent reason to do so."

Donovan chuckled. "And what would an excellent reason be?"

"If someone he cared about or who he'd taken under his protection was in danger." Morgana wrinkled her nose. He might also betray her if he thought it would lead to a more interesting outcome. Or if it was Tuesday and he felt cantankerous. But Donovan didn't need to know that. If he thought Paska was a weak link, he might try to neutralize him, and that would not end well for Donovan. Paska was the only living person Morgana knew who could potentially best her.

"Do you think Paska would be capable of murder?" Donovan asked, his eyes suddenly hard and serious.

Morgana shook her head decisively. "Did you not hear what I said earlier? Anyone is capable of murder. Paska is as old as I am, and he takes an even longer view than me. He has killed before and likely will again. His morality is less...modern than yours. But if you're asking if he's the serial killer we're looking for, no."

"Why are you so certain?" Donovan asked.

"There is no reason for him to do it. He has all the power he needs."

The server appeared and deposited Donovan's beer with a flirty smile. "Does your...sister need another drink?" they asked him.

"I am not his sister, and I am perfectly capable of answering that question myself," Morgana said acerbically. "I would like another drink, but not this wine. Please bring me a glass of your best Irish whiskey, neat, and a glass of your darkest beer—Guinness, if you have it."

The server glanced at Morgana, turned back to Donovan, and asked, "Anything else?"

"You heard the lady," Donovan said easily, then winked. "Thank you very much."

After one more hard look at Morgana, the server stalked away.

"You were rude to them," Donovan observed. "Why?"

"I dislike being talked about as if I didn't exist. That doesn't happen when I am allowed to dress as myself." Morgana glared after the server.

"You don't wear your disguise well if you can't act the way that fits with your look. Shouldn't you be quieter and more acquiescent? If you'd let me speak, I would've informed them that you were my secretary and not my sister and ordered you another glass of wine. Or perhaps a cosmo. Either of those drinks would match who you're trying to be." Amusement danced in his eyes. "I think you were jealous."

Morgana scoffed. "The only thing I'm jealous of is you getting the respect that I deserve."

"You tell yourself the stories that help you sleep at night, sweetheart." Donovan looked up as the server approached and smiled broadly at them, then looked pointedly at Morgana.

She pasted a smile on her lips and took a deep breath. When the server set the whiskey and beer on the table, none-too-gently, Morgana said, "Thank you so much, and I apologize for my temper earlier. My colleague and I were having a disagreement, and I shouldn't have taken it out on you, no matter how relieved I am to not have to see him at family reunions."

The server smiled at Morgana, and the expression lit up their face. "Apology accepted. I totally get it. Work conflict can be a pain in the ass, for sure." They dropped a piece of paper on the table in front of Donovan and walked away.

Donovan unfolded it and grinned. "They gave me their number."

"You're old enough to be their father," Morgana pointed out, the edge back in her voice.

"Which is why I won't be calling them. But it's nice to know that an old man like me can still get a couple numbers." Donovan took a long drink of his beer, then looked down at the folders they'd closed while ordering their drinks. "How do you want to work this?"

Morgana pursed her lips. "I wish you were still in Europe. I know you think Hazel will be too great a lure to resist, but the last string of murders was all in Ireland. It would be good to have you following up those leads."

"A colleague of mine is in the area and will let me know if anything comes up there. It won't be unwatched. And neither will you." Donovan leaned back and crossed his long legs at the ankle.

"I'd like to find them before anyone else dies. And as much as I hate to agree with you, Hazel is our best bet. So, how do we keep an eye on her without putting off any potential killers?" Morgana took a drink of her whiskey but didn't take her eyes off Donovan.

"I think there's really only one way. You'll have to move in with me so we can have a torrid affair. That should throw the killer off their game," Donovan said seriously.

Morgana paused with her drink halfway between her mouth and the table. "How would pretending to have a torrid affair throw anyone off their game?"

"Obviously pretending wouldn't work. We'd actually have to spend a lot of time in bed doing unspeakable things to each other." He licked his lips, and Morgana couldn't help following the path of his tongue.

"I think you are completely out of your mind." Her voice was huskier than it had been a couple minutes ago, and she felt an unwelcome flush rising from somewhere deep in the pit of her stomach.

Donovan shrugged. "It was worth a shot. Our best bet is to be a little too obvious about our investigation. Make whoever might be watching feel overconfident. I'll ask a lot of loud questions about strangers in town and buzz around the tourists asking if they've ever had any mysterious and unexplainable phenomena happen in their vicinity. You should alternately hover over Hazel and glare at anyone who comes near her and leave her completely alone."

"That's a good start, anyway," Morgana said. "But I'd like to develop something more concrete. We're not dealing with a random opportunist. We are dealing with someone ruthless enough to hunt women, drain their blood magically, and carve them up."

"I think you mean carve them up and then drain their blood. They'd have to be alive when the ritual started or the power wouldn't transfer with the blood," Donovan said.

Morgana knew that, but she hadn't wanted to say that out loud, even though avoiding the fact made her a lot less practical and pragmatic than she wanted to appear. "Of course. My point is, the person we are targeting is not an amateur, and they will have a lot of power at their disposal. I feel confident in my ability to stand against them unharmed, but I am less certain of yours."

"Sweetheart, you wound me," Donovan gasped, placing his hand over his heart. "I think I'll surprise you someday when you see how truly powerful I can be."

"I wait with bated breath," Morgana said with a smile. "But in the meantime, you'd better stay close."

"I love that we're back to my original plan of confusing the enemy with lots of wild, monkey sex."

Morgana stood, dropped a couple twenties on the table, and walked out. Donovan's laughter followed her out of the pub and to the parking lot.

fourteen

"I need a job."

Morgana looked up from the needlepoint she was pretending to do in Antonia's tea shop and stared at Hazel. "Why?"

"I've been here for two weeks. No one's tried to murder me, and I'm bored. Besides, if I'm going to stay with you for a while, I'd like to be able to contribute something." Hazel looked around the tea shop. "I wonder if Antonia needs a part-time assistant."

"I don't dear. I'm so sorry," Antonia called from the back of the shop.

"Ears like a bat," Morgana muttered. "Pretty good for an old lady."

"I heard that, Morgana," Antonia laughed. "Of course you knew I would, didn't you?"

Morgana laughed. Out of all the mundane folks in Oracle Bay, Antonia was her favorite. They'd spent hours together drinking tea and making the kind of small talk that revealed a lot more about a person than one would expect. She turned her attention back to Hazel. "If you want a job, we will find you a job. Do you want to work in the service industry? I suspect Bill is ready to hire another barista now that the tourist season has begun. There is also bartending and waiting tables. Both the Sleeping Inn and the Pour House have room for more employees."

"I have experience in bartending," Hazel said. "But I'd prefer to find a job that had fewer drunk men trying to grab my ass."

"I do not know if that would be a likely occurrence at the Sleeping Inn. We could certainly ask Russell about his experience. But there is no way that would happen at the Pour House. Something about that bar brings out the best behavior in everyone."

"Wasn't Ceri stabbed there?" Hazel asked.

"In almost everyone," Morgana amended. "You will not be touched inappropriately."

"No sexual harassment but possible attempted murder. Still better than some jobs I've had." Hazel cracked a grin. It was the first genuine smile Morgana had seen since they'd arrived.

"And what will Bridget do while you're busy at work?" Morgana asked.

"I suspect she'll be sitting wherever it is I'm working and pretending not to watch me whenever you take a break from watching me." Hazel picked up her tea and stared into the cup. "I'd like you to read my fortune, Morgana. Could you do that here?"

"Not with that cup. Antonia's tea leaves stay firmly in the tea strainer where they belong. But if you truly want me to, I can make you some tea back at home and see what the leaves tell me." Morgana eyed Hazel cautiously.

Many people with magical powers liked the idea of tasseography in the abstract but became nervous when the plans became more concrete. It was less exciting to know one's future when one could feel the shifts and eddies of the world around them. Those with the power to understand the truth of a reading usually felt compelled to use that power to change their future. Even knowing there was nothing to be done, they would still look for magical solutions, driving themselves mad with impotence and driving themselves closer to the very future they were trying to avoid. "It is unlikely we will see who is responsible for the murder of your girlfriend. Nor will the leaves tell you if you will remain safe in Oracle Bay."

Hazel waved Morgana's caveats aside. "I've thought about approaching each of your friends. It seems to me that Ceri would have the best shot at seeing who was after me, at least if they were going to show up in my future. Scrying is the most visual, isn't it? That's not to say the other things are vague. Just..." She held her hand up palm down and wobbled it back and forth.

"And you don't want to see?" Morgana asked.

"Oh, I very much do, but Ceri said she's not doing that very much right now. I'm guessing that's primarily due to stabbing recovery. I didn't want to ask again." Hazel toyed with the small napkin that'd come with the small cakes they'd ordered with their tea.

"Drew would be another visual seer you could ask," Morgana suggested.

Hazel wrinkled her nose as she thought. "I'd forgotten about him."

"He would be devastated to hear that," Morgana said. "Out of all of us here, he is the one who most enjoys attention."

"If you think it'd better to ask him..." Hazel let her voice trail off.

"I have no thoughts on what would be better or worse. I only want you to think through your options. After all, there is nothing stopping you from asking each of us and seeing how the predictions intersect." Morgana drained her tea.

Hazel grimaced. "I could, I suppose. But I don't think I have enough money to pay for more than one. Another reason I need a job. I didn't have much saved up from my last job yet."

"I won't charge you. I can't speak for the others, but I don't think they would, either." Morgana would talk to them ahead of any contact Hazel made and tell them not to. She could, and she would insist upon it, cover the cost of whatever services Hazel wanted.

"That doesn't seem fair," Hazel protested.

"We are colleagues. It is a fair exchange. I will read for you, and at some point, I might need your magical abilities to come to my aid."

"You'll be waiting a long time. I don't have much in the way of magical abilities at all. All I can really do is change my face when I'm scared, and sometimes make people's clothes fall off. I just thought I was a weirdo." Hazel's smile was wry, but there was pain in her eyes that was older than the recent sting of loss.

This was new information and something that should've come up before. "How did you discover you were more than a 'weirdo'?"

Hazel laughed nervously. "It's funny, actually. I went to have my fortune told at a little booth at a fair in Galway when Rowan and I were visiting. The gentleman was a palm reader, and he gave me the usual stuff. You know, 'You'll meet a tall, dark, and handsome stranger who will sweep you off your feet, live a long time, have a good love life, and give birth to a million babies.' When I walked out, I told Rowan that he was a fraud who should be ashamed, and he'd better hope he was never exposed for being a charlatan. His booth fell down around him, and his clothes disappeared."

"Exposing him to everyone around him." Morgana laughed. "That is a wonderful story."

"There were a bunch of nuns on the street, and the poor man was even more embarrassed at that. The nuns came over and told me that was one of the best things they'd seen in a long time. I didn't understand why they were telling me until one of them pointed out that I'd made it happen." Hazel grimaced a bit.

"And you didn't believe her?" Morgana guessed.

"Why would I?" Hazel's eyes darted around the room, and her voice dropped to a whisper. "Should we be talking about this here? Antonia…"

"You don't have to be shy around me, dear." The elderly woman's voice floated serenely from the back of the shop. "I've lived in Oracle Bay my entire life. I know the truth."

"Was it Bridget who spoke to you?" Morgana asked.

Hazel shook her head. "No, it was Sister Mary Joseph. She's not a member of Willow Grove, but all the nuns at the convent know about it and about magic. I don't even know if Bridget was on that trip. The nun gave me a business card and said that if I was ever in the area to give her a call and come visit. She had some people she wanted me to meet."

"And since the convent was close to where you lived in Carrick-on-Shannon, you did so." When Hazel nodded, Morgana continued. "I am interested in the tale of how an American girl from Las Vegas ended up in a tiny town in the middle of Ireland. I wonder if it has any bearing on this story."

Hazel shrugged. "It isn't a very interesting story. I met a girl who was in Vegas for her friend's bachelorette party, and I followed her back to Ireland."

"That was Rowan? I didn't realize you'd met in the States." Movement in the street on the other side of the large plate-glass window caught Morgana's eye, and she sighed in resignation as a tall man wearing tight blue jeans and a tighter red t-shirt saw her and changed direction.

"It wasn't," Hazel laughed. "It was another woman from an even smaller village in County Leitrim. When things didn't work out, I hitchhiked to Carrick-on-Shannon and used the last of my money to take a place at a boarding house and get a job at the supermarket. That's where I met Rowan."

The bell over the door tinkled lightly as Donovan walked in.

"Morgana, Hazel. What a surprise to see you both here!" Donovan grinned broadly at them, then pulled a chair close to their table and sat down.

"We were just leaving," Morgana said. She didn't despise him as much as she had when they'd first met, but he had a way of getting under her skin and raising a blush, and she wasn't interested in showing him or Hazel how much he affected her.

"That's a real shame. Can I offer to escort you ladies to your next destination?" His grin was free and easy, but the wink he aimed at Morgana made her toes curl in a most unbecoming manner.

"That won't be necessary, Chief Davies," Morgana said, trying and failing to keep the bite out of her voice.

Hazel stood and held a hand out to Donovan. "Morgana is being stubborn. We'd love your company. We were going to Title Wave to see how the new owner is coming along." She glanced at Morgana. "Maybe they're hiring? I've always wanted to work in a bookstore."

"If it's a job you're after, I could use some help in the police station," Donovan said. "The officers that are currently employed by the town are next to useless, and it would be wonderful to have someone help me go through the paperwork to see if I can figure out what's been going on here."

Hazel wrinkled her nose and slipped her arm through Donovan's. "Thanks but no thanks. I'd rather deal with drunken groping than paperwork. If the bookstore doesn't pan out, I'll see if the Pour House is hiring. The people there seemed pretty nice, and what are the chances there'd be another stabbing there so soon?"

"Suit yourself," Donovan said. "I don't know why a person would rather pour drinks than dig through police files, but we can't all like the same things."

Hazel laughed again. "I'm a weirdo, all right. Now, let's go look at the books."

Morgana and Donovan sat in the Pour House alcove, surreptitiously watching Hazel's first day behind the bar. Morgana wouldn't have hesitated to threaten Andy into hiring her if it'd been necessary, but Brandy had already decided to expand the staff again and was more than happy to hire someone with experience waiting tables in Vegas casinos.

"Are you expecting the rest of your band of misfits?" Donovan asked.

Morgana nodded. "They should be here any moment. I'm surprised no one is yet. They are the nosiest group of humans I have ever met."

"If they can see the future, why bother being curious? Can't you just look at a card or a hand or the stars and find out without ever leaving the comfort of one's home?" Donovan's voice held a teasing note, so Morgana obliged him by rolling her eyes at him.

"Some of us like leaving our homes," Misty said, sliding onto the chair next to Morgana. "And reading the future of my own life and timeline is confusing. When I'm looking at my own...hands, my mind is jumping from potential future to potential future, and I can't get a fix on anything. It's easier when it's a stranger—they can't see what I'm seeing, only what I'm telling them, so they fixate on my words instead of possibilities."

"That makes sense," Donovan said. "I wouldn't have thought of it that way."

"Psychics tend to be loath to use their powers to read their friends and acquaintances," Morgana said. "We seldom do, and never without explicit permission."

"It's not unlike spying or eavesdropping," Paska said. He crowded in on the other side of the table, pushing Donovan closer to the back wall. "And we all know that spies and eavesdroppers are some of the worst folks around."

He didn't look at Morgana when he said it, but she saw the corner of his mouth quirk up. He did know who she was working for, and probably what was going on right now. If it was completely up to her, she'd pull him into her confidence. Paska saw more than anyone she knew and would probably spot the black magic user in seconds if he could be arsed to look.

Donovan's expression went from curious and amused to tense. "That's an interesting turn of phrase," he said to Paska.

"It's all just words, boy. Words don't mean anything more than you think they do." Paska looked at Donovan, his eyes wide in innocent amusement.

Hazel interrupted what threatened to become a tense exchange by popping into the alcove. She placed a bottle of wine and a single glass in front of Morgana, a bottle of Scotch and a pitcher of beer in front of Paska, along with a tumbler and a pint glass, and a pint of beer in front of Donovan. Then she looked at Misty. "Sorry, Zeke didn't know what you'd want. I can take your order now if you'd like."

Misty pursed her lips. "Is the Pearly Gates Pale still on tap?"

Hazel nodded. "Along with the Broken Halo Bitter, St. Peter's Pilsner, an Inferno IPA, Storm Clouds Cream Ale, and Eve's Bite cider."

"Why don't you bring a couple pitchers of the pale along with eight pint glasses. I'll share with the next few people who show up, and we'll order more if we need it." Misty eyed Paska's bottle and pitcher. "Unless Paska feels compelled to share what he has."

"This is my order. You'll have to make do with your own." He filled the tumbler with Scotch and took a healthy swig, then followed it with the stout.

"You can bring a couple more wine glasses, too," Morgana said. "I don't mind sharing."

Hazel smiled. "Two pitchers of the pale, eight pint glasses, and two wine glasses. Can I assume waters all around as well?"

"That'd be great," Misty said. "Thanks."

"No water for me," Paska said. "I don't want anything diluting what I'm drinking."

Donovan's eyes were wide, and he looked between Paska and Morgana as if to confirm what he was seeing.

Morgana hid a smile behind her hand as she poured herself a glass of wine. It's not that Paska didn't typically have this order at the Pour House, but he always ensured that he made a production of it in front of new people.

"You must have an interesting bar tab," Donovan finally said.

"New person pays for the table," Paska said. "And you need to know that Morgana and I only drink the top shelf stuff."

"Stop teasing him, old man," Ceri said, sliding in beside Paska, who obliged by scooting closer to Donovan, who was forced to shuffle his chair a little further over. She looked at Donovan but didn't quite meet his eyes. "We drink free in the Pour House, a fact that Paska continually takes advantage of because he's a cantankerous old man."

"Aw, lassie. You say the sweetest things." Paska raised his pint glass in a toast to her. "You always know the way to my heart."

Ceri grabbed his glass of Scotch and took a drink, then shuddered. "I don't know how you drink so much of this stuff."

"You develop a taste for the good stuff as you get older. Maybe someday you'll spend less time with cheap whiskey and cheap men and give me a second glance." Paska winked broadly at Ceri, and she laughed.

"Keep dreaming, old man. That age gap doesn't work for me, though."

"How old are you?" Donovan asked.

Paska's jovial mask slipped. "You might be young, but you should know better than to ask that question when you're among the magically inclined."

Donovan's already russet skin reddened even further. "You're right, and I'm sorry. I mostly work with people who are the age they appear and hearing her—" he pointed with his pint glass at Ceri, who flinched and tried to cover it with another swig of Paska's whiskey "—call you 'old man' threw me off for a moment."

Drew and Jezebel arrived in the moment of silence that followed Donovan's apology.

"Hey all," Jez said, looking around. "Are there drinks coming?"

"Right behind you," Hazel announced.

"Let me get out of your way," Jezebel said. She grabbed the chair next to Misty while Drew sat next to Ceri.

"Who are we still waiting for?" Donovan asked while Misty, Drew, and Jezebel filled their glasses.

"Russell and Sandy," Misty said. "Sandy texted me a couple minutes ago to say she was going to be late. And Russell is almost always the last one here. I think he does it just to tweak Morgana."

"I resent that very much," Russell said.

"I feel like I'm at the beginning of the Hobbit," Donovan muttered.

Misty smiled and leaned forward. "Yes! More just keep popping in without a by-your-leave."

"And it wouldn't be out of the realm of possibility to have an ancient wizard show up," Paska said.

"You're the ancient wizard," Ceri said. "Take a vacation to somewhere mundane, grow yourself a beard, buy a bathrobe, and you'd fit the part perfectly."

"Why would he need a vacation?" Donovan asked.

Ceri licked her lips, then grabbed an empty pint glass and filled it from Paska's pitcher. Morgana watched the exchange. Paska didn't protest the way he would've if anyone else had done it. Something had changed between Ceri and Paska during Ceri's recent near descent into madness. They'd developed a deep friendship. Morgana wasn't sure she'd ever seen Paska have such an easy friendship with anyone. At least not for a millennium and a half, anyway. It was good for him to have this, and she was happy for him.

Donovan looked around the table at the psychics who were all busy filling glasses, checking phones, and looking out into the main bar.

"Another sensitive question," Donovan guessed. "Maybe someday you'll let me in on a few of your secrets."

"Maybe someday you won't be a cop and a witch hunter," Drew said with a shrug. "You might be sitting with us, and maybe Morgana vouched for you, but you're not one of us."

"Ouch," Donovan said easily. "But don't worry, Drew Hardy. I'm here on a limited-term contract. And once I've saved the girl and earned the town's gratitude, I'll be heading out on the next stagecoach."

"Sorry I'm late!" Sandy said, hopping up the single stair into the alcove and shoving into the space next to Jezebel.

This caused a dominoes effect of pushing everyone a little further around until Morgana felt herself pushed up against Donovan.

Morgana stiffened a bit, then saw Paska's smirk from across the table. She forced herself to relax and ignore the frisson of electricity that jolted her system from where her thigh pressed against Donovan's. Attraction was a normal part of being alive, and there was no reason to feel uncomfortable. He was a good-looking man, and it was natural that she'd notice. She didn't have to do anything about it other than enjoy the moment.

Sandy opted for a glass of wine, then looked around the table. "So, what are we talking about?"

MORGANA PUSHED HERSELF AS FAR BACK INTO THE CORNER AS SHE COULD, snagging the bottle of wine off the table and refilling her glass. Donovan joined her with a glass of water.

"How do you stay so sharp after that much wine?" he asked quietly under the sound of the chatter around the table. "I had two pints of beer and felt guilty, even though I'm not on duty right now."

Morgana took a sip. "Practice."

"Let me guess, another Oracle Bay secret?" Donovan sighed. He adjusted his position on his chair, and his arm brushed against the side of her breast.

She inhaled sharply, then cursed at herself. There was no way she was going to be able to explain the reaction away.

"Sorry," Donovan said. "I didn't mean to...bother you that way."

"It's forgotten already," Morgana said evenly.

"That's a shame. I'd hope I could make a more lasting impression on you than that." The flirtatious, teasing note that'd been absent the last couple weeks was back in his voice.

Morgana didn't take the time to think about what she wanted to say and went with the impulse she seldom gave into. "If you want to make a lasting impression, it'll take more than an accidental brush."

Donovan didn't answer right away, and the silence between them was filled with the sound of oohs and ahhs from the table, signaling that Drew was showing off pictures of his kittens.

Morgana started to think she'd read the situation wrong and offended him. She took a risk and looked up. He was looking down at her with a hot, hungry expression. The frissons of electricity that'd been taking periodic trips through her body every time they'd brushed against each other centered low in her core, and for a moment she thought she had to be glowing from the heat it generated.

"I'd like nothing more than to create a lasting impression," Donovan said in a deep, husky voice that expertly plucked the strings of her desire.

Morgana's pulse increased. "I have houseguests," she said.

"I don't. My apartment isn't much, but it is empty." His eyes focused on her lips, and she licked them unconsciously. He groaned softly. "If I'm not going to embarrass myself, I need to get out of here soon. Join me?"

Morgana looked around. No one appeared to be taking any notice of their quiet conversation, but she knew she would not be that lucky. Every single person at the table, with the possible exceptions of Sandy and Misty, knew exactly what was happening between Morgana and Donovan. She decided she no longer cared. To hell with discipline and appearances, at least for a little while. Fear and excitement gripped her, quickening her pulse even more, as she opened her mouth to ask the question that would mean she was giving in to the desire rather than maintaining control. "Later?"

"What, don't fancy rushing out of here like a couple teenagers who can't control their hormones?" He laughed. "Or is it that you don't want people to think you'd stoop so low as to run off with me?"

Shattering glass reverberated through the alcove, saving Morgana from having to answer.

"Hazel," Sandy gasped. "She's... Is she?"

Morgana was on her feet and trying to shove past the people blocking her in before Sandy finished her sentence. Donovan didn't even try to get by the psychics. He hopped onto the table and was across in one long step without disturbing any of the drinks or spilling a drop.

Hazel was standing in the middle of the floor surrounded by three perfect concentric circles. The middle circle was comprised of broken pint glasses that'd been pulled into an ellipse of broken glass and spilled beer. The outer circle was inch-high flames flickering without any fuel. The inner circle was nearly invisible. In fact, Morgana suspected it was invisible to anyone who didn't have the ability to see into the next plane.

In the center, Hazel was shaking with tears running down her face. Every single person in the packed bar was staring at her with mouths open.

"Holy shit," Russell said. "I always wanted to know what would happen if a server dropped a tray full of Flaming Dr. Peppers, and now I know." He beat Donovan to her by half a step and earned glares from both the new Chief of Police and the bar manager. He didn't touch Hazel, though, and neither did Donovan.

The fire disappeared as fast as it'd sprung up, and Andy strode across the room. "I've got this Brandy," he said to his bar manager.

The rest of the psychics had gathered in the opening of the alcove, and Morgana could feel their alertness vibrating against her. Ceri walked forward to stand next to Andy. She slipped a hand into his. "You know, last time you had a server break a lot of glasses, she tried to stab me."

Morgana shook her head. "You will not get stabbed today, Ceridwen." She passed Donovan and Russell and reached past the barrier around Hazel and put an arm around the young woman. She felt the moment Hazel let go of the shield that'd sprung up instinctively to protect her. "Why don't you come sit with us for a moment? Russell and Zeke will clean up this mess while you gather your composure."

"I don't work here, you know," Russell said as he headed towards the bar.

"But you're good at cleaning up bar messes," Morgana said, leading Hazel towards the alcove. "Stop by when you're done. I think you're going to be more help than I'd anticipated."

Hazel sat down. Her arms were trembling so badly, she couldn't hold the glass of water Donovan pushed in front of her. She wrapped her arms around herself, pushing up her sleeves in the process.

Morgana grabbed her left wrist and pulled her arm out straight.

In the space between her wrist and elbow were rapidly fading runes. "Someone take a picture," she snapped.

Three cellphone clicks followed almost immediately.

"Send them to Morgana and me," Donovan instructed, then met Morgana's eyes. "Guess I was right."

Guilt flooded Morgana's system. Donovan had been right, not only that the killer would follow Hazel to Oracle Bay, but that they'd be cocky enough to try to take her in front of Morgana and Donovan. If she hadn't been seducing the witch hunter, they might've been able to prevent this attempt—or at least follow the attack back to the source. The blood witch wasn't the only one who was overconfident.

She wouldn't make that mistake again. She glanced at Donovan. His attention was focused on his cellphone, probably studying the pictures. No. She wouldn't make that mistake again, no matter how much she wanted him.

sixteen

Donovan and Morgana flanked Hazel at Morgana's kitchen table. A pot of herbal tea sat in the middle of the table steeping, and no one talked.

"Hi!" Bridget called, sweeping into the room. "I've had the most marvelous day trip. Thank you for lending me your car, Morgana, although I just about abandoned it to try to learn how to fly a broomstick when I got to that horrible bridge across the Columbia River. I hate the water so much, but Astoria was worth it."

She skidded to a stop and took in the grim faces around the table. "Is something wrong?"

Hazel laughed, and there was more than a light note of hysteria in her voice. "I'm the best bait, it turns out."

Bridget swung her gaze to Morgana. "She was attacked? Where?"

"At the Pour House," Morgana said shortly. "Right in the middle of the bar."

Bridget gasped. "How is that possible?"

"I don't know," Morgana said. And the truth of that statement galled more than anything.

Donovan stood and paced the length of the kitchen. "We vastly underestimated the power and sheer cockiness of the blood witch. We weren't even supposed to be at the Pour House. I was invited to a psychic mixer, and at the last minute, the venue changed from Drew's house to the Pour House."

"It's a good thing it did," Morgana said. "And that's one of the many benefits of having a bunch of psychics around. A lot of times we're in the right place at the right time because someone had a weird feeling."

Hazel laughed again, although this time it was steadier. "Wherever the fire came from was the big help. I could feel something cold closing in on me, and it was starting to get through whatever it was that I wrapped around myself, but the flames just burned the cold away." She shivered, then her eyes widened. "Do you think I'm fired?"

"I doubt it," Morgana said. "Andy hardly ever fires anyone. In fact, I think the only time he did was when one of his servers stabbed his girlfriend."

"So as long as I don't kill anyone while I'm on the clock, I'm okay?" Hazel asked.

Morgana could tell she was trying to pull the conversation back to lighter topics, and for now, that was okay. "You might be able to kill a lot of people without getting fired. Just don't kill Ceri. Or Brandy."

"Will you lot be serious?" Bridget demanded. She dropped into a chair and poured four cups of tea. "Tell me about what you wrapped around yourself, and I definitely want to know more about the fire. Maybe we've made a mistake keeping her untrained. If you're right, and she'll be a target regardless, there's no reason she shouldn't be able to defend herself with more than luck and instinct."

Morgana nodded. "You're right. Do you want to work with her on some rudimentary shielding and defense? When you think she's come along far enough, I'll take over with some of the more advanced training so she can follow the magic back to the caster."

"That's dangerous," Bridget objected. "If it goes wrong, she could open herself up to further attack."

"That's why it's advanced work," Morgana retorted. "And that's why I'll teach her instead of you."

Bridget inhaled sharply, and Morgana watched tears form at the corners of the other woman's eyes.

"I'm sorry," Morgana said. "I shouldn't take my ire at myself out on you. You're correct that any offensive magics would be counterproductive to our goal of keeping Hazel safe. Why don't you work together tomorrow morning. I know you'll do an excellent job."

"Um, hi. Do I get a say in this at all?" Hazel asked timidly.

"Of course," Morgana said at the same time Bridget snapped, "No!"

Hazel looked back and forth between them.

Donovan stopped pacing in front of Hazel and squatted down. "You do get a say, but if you're going to turn down the training, I think we'd all like to know why."

"I wasn't going to say no. I just hate being talked about and decided for when I'm sitting right here." Hazel stuck her tongue out at Morgana.

Morgana was pleased Hazel felt comfortable around her, but this was a level of familiarity she wasn't used to.

"It is decided then," Morgana said. "Why don't you stay here for the rest of the day. I will head back to the Pour House to see if I can find any other sign of who attacked you. You'll be safe here with Bridget as long as neither of you leave the house."

"Why?" Hazel asked.

"It's warded," Donovan said. "Maybe your first lesson should be figuring out how to sense that. Bridget, you can feel it, right?"

Bridget nodded uncertainly, and Morgana had to resist the urge to roll her eyes.

"If you can't, you need the practice as much as Hazel does," Morgana said. "You're certainly powerful enough to feel it." At least the main one. Morgana had so many shields and wards layered on her house, and only one was magically overt enough to be sensed. The rest would go completely unnoticed by all but the most powerful witches, and the two that protected her basement workspace and backyard sanctuary would only be felt by someone of ill-intent. They were higher-powered versions of the spell she'd cast in Kilnamanagh six hundred years ago, and rather than being tied to the land, they were tied to her.

"Do you want me to stay with you and Bridget while Morgana goes on her magical fact-finding mission?" Donovan asked.

"No, you're the cop. You should probably be at the scene of the crime," Hazel said. "I'll be safe enough with Bridget here in Morgana's magically impregnable house."

"It's not impregnable," Morgana said severely. "Just nearly so. Don't get cocky."

"You got it, boss!" Hazel said, shooting finger guns towards the older witch.

Morgana shook her head but let a small smile slide across her face. She turned and walked out of the kitchen, calling back over her shoulder, "Are you coming, Donovan Davies?"

MORGANA CURSED AT HER STUPID SKIRT AND STUPIDER SHOES AS SHE TRIED to walk quickly along the sidewalk back towards the bar. Donovan pulled up beside her in the pickup he'd driven her and Hazel back to Morgana's house in.

"Do you want a ride?"

"I'm fine," Morgana said. Her heel wobbled on a crack in the sidewalk, and she cursed. "Yes, I'd like a ride. These shoes are not made for walking." She opened the door and climbed up into the cab.

"What do you want to do about where things were headed earlier?" Donovan asked.

Morgana stared straight ahead. "Nothing. It was a moment of

weakness, and my inattention—our inattention—nearly got Hazel killed."

"Even if we hadn't been flirting in the back corner of the bar, I don't think either of us would have seen the attack before it happened." Donovan looked over at her, then pulled out onto the street. "You want me."

"It doesn't matter," Morgana said, dismissing his words with a wave of her hand. "I want a lot of things that I don't give into. And you don't know that I wouldn't have been able to stop the attack and figure out where it was coming from if I'd been paying attention."

Donovan sighed. "You're killing me, Morgana. Life is short—why not do the things that'd make you happy?"

Morgana barked out a laugh. "My life is anything but short. I'm sixteen hundred years old, Donovan Davies. You can't talk me into bed with my imminent mortality. Save that for a woman on her first lifetime."

Donovan slammed on the brakes, bringing the pickup to a screeching halt. He pulled over to the side of the road and twisted to look at Morgana. "I'm sorry, did you say sixteen hundred years? That's not what you told me before."

"I said over a hundred," Morgana reminded him. "And sixteen is more than one. Does that help you bury your desire for me?" Morgana wasn't sure why she was so upset at the thought of her age being a deterrent. After all, this was what she wanted, wasn't it? To get him to stop looking at her like he did and melting her tenuous resistance.

"And you said Paska is the same age as you. Are the rest of them that old, too?" Donovan sounded dazed.

Morgana smiled sympathetically. Finding out lifespans weren't necessarily as cut and dried as you'd always believed tended to be a bit of a shock. Donovan might've been willing to believe she was a hundred and ten years old—witches had the ability to extend their lives, often even doubling them—but sixteen hundred years was nearly incomprehensible.

"No. I will not give you a rundown on everyone's ages, but there are a couple in the group who are exactly how old they appear to be, and a couple who are older, but none of the other psychics are as old as Paska and me."

"Why are you here?" Donovan asked. He turned off the ignition and stared at the steering wheel.

"Do you mean here with you, here in Oracle Bay, or here on earth still alive?" Morgana asked.

"All three, I guess. It sounds impossible, but I don't know why you'd lie. If you were trying to reject my advances, there'd be a lot easier ways to do it. Like tell me you're a chlamydia-riddled vampire." Donovan laughed softly at his joke, then turned to look at Morgana. "Are you immortal? Are you a vampire?"

Morgana pointed at the sun. "Not a vampire. And I'm not immortal, as far as I know. It's been a long time since I was close enough to death to wonder if this is the time I'd lose. I don't know why I'm so old. At least not exactly."

"You don't trust me with your secrets," Donovan said bluntly. "It's fine. The amount of time you've known me must barely register on your timeline."

"I'm in Oracle Bay because it's a haven for psychics. I feel at home here. The Washington coast reminds me a lot of where I grew up. Wild storms and rocky coasts soothe my soul. And I'm in your pickup because you offered me a ride to the Pour House so we could continue our investigation." Morgana tried to catch his eye, but he turned away from her and started the car.

"Right. Back to work." Donovan drove the rest of the way to the bar without saying anything.

After parking in the nearly empty parking lot, Donovan said, "I'm glad you told me. It's weird. Like really weird. But I want you to know that as long as you're not a chlamydia-riddled vampire, my offer still stands." Heat blazed from his eyes, melting away Morgana's defenses. He really was a beautiful man, and it'd been a long time since anyone looked at her like that.

Before she could think about what she was doing and talk herself out of it, she unbuckled her seatbelt and slid across the bench seat until she was pressed up against his side. She licked her lips and slid one hand up his chest, across his shoulder, and then cupped his face.

He leaned towards her and brushed his lips over hers.

Morgana threaded her fingers into his hair and held him in place when he tried to back away.

"Don't start anything you won't finish," Donovan whispered, his lips brushing hers with each word. "I won't do anything you don't want me to do, but if you kiss me again, I can't promise we won't be making out in a pickup like a couple teenagers within thirty seconds."

"Do you think so little of my self-control?" Morgana asked.

He didn't answer. Instead, he parted his lips and delicately traced the shape of hers with his tongue.

A dam burst in Morgana. She'd spent centuries holding herself back—even when she was in the throes of passion, she was always in control. She no longer wanted to be in control, not for a little while, anyway.

She pulled herself onto his lap with her free hand and pulled his face closer with the hand still tangled in his hair. She brushed his lips, then opened her mouth and deepened her exploration.

There was no control, no gentleness, in their kiss. It was heat and passion and rough mouths exploring each other.

Donovan's hands found her hips, and he pulled her against him.

She groaned and leaned back to slide one leg across his lap until she was straddling him. Ripping fabric had her cursing against his lips as a seam in her too-tight skirt tore.

Donovan pushed her skirt up until it bunched around her waist, then pulled her closer to him, rocking her against him.

Morgana fumbled at the hem of his t-shirt, trying to lift it out of the way. She leaned back, breaking their kiss and making him groan, to give herself more room to work, and leaned directly into the horn on the steering wheel.

The loud honk pulled her back to her senses, and she dropped his shirt.

"Oh my goddess," she whispered. "What are we doing?"

"Making out like a couple of teenagers in the front seat of my pickup?" Donovan asked. "I warned you this was likely to happen." He shifted under her, and the evidence of his desire for her made her moan.

"It's broad daylight. Anyone could walk by and see us." Morgana slid off his lap, brushing over his erection with her panty-hose clad leg.

It was Donovan's turn to moan. "This isn't finished. Please tell me this isn't finished."

"This is finished. For now," Morgana said. "But when we're done here, I want a tour of your bedroom and every other room in your apartment." She pulled her skirt back down and winced when she saw the seam that'd split.

"You managed to make that skirt sexy," Donovan said. "It's going to be hard to keep my mind on the job when you have that much leg on display."

Morgana rolled her eyes at him, then ran a finger along the seam. The tear disappeared.

"Nice," Donovan said. "Although I did like it the other way better."

"Are you ready to go in?" Morgana asked, ignoring the leer he was directing her way.

Donovan glanced down at his lap. "Not quite yet. But that'll give you time to fix your lipstick. I hope you have some tissues in your purse, because if your lipstick is that messed up, I'm willing to bet I'm wearing at least a little of it."

Morgana pulled out a small compact, a handful of tissues, and her shell-pink lipstick out of her purse and set about fixing her face. The pink might not be her preferred color, but it was a lot easier to clean up than her typical red.

She reached across the space between them to wipe the traces of lipstick from Donovan's mouth. He caught her wrist and kissed her palm. "You're an amazing woman, Morgana. Even in that get-up, you're the sexiest thing I've ever seen."

Morgana blushed a little, then pulled her hand back. "Thank you. You're not bad yourself, Donovan Davies."

She opened the door and hopped down, then followed Donovan into the bar.

seventeen

Most of the mundane customers who'd been in the bar when they'd left to take Hazel home were gone. The psychics had regrouped in the main seating area.

Paska caught her eye when she got close, flicked his glance between her and Donovan, then frowned.

"I'm going to look around," Donovan said. "Why don't you do your thing, and we'll regroup far away from your nosy friends."

"I'll 'do my thing' with my nosy friends. You may join us when you're done. If you're good." Morgana smiled up at the man towering over her, and her pulse sped up again.

"Oh, I think you know I'm good." Donovan smirked down at her.

Morgana shook her head sadly. "If that's all it took for me to render a judgment, I wouldn't be following you home later. I hope that wasn't the best you could do."

"Sweetheart, you have no idea how much better it's gonna get when I have you alone and out of those blasted shiny tights." Donovan winked and turned around, heading to the bar where Brandy sat in her customary spot on her laptop.

Morgana pushed down the flames of desire that were licking the edges of her consciousness. She glanced around. Donovan was busy questioning Brandy, and the psychics, although aware of her presence, weren't paying any attention to her.

She took the chance to walk back into the middle of the bar and look one more time for anything they might have missed.

Nothing appeared out of the ordinary. Then, she closed her eyes and reached out with her other senses and repeated the rotation, this time making sure she looked at the ceiling and floor. She was just about to walk away satisfied, when a shimmer at the end of the bar caught her eye.

She walked closer and opened her eyes, examining it on the magical and mundane planes at the same time. It looked like a... piece of glass. A glass bead, maybe?

Morgana crouched and examined it. It was a bead, but crystal, not glass. She'd have to examine it in the light, but she was pretty sure it was crystal quartz, and it glimmered with power.

Morgana pulled it out from where it was wedged into the wood, slipped it into her pocket, then did another sweep through the bar. When she didn't see anything else, she walked over to where her friends were scattered loosely around one of the big communal tables in the center of the bar.

"Did you find something?" Russell asked.

"Nothing worth mentioning," she replied. "Just an old bead that's probably been under the bar for ages."

"Is Hazel okay?" Sandy asked.

Morgana smiled at the young woman, grateful for the quick subject change. "She is. Bridget is back from her sightseeing trip and staying with her while Donovan and I see if we can figure out how it happened." Morgana flushed a little when she said Donovan's name and hoped no one else noticed. She wasn't ashamed of what she was doing. Not exactly. It just wasn't a good marker of how seriously she took this if she was making out with the chief of police in his pickup while they were mid-investigation. Mixing business with pleasure was something she'd never done in the entirety of her sixteen hundred years of life.

"None of us felt anything before she dropped the tray," Misty said. "We've gone back over the events in the last five minutes before Hazel was attacked. I took notes." She shoved them across the table to Morgana.

Morgana scanned the notes. There was nothing in there noteworthy except for one footnote. "Morgana and Donovan were flirting in the back corner and probably assuming no one noticed." Her lips tightened, and a ripple of laughter went around the table.

"She read the footnote," Sandy giggled. "It was mean to put it in."

"Mean but funny," Russell said. "My specialty."

Ceri heaved a dramatic sigh. "Now that you're here, we can get down to business. Andy's on his way down. Obviously, he's the only one who realized what was going on in time to actually do anything about it, so I assumed you'd want to talk to him."

"Most of us didn't feel anything even after we were alerted that something was happening," Paska said. "Russell felt something, and I'll let him tell you about it. I didn't notice anything until after you'd left. But a few minutes after you and Hazel walked out the door, I was probed by a dark, hungry power."

"I don't think we need to hear about your probing," Drew said seriously. "You have jumped across the TMI line and need to scurry back."

Paska didn't even look at Drew, although his statement elicited another chorus of giggles from everyone but Paska, Russell, and Morgana.

"I couldn't tell if it was looking at anyone else but me, but whoever or whatever this is, it's not just after Hazel anymore. I think they realized they're first in line at the buffet and are ready to start filling their plate." Paska looked around the table. "All of you could be in danger, but if I was going to pick the mostly likely to be targeted, I'd go after Ceri and Misty."

"Why me?" Misty asked. "I'd go after you and Morgana. I'm nowhere near as powerful as you two."

"Of course you're not," Morgana said smoothly. "But Paska and I are too powerful to be targeted."

Paska smirked. "I have more magic in my—"

"Stop," Ceri said. "I don't know what you were going to say, and I don't want to know. I know why it'd be me. I'm old and have had plenty of time to build up my reserves. A couple months ago, when I was drained, I wouldn't have been so defenseless, but now…"

"It'd actually be great if they went after you," Paska said, looking thoughtfully at Ceri. "I'd like to see them try to drain you."

"I wouldn't like that at all." Ceri glared at Paska.

"But when they got to the bottom of your well, think about what they'd pull next. There's no one here who could take a drink of infinity and survive. Not even your fallen angel." Paska's voice took on a dreamy quality, and not for the first time, Morgana wondered if he was dipping towards insanity.

"Okay, we've covered Ceri, but why me?" Misty asked. There was a thread of fear in her voice, and Morgana silently cursed Paska for saying anything. "Wouldn't Drew be a better choice?"

"You not only have your own power, but are connected to the magic of Oracle Bay," Morgana said. "When I look at you, you glow with the magic of both, and if I didn't know better, I wouldn't see the separation between the two. I don't worry about any of you, though. You are all shielded well enough, both by your own practice or instinctive shields and by the town. Oracle Bay has claimed each of you, and it will not easily give you up." Morgana looked around the room in time to see a young woman walk through the front doors.

The woman looked vaguely familiar, but Morgana couldn't place her.

She looked around, and when she spotted the group in the center of the room, she made a beeline for their table.

"Violet?" Sandy asked when the woman got closer. "I thought you were leaving town."

Violet smiled broadly. "I was going to leave today, but then I decided to hang out a while longer. It's such a cute town, and everyone is so friendly! And I love that all of you are friends and not competitors."

Morgana regarded the woman with narrowed eyes. She needed to get Donovan over here so he could look at Violet and see what untapped powers she had. "Violet, did you visit all of us?"

Violet nodded enthusiastically. "Well, you and Sandy, Misty, and Drew. The scrying shop has been closed, and I didn't know there were more guys besides Drew! Can I make appointments with the rest of you?"

"I'm not seeing clients right now," Ceri said. "I was recently ill and am not yet back into fortune telling shape."

"I don't see anyone without a five-thousand-dollar down payment and a background check." Paska looked her over. "Not even for someone trying to fill out her stamp book."

Violet's face fell, then she turned to Russell. "What about you? What do you do?"

"You can come see me whenever you want," he replied. "I'm a bartender at the Sleeping Inn. I work Wednesday through Sunday from five p.m. to close, and I can make you a fabulous cocktail."

"You're not a psychic?" Violet clasped her hands in front of her.

"Nope. Just a bartender. This group lets me hang out with them because I give them half-price martinis on Thursdays." Russell's grin was wide, and there wasn't a hint to betray his lie.

Violet pouted for a second. "Oh, well. I wanted to get a feel for what all of you could do, but I guess I'll have to settle for what I have. I really am hoping to get rid of my nightmares. You all gave excellent advice, and it was remarkably consistent. But now that I know you're all friends, maybe you had a phone tree to share information."

"I can promise you we do not have one of those," Morgana said. "There's not exactly client/psychic privilege, but we seldom discuss the querents we've seen."

Violet nodded solemnly. "Because it would violate the spirit of the visions."

Paska snorted. "No, because we see a lot of people, and when we're gathering like this, we prefer to talk about our own lives."

"Oh." Violet flushed and looked like she was going to burst into tears for a second.

"Don't be mean," Ceri said, then turned to Violet. "He isn't wrong, no matter how terrible his delivery is, though. It's exhausting to look into the future of so many people, and when we're not at work, it's easier and more restorative to talk about the other pieces of our lives, like our families, weekend plans, favorite new television shows."

"That makes sense. Listen, I'm meeting my husband here, and he just walked in. Sorry I bothered you, but I wanted to say hi again before we went back to Long Beach and the real world. It was so nice to meet you!" She waved, then hurried back to the bar where she slipped an arm around a red-haired man of medium height and build, then jumped on the barstool next to him.

"She was...friendly," Drew said.

"Too friendly," Paska growled. "Too many questions."

Misty rested her chin on her hand and tapped the side of her face. "Do you think she could possibly be our bad guy?"

"The timeline fits. She came to visit right after I returned with Hazel, and she's been to see all of us. She's from Long Beach but never drove the ten miles to Oracle Bay before now. And she's staying here, even though our towns are so close together. Also, she was in Ireland when Hazel's girlfriend was murdered. She doesn't feel like she has enough magic, even in potential, to steal other people's, but if she's been doing this long enough, she'd be able to mask it pretty well." Morgana looked thoughtfully at the woman's back.

"Could it be her husband?" Drew asked. "Or the two of them working together? She is too friendly, and he is just as obviously not friendly enough."

Morgana paused to think about it. She'd all but dismissed the idea of a man being the culprit—most cis men didn't cultivate the ability to sense the earth's magic, much less harness it, preferring to dismiss it as "women's magic." But working in tandem with someone? "It is unlikely," she said at last. "But according to Violet, he was the one obsessed with the mystical sites in Ireland. He could have been looking for witches. And it wouldn't be the first time an ordinary man has taken control of a woman, magical or not, for their own purposes. I can't rule it out, and this isn't something I want to be wrong about. If he is part of this, she might be in just as much danger from him as Hazel is from her."

"I'll keep an eye on her," Russell volunteered.

"I'm sure you will," Drew snorted. "We all saw the way you flirted with her."

Morgana tracked the way Russell's gaze darted to Brandy, then back to Drew. "Her virtue is safe with me. Besides, I'd never flirt with someone in a relationship."

"Don't be ridiculous," Ceri said. "I'll tell her she can schedule an appointment with me."

"You most certainly will not," Andy growled, stalking across the room and pulling a chair up next to Ceri.

Morgana leaned back and smiled. She enjoyed watching Andy try to tell Ceri what to do "for her own good" almost as much as she liked the idea of locking herself in her house with a bottle of wine and zero people for at least a week. Well...maybe not zero other people.

"I'm sorry. Are you trying to tell me what to do?" Ceri asked sweetly. "Is it because I'm 'your woman' and you need to protect me from the big, bad world?"

Andy's shoulders slumped. He'd already lost. "I just don't want you to do anything to strain yourself. You know what the doctor said about trying to see too much."

"Andy, Barachiel is an angelic himbo, not a doctor. And I'm not looking past any veils for Violet. I save the dangerous bits for my friends." Ceri patted Andy's cheek, and the look he gave her could've melted the whole table. Ceri stood and walked across the floor, had a brief conversation with Violet, then returned.

"I told her I could see her the day after tomorrow. She's now extending her stay, and I think her husband hates me. He doesn't think it's quaint here." Ceri shrugged. "I enjoy sowing a bit of chaos from time to time, so I don't mind. Now, figure out if it's her or not before she gets a chance to see me do my stuff."

"Should I be more worried? Should I lock up the magic goats and move in with you, Morgana?" Misty asked.

"No. Do not be more worried. You are surrounded by the town's magic as well as an ancient Etruscan's goat magic. You're probably the safest one here. And no one else is moving in with me." Morgana took a deep breath. "We got sidetracked by Violet's appearance. Russell, you felt something before Hazel was attacked?"

Russell nodded. "Right before she dropped the glasses, it felt like the veil dropped. It was a little like the way your stomach feels during severe turbulence or a rollercoaster. It dropped, and the room filled with the dead desperately trying to grab on to this side. As soon as Hazel dropped the glasses, though, the veil snapped back up."

"That's probably when her shields and Andy's fire sprang up," Morgana said. "And speaking of fire, how did you know what was happening and how to counter it? Hazel said the fire burned away the ice that was freezing the blood in her veins."

"I felt the veil disappear, too. When Hazel dropped the tray, the beer froze in mid-air before it hit the ground and shattered with the glasses. Fire seemed like the way to go." Andy shrugged. "Do Hazel or Donovan know it was me?"

Morgana shook her head. "No. They don't know who it was or what you are. For that matter, Bridget doesn't either. Some things are better held back."

"And if we are going to continue to hold some things back, we should change the subject now. Morgana's friend is returning from his investigations." Paska shot a look at Morgana that she couldn't interpret.

It wasn't the teasing mockery she'd seen earlier when she walked into the bar after making out with Donovan in the car. This was something darker, angrier.

"Do we need to chat, Paska?" Morgana asked quietly.

"It's been a while since we've had a heart-to-heart. Maybe you should stop by tomorrow morning before you head home," he replied in the same low tones.

"Before I head home from where?"

Paska glanced over his shoulder, and Morgana followed his gaze to Donovan. "You'll have a wonderful time, nothing bad will happen while you do, and then you'll come over for your penance tomorrow."

"I don't pay penance to you, Paska Cooper. My debt to you was paid eons ago." Ice built in her chest. "And now is not the time to talk about it."

"You are correct about the latter, and we can talk about the former in the morning. Go have your fun, Morgana. Your clock won't start ticking again until tomorrow." Paska stood and walked out of the bar without another word to anyone.

Morgana shook her head, suddenly feeling every one of her sixteen hundred years settle on her shoulders, and tried to let the dread at Paska's words settle below her subconscious. She hadn't lived this long to dwell on things that hadn't yet come to pass. "Everyone stay safe. Don't be alone. If you have a place that's warded or shielded, go there."

"I have three guest rooms at Joseph's place," Misty said. "And an Etruscan goddess who treats me like her daughter-in-law. If Morgana is right, that should be enough to protect us."

"If you don't mind, Vincent and I would love to come visit for a couple days," Sandy said hesitantly.

"Of course, that's why I offered. Jezebel, you should come too. Natalie's welcome if you want to invite her, of course."

"Natalie who?" Jezebel asked too quickly.

"Don't be ridiculous, everyone in this town knows Natalie,"

Misty said. "Besides, it's almost impossible to do anything in a town this size without being seen, much less when all your friends are psychic. Bring the butcher, but don't let Joseph catch her eyeing his goats."

Jezebel laughed ruefully. "I guess we can stop sneaking around, then. I wonder what the shelf life on a secret relationship is in this town."

"About fifteen minutes," Drew said with a sidelong look at Morgana.

"Andy and I will stay with Drew at Bill's house," Ceri announced.

"We will?" Andy asked. "Are you making decisions for me without consulting me first?"

"You will?" Drew asked. "And same question Andy just asked."

Ceri shrugged. "I'll apologize later. But for now, Andy and I are going home to grab our things. We'll be at Bill's by dinner time. Don't forget to let him know." She grabbed Andy's hand and pulled him out of the bar.

Drew shrugged. "That's us sorted, then. I'll check back in with everyone tomorrow." He followed Ceri out the door, passing Donovan as he returned to the table.

"Russell, you're obviously staying with me tonight," Misty said. "Don't argue. You're family, and I'm keeping you close. Besides, you're almost as useful as…" She glanced at Donovan, and her words trailed off. It didn't take her long to recover, and she continued, "You're almost as useful as Andy at a sleepover."

"Thanks, I think," Russell said. "Is this your way of hinting you want me to make you a cocktail when I show up at the farm?"

Russell, Sandy, Jezebel, and Misty walked out of the bar, the sound of Russell's and Misty's good-natured bickering following along.

"Was it something I said?" Donovan asked as he watched the rest of the psychics disappear. "Usually, I don't clear a room quite that quickly."

"I'll catch you up on everything, including our potential new suspect," Morgana said to Donovan. "But now, let's get out of here."

Donovan bowed slightly, and when he glanced back up at her, there was a twinkle in his eye. "I do like a woman who knows what she wants, and there is no shortage of those in this town."

"As long as you're keeping your eyes on me, at least for the time being," Morgana replied.

"You're all I see, sweetheart. You're all I see."

eighteen

Donovan pulled into the parking lot of the small apartment building where he was staying, and Morgana's nerves chose that minute to show up.

What was she doing? She couldn't remember the last time she'd jumped into bed with someone, much less after such a brief acquaintance.

"Second thoughts?" Donovan asked.

"At least," Morgana replied. "Although it is unlikely, it is still possible that you're the murderer in all this, and I am about to place myself in a very vulnerable position."

"You don't have to do anything you don't want to. I'm not going to hold you to it. If you want to watch some Wrestlemania and drink a Budweiser, we can do that as well." Donovan opened the door, slid out, then walked around the pickup to open the door for Morgana.

"I would almost rather be a victim of blood magic than take you up on that offer. Wrestling and American lager are not particular interests of mine." Morgana grinned tightly and accepted the hand he offered to help her out of the pickup.

"You're nervous, though," Donovan said.

"Not nervous, just cautious," she corrected.

"Nope. You're nervous. Your speech gets even more formal when you're uncomfortable. When you're around your friends, you almost relax. And earlier, when we were in the pickup together, you were downright casual." Donovan took her hand and tucked it through his arm, leading her towards his apartment.

"My speech patterns do not change based on my mental state," Morgana retorted. "I have a more formal mode of speech because I have lived for centuries, and I don't choose to pick up the various slangs that come and go."

Donovan smiled down at her. "Okay, sweetheart. Maybe after I make that lasting impression I promised, I'll teach you some of the good slang."

Almost against her will, Morgana found herself smiling back up at him. "You can try, but I think you're a little young to be teaching me anything. It'll probably be the other way around."

"Whatever tricks you can teach me are welcome." Donovan unlocked the front door of the complex, then ushered her inside.

His apartment was on the third floor of the three-story building, and she looked around curiously while he sorted through his mail. It was sparsely furnished, and what furniture there was looked worn but comfortable.

"I'll have to find my own place," Donovan said. "And get my own furniture. A fully furnished apartment sounded like a good idea until about five hours ago when I realized I'd have company."

"It is only stuff. The appearance and wear doesn't matter. As long as you are comfortable. And clean, of course." Morgana sat on the overstuffed couch and tucked her legs underneath herself. A loud rip accompanied the movement. "Dammit. I forgot about this horrible skirt. I cannot wait until I can get rid of it."

"You can take it off whenever you want," Donovan said with a friendly leer, then continued with a more serious tone. "Would you like a robe and a glass of wine? That way you can get out of those clothes and relax a bit while we talk about the investigation. Then, if you're still up for it, you'll be mostly naked already."

"Convenient," Morgana said. She stood and held the seam of her skirt where it was nearly falling off.

"Efficient," Donovan countered.

Morgana shuffled towards where she assumed the bathroom was. "A robe and a glass of wine would be most appreciated. I'd love to hear if you discovered anything, and I'll share with you what information I put together after talking to the rest of the psychics."

"Your wish, my command." Donovan brushed past her and opened one of the two doors off the small hallway, returning moments later with a long, black robe.

"This is not what I expected you to have," Morgana said, taking the silky garment from him.

Donovan shrugged. "I like to be comfortable, and I like luxurious fabrics against my skin. Wait until you touch the sheets."

Morgana smiled and gestured towards the door behind her. "Is that the restroom?"

"It is. Take your time. I'll have a glass of wine waiting for you whenever you're ready."

Morgana disappeared into the bathroom and closed and locked the door behind her. She leaned against it briefly, taking in her reflection. She was even paler than usual except for two bright red spots high on her cheeks. She draped the robe over her arm and pressed her hands against the flush, trying to cool herself down.

This wasn't right, but she wanted this, and it'd been a long time since she'd done what she wanted without considering every possible repercussion. There might be impacts even she could not predict, as Paska was only too happy to remind her, but she would not fall in love with him—anything else she could control.

When her face cooled and the butterflies in her stomach subsided again, she stripped out of her ruined skirt, peeled off the hated pantyhose, and shed her sweater set. She slipped the robe on over her bra and panties and tied it around her waist. It was almost sinfully comfortable, and she sighed in pleasure. A weakness for soft fabrics was one thing she had in common with Donovan.

One more glance in the mirror had her wrinkling her nose. The hair... It wasn't the right hair for a tryst. Even without the sweater set, it looked too normal. She'd dropped her purse in the living room, or she could take care of it immediately, although that probably wasn't the best idea.

The only other reminder of who she was pretending to be was the double strand of pearls around her neck. A wicked grin flashed across her face. She opened the door and called, "Please close your eyes and don't peek. I'm not naked, so you don't have to worry that you're missing something. I just need to grab my purse."

"Why don't you stay in there, so I'm not tempted. I'll grab your purse and leave it right outside the door." Donovan's suggestion was followed by the sound of him walking towards her.

Morgana closed the door and waited for him to walk away. Then she pulled her comb out of her purse. Moments later, shiny black hair fell midway down her back. Then she took off the double strand of pearls, ran her hands over it, and put back on the longer single strand. She tucked it under the robe. It could be a sexy surprise for later if she decided there would be a later.

She shoved the pantyhose back in her purse, neatly folded her clothing, and carried everything out to the living room.

"May I look now?" Donovan asked. He was in the kitchen with his back to her, holding two glasses of wine.

"You may." Morgana settled back onto the couch, pulling her legs up under her and enjoying the ease with which she did so.

Donovan turned around. His jaw dropped, and one of the wine-glasses slipped out of his hand. He caught it before it hit the floor, and not a single drop spilled.

"Wow. Those are some impressive reflexes," Morgana said. She accepted the glass he handed her and leaned back into the corner of the couch.

"It's one of my few gifts," he said. "You've never asked if I had more than power-sensing; I thought you might."

Morgana took a sip of wine. "I've spent a very long time around people with a variety of magical abilities and gifts, and I've learned not to ask too many probing questions. It is a very personal thing, after all. However, considering circumstances, I would appreciate it if you'd share with me."

Donovan settled into the opposite end of the couch, stretched out his legs, and crossed them at the ankle. "I am connected to the natural world in a different way than most elemental witches. My powers are small, but effective in their own way. I can draw on the abilities of animals I've connected to. I have excellent reflexes, night vision, and hearing. Oh, and fantastic stamina."

Morgana rolled her eyes. "How do you create and maintain the connection, if you don't mind me asking?"

Donovan was silent for a long time, and Morgana watched him take several long drinks of wine.

"You don't have to share," she said after a couple minutes. "There are many things about myself that I'm not prepared to discuss."

"I want to tell you, but I'm not sure the moment is right. I mean, I trust you enough to take you to bed with me, but I don't know if that extends to sharing a piece of my soul." Donovan grimaced. "That sounds like a stupid excuse, and I'm sorry."

Morgana shook her head. "It sounds perfectly reasonable. Why don't we leave it at you have amazing abilities you've obtained via a magical connection with animals, and if you ever want to tell me more, I would be more than delighted to learn about this hitherto unknown branch of magic."

"You are really nervous now, aren't you?" Donovan asked with a wink. "You're one 'prithee' away from a tension headache."

Morgana smiled. "Honestly, I am a little nervous. There are a lot of things going on, and I am worried about any number of the decisions I've made today." She started ticking them off on the fingers of the hand holding the wine glass. "I left Bridget and Hazel alone after an attack nearly killed the young woman, my friends are scattered to disparate houses where they could be targeted without you or I there to counter any attacks, and although they are shielded to the best of my abilities, those shields are less foolproof than the ones on my home. I am uncertain if you will be a target now that I know you have a deep wellspring of power that is likely more than you're going to admit, and I'm not sure how you will be able to stop an attack in progress without getting yourself killed."

Donovan grabbed her free hand and held it tightly. "Two of those bullet points were about my safety, and since the other two were how you were leaving people unprotected by your absence, you must admit that I'm the safest of them all, right?"

Morgana glared but didn't pull her hand away. "No, Bridget and Hazel are the safest. My house is shielded and warded more extensively than anywhere else in this town. No one is getting through that."

"That's three of your four worries gone. The last one is your friends. Is there a reason besides your uncontrollable desire to get in my pants that you didn't suggest a giant sleepover with the requisite pillow fights and games of Truth or Dare?"

Morgana bit her lip. Andy could keep Drew and Ceri safe if they were even in danger. They were both old enough and experienced enough to not be an easy target. Russell had felt the attack before anyone else, but that didn't mean he could protect against it. But he'd learned a lot about his power and how to use it in the spring, and she didn't think he'd be an easy target, either. Misty might be tempting, but she had a goddess on her side in addition to the entire well of the town to draw on, and if she didn't quite know how, the town would probably rise up to defend her if it came down to it. But those reasons were all things she wasn't quite ready to share with Donovan.

"Most of them can protect themselves, and those who aren't are with people who can protect them as well as I can. It would be better if Paska would stay at Misty's, but I don't think that is likely to happen," Morgana said, choosing her words carefully.

"Why don't you ask him? The worst he can say is no, right?" Donovan let go of her hand, and the absence of it left her shockingly cold.

She considered for a moment, then silently handed Donovan her wine. She leaned over to dig her phone out of the ridiculous purse and heard a strangled gasp behind her. When she turned back around with raised eyebrows, Donovan was staring at the ceiling.

"What is your problem?" she asked, unlocking her phone and opening the messenger app.

"Your robe is a little...loose in the front." Donovan said.

Morgana glanced down. The robe had gaped open when she'd leaned over, putting her bra-clad breasts on full display. She pulled it closed and tightened the belt, then texted Paska. *Misty is hosting Sandy, Russell, and Jezebel and partners at the farm. You should go keep them safer.*

Three dots appeared almost immediately, followed by a grumpy cat .gif that simply said "No!"

Morgana turned her phone to Donovan to show him. "As I predicted."

"He sent another text." Donovan's voice was strangely flat.

Morgana turned her phone back around and read Paska's follow-up text.

You're close to the edge, and you'll fall off if you're not careful. Don't gamble your life for one night of animalistic passion.

"What does he mean?" Donovan asked with a stiffness in his voice Morgana hadn't heard before. Donovan knew exactly what Paska meant, and he did not want to talk about it.

That was okay. There would be time to discuss Donovan's magic beyond his ability to sense power.

Morgana dropped her phone back in her purse. "It is often difficult to know what Paska means at any given time. I wonder sometimes if he is becoming senile in his old age."

"Didn't you say you were the same age?" Donovan demanded.

"Let's not talk about Paska and his cryptic messages." Morgana smiled, took another drink of wine, and untied the belt of her robe. "There will be time enough for consequences in the morning."

nineteen

Morgana stretched and sat up. Sunlight streamed through the cracks in the blinds, and the red digital clock on the bedside read six a.m.

Donovan was softly snoring beside her, and the sheet was positioned low enough that she could see he was still nude. For that matter, so was she.

Morgana snagged the robe from where she'd left it on the floor and headed into the bathroom. She stepped into the shower, then wrinkled her nose at the bath products. She pulled her hair back and twisted it into a loose makeshift bun. It wouldn't hold past the first time she bent over, but it was out of the way for now.

The bathroom door opened, and Donovan's husky voice asked, "Is that a private shower, or is there room enough for me?"

Morgana rolled her eyes. "This is a private shower. There's physically not room for both of us in here, and I am finished anyway."

"No shower sex, then?" His voice was more amused than disappointed.

"No. I find shower sex to be awkward and less fun that it

sounds." Morgana turned off the water and opened the curtain. "Can you hand me a towel?"

Donovan reached behind him, opened the small linen closet, and grabbed a towel, all without taking his eyes off her. "You are beautiful."

"I know, but thank you all the same." Morgana smiled at him, then dried off. "I wish I had clean clothes. It'll be uncomfortable to put on yesterday's clothing."

"Can't you just magic some up the way you change your hair and fix the tears in your skirt?" Donovan asked. He reached around her and turned the water back on.

"I could, but it's more work than I prefer to do. Magic isn't free, you know. It doesn't cost me as much now as it did when I was younger, but there's no point in using it unnecessarily. Although clean underthings might be a necessity." Morgana wrapped the towel around her and watched Donovan step into the shower. He was a well-built man, and age looked good on him.

"Like what you see?" Donovan asked. He didn't close the curtain.

"Obviously, or I wouldn't still be looking." She leaned against the counter and watched him shampoo, then lather up a washcloth and run the soapy water across the planes of his body.

When he finished, it was her turn to hand him a towel. "I'm going to get dressed. I told Paska I would stop by his house in the morning, then I need to check on Bridget and Hazel before going to the shop. It's Saturday, so I suspect I will be busy."

"Do you have to leave now?" Donovan wrapped the towel around her back and pulled her close. "Your speech patterns are almost relaxed, and I'd love to see if I can get you to throw in some slang. An 'awesome,' maybe. 'Far out' would work. If you dropped a 'sike,' I might die a happy man, secure in the knowledge that no one else's bedroom prowess has ever surpassed mine."

The sensation of his rougher skin against hers almost caused her to lose her resolve. "I do have to go, no matter how much you want to boost your ego." The next words almost stuck in her throat. She expected to have an enjoyable time with him, but she hadn't anticipated how difficult it would be to walk away. "I had a wonderful time, but I'm not sure we can repeat the experience."

She slipped past his towel and walked out of the bathroom, refusing to let the emotions that were threatening gain purchase. Morgana regarded the rough pile of clothes on the floor and grimaced. She closed her eyes and concentrated, pulling into her the energy of the sex magic they'd inadvertently created, envisioned what she wanted, and softly snapped her fingers. When she opened her eyes, matching panties and bra were on the bed in front of her. The rest of the outfit could be salvaged. She once again mended the tear in the skirt, then used the same low-level magic to change the color of the sweater set to coral. Once she'd fixed her strand of pearls to its previous condition, she was ready to go. There was no way on the goddess's green earth she was going to put pantyhose on this morning.

"At least have a cup of coffee before you leave." Donovan, still nude, was leaning against the doorframe. "Coffee and an explanation would be a great breakfast."

Morgana sighed. "Thank you, but no. And you are, of course, owed an explanation. I will find the right words to give it, but not now." She stood on tiptoe and brushed a kiss across lips. "I will check in soon, so we can determine the next steps to take in our witch hunt."

She grabbed her purse and walked to the front door. Just as the door swung closed behind her, she heard him say, "Wait! Your hair!"

Morgana cursed under her breath. Months of being careful, and she almost lost her head—or at least her hairstyle—for the chance to look a little more attractive to a man who had already been a sure thing.

She stepped back into the apartment. "Thank you. It would not do to lose my disguise now." She pulled the comb out of her purse and slowly ran it through her hair until she could no longer feel any hair lower than her shoulders.

"I will see you later," Donovan said. "Now that I've found you, don't think you can get away from me so easily."

She smiled sadly at him, then slipped out for the second time.

MORGANA PUSHED OPEN PASKA'S FRONT DOOR AND WALKED INSIDE WITHOUT knocking. His door was unlocked, and he was expecting her—had basically commanded her to show up—so he didn't get the niceties of announcing her presence.

"I'm in the kitchen," Paska said.

"Where else would you be?" Morgana strode into the kitchen and put two to-go cups of coffee on the table.

"Black coffee?" Paska asked.

"Don't be ridiculous. It's a flat white for you. I'm having a London fog." Morgana settled onto the chair across from him and pulled her tea close.

"You look well, considering how little sleep you likely got last night," Paska said.

Morgana smiled coldly at him. "If it was my one chance, I wanted to enjoy every last second of it."

Every hint of friendly banter left Paska, and his voice turned low and dangerous. "Does he know who you are?"

"No. I've told him very little about me. He knows I practice tasseography. He knows I'm a powerful witch. He knows how old I am. That's all." Morgana took a sip of her tea and tried to match the coldness in Paska's voice.

"You mean he knows how old we are. You told him we were the same age." The accusation in his voice made Morgana cringe.

She wanted to ask how he knew, but that sounded too defensive, so instead she answered simply. "I did."

"I did not give you leave to share." Paska pulled the leather pouch off his belt and dropped it, spilling bones with runes carved and stained into them out onto the table. "How long can you spend time with this man without giving him more of the truth? How long until you feel that you are living a lie and in a moment of bedroom weakness give him your true name—and mine?"

Morgana stared at the runes. She read tea leaves now because she really liked tea, and it was easy to see the pictures of the future in a cup, but she'd learned divination at the same time Paska had, and she could read their future on the table. Grief and fear warred inside her. She had to take a breath to steady her voice. "Before I left him this morning, I told him it was a lovely experience that would not be repeated. I will not trigger the curse that lies on us, especially not for a man."

Paska nudged the three runes that were in the center of the table. Two had landed together, forming an upright triangle that framed the third. "Do you know what you see here?"

Naudhiz, Hagalaz, and Wunjo. Trouble and deliverance. Disaster and healing. Joy.

"Hope," Morgana said finally.

"Destruction," Paska replied. "Happiness brought down in a moment of ecstasy. Hagalaz, the great wheel, is going to turn again, Morgana. And you are the one who pushed it into motion."

"That is unfair. We've both taken any number of lovers over the centuries, and never before have you been so fatalistic." Morgana said the words, but she couldn't take her eyes off the runes making a bony house of cards between them.

"We have both taken *mundane* lovers over the years," Paska corrected. "And now you have shared your breath and life with a being that is different."

"Hagalaz can just as easily represent primal mystery and magic; it leans against Naudhiz—manifestation—and together they create a perfect triangle with Wunjo, joy and balance. It is magical balance. Hope. Transformation." Morgana wanted very much to believe her interpretation to be the correct one, but there was a flaw.

"Wunjo is separate from the others and does not touch them. Change is coming. And when the serpent swallows us both, remember who it is that is to blame." Paska gathered the runes back to him and slid them into the pouch made of the skin of a man they'd once both called friend.

"He's just a man," Morgana said.

"He is so much more than just a man. You have always seen too little when your heart—or your lust—gets in the way."

"And you have always found too much destruction when a little love could heal more than a sword in the dark." Morgana stared at him, willing him to stop talking. To admit he might be wrong. To tell her she was in no danger of invoking the curse that kept them alive and together until one of them lost their heart.

"Do you wish to die, Morgana? After all these years, have you wearied of this life?" Paska leaned forward, and the intensity in his question fed the air between them until it crackled with static electricity.

"I do not, and I have not. Fixating on death is your province. Perhaps it is you who is ready to sleep." Morgana cocked her head and regarded him. "Tell me why you think Donovan Davies is more than a man. He may have some power, but he is still human, if not mundane. Would you be carrying on so if I were having a fling with Drew or Russell?"

The corner of Paska's lips quirked up for the barest moment before he narrowed his eyes at her again. "I would be concerned you were having an affair with Drew for very different reasons, as I don't believe you are his type at all. But no, neither of them are other in the way Donovan is. They are human."

Morgana stood and didn't bother trying to hide her shaking hands. "Is this why you wanted to see me? To tell me I'm killing us both because I had sex with a man you don't like?"

"It's not about me liking him!" Paska roared.

Morgana took a couple steps back, her eyes widening.

"It's about the curse Vortigern laid with his dying breath. You know as well as I do that you are creation, and I am destruction. Our lives are bound together outside of time, and when love comes between us, our time is up.”

“Having a physical relationship with a man who possesses magic is not love, nor is it something that could ever come between us.”

“You haven’t been in love in over sixteen hundred years—until now. It’s only a matter of time before he breaks the bond between you and me, and when that happens, we will die.” Paska took a drink of his coffee and grimaced. Then he turned, grabbed a bottle off the shelf behind him, and poured in a generous glug of Irish cream.

Morgana knew better than to raise an eyebrow at his drink. She wasn’t sure if she’d ever known him to be one hundred percent sober, and she was positive it would be a bad sign if it started happening now.

“If you have nothing else, I need to get home to see how Bridget and Hazel are doing and connect with the rest of our friends. The blood witch failed yesterday, but it will not take them long to regain their strength for another try. I will keep Hazel home today, but she is young and head-strong, and I cannot keep her prisoner forever. Maybe instead of looking for reasons you might die, you could look for a way to keep someone else alive.” Morgana’s voice had risen steadily until she was nearly shouting. She closed her eyes, picked up her tea, then opened her eyes to look at him. “Do you wish for me to spend another sixteen hundred years alone just for the sake of prolonging our lives? Do you wish that for yourself?”

Paska sighed and scrubbed a hand over his eyes. “Yes. But you’ve never been alone. Haven’t I always been beside you?”

Morgana smiled at him sadly. “You have never truly loved and never truly experienced loss. I have done both, and do not wish to exist indefinitely without them.” She turned and walked towards the front door.

“You’re wrong.” His voice was almost too quiet to hear.

Morgana stopped and turned around to see if he would continue.

“I have loved deeply. And I have lost almost everything. I killed my dearest friend at your behest.”

Morgana held her breath. He hadn't brought that day up even once since she'd watched him greet Vortigern with a hug and a knife to the gut.

Paska continued, "I would have done anything for him at one time. He had only to ask. He wanted so much."

"He wanted Elaine," Morgana said flatly, unable to keep her silence anymore. "He wanted my daughter."

"He didn't get her," Paska replied. "Not in the end."

Rage rose in Morgana. "She threw herself off a cliff to escape him. He did not have her, but he destroyed her, destroyed me."

"And that's why I greeted him as a friend and gutted him like an enemy," Paska said. "His excess turned him from the man to whom I pledged my service to the bastard who betrayed everyone who ever loved him. I did what I thought was right—for Elaine, for you, and for me. And that is why we are bound. It would've been better to exile him."

"But then we would have been dead all the sooner, and you would not have occasion to remonstrate me for my choice of lovers potentially ending your life now." Morgana drooped a little. She was tired. Paska was right; she hadn't slept much the night before, but it was more than that. "The years weigh heavy sometimes, and joy can make them light, even if only for a little while."

Paska sighed and walked into the room where she was standing. "I knew it would do little good to warn you, but I had to anyway. I have finally found people to live for, and I am not ready to walk away from that."

"I will not go back to him," Morgana promised. "I will keep our secrets and our lives whole."

"If you ever loved me, Gwenddydd y Dylwythen Deg, you must swear it to the earth and moon."

She shook her head sadly. "I will not swear it. One binding cannot keep another. But I would never willingly do anything to hurt you. You have been by my side since the beginning, and my loyalty is always first and foremost to you, Myrddin y Doeth."

"The mad, you mean. The histories agree on that, at least." Paska slumped into a nearby chair.

"Never mad. Eccentric only, as is a common idiom of the time. But I must go now. I'm already later than I wished to be." Morgana turned back towards the door.

"You should relax before you get home. You sound practically archaic at this point. Would you like some whiskey?"

Morgana shook her head at the sound of a bottle opening. "Not today, old man."

"Next time, then, sister. I'll always have a glass ready for you."

twenty

Morgana hung her keys on the hook just inside the front door and grimaced at her shoes. Beige pumps, no matter how sensible the heel, were no match for three miles of walking in the often-rainy May Pacific Northwest. She'd initially been grateful that Donovan hadn't seemed to remember he'd driven yesterday, and she didn't have a car, but after the trek out to Paska's, then back to her place, her feet hurt and her shoes were scuffed, filthy, and possibly structurally unsound. She toed them off and slid her feet into the lambskin lined slippers near the door.

"Hazel? Bridget?" she called as she walked towards the kitchen. Her stomach growled, reminding her that all she'd consumed that morning was a large London Fog and an enormous amount of guilt and trepidation.

There was no answer. A wrinkle creased her brow as she drew her eyebrows in and paused to listen for any sign of other people.

The house was silent. Her pulse increased. They'd been fine this morning. Morgana had texted them as she walked to Paska's house to let them know where she was, to ascertain their safety, and to let them know what time she expected to return.

The faint sound of metal against metal caught her attention. What would make that noise here? And where was it coming from?

Morgana held her breath and slowed her heart rate so she could listen between beats. Metal against metal again caught her attention, but this time, she could better pinpoint its origin. It was... underneath her?

The worried crease in her brow gave way to a tight, angry glare. She toed off her slippers—they were comfortable, but the rubber grip soles could be noisy—and padded to her herb room. The door opened at her touch. She never locked it. She'd never needed to before. Once inside the herb room, she breathed deep and let the smell of the drying herbs hanging from strings on the ceiling soothe nerves she hadn't even realized were tight. This was her refuge, and the only people who'd ever been in here were the women who were mysteriously missing right now and Paska.

Paska scoffed, of course. He liked to say kitchen and earth witchery were the province of women while men controlled the greater magics of fire and air, but the truth was, he'd never developed his connection to the earth the way Morgana had. And instead of looking for that path, he swore his allegiance to fire and air, leaving the moon, the earth, and the tides to her.

If he ever agreed to work with her again, they'd find the balance that had eluded them since he'd killed Vortigern to avenge Elaine— his niece and Morgana's daughter. But now wasn't the time to regret the distance that held them apart and the curse that bound them together. Now was the time to find two wayward witches, make sure they were alive, then flay them for the violation of her boundaries, secrets, and home.

The soft, deep, black rug in the center of the room that kept her feet warm when she was creating new tea blends was shifted to one side, exposing a trapdoor. Morgana walked down the narrow, spiral staircase she kept meticulously maintained and luxuriously padded to eliminate all possible noise. The air cooled noticeably once she'd descended far enough, and the energy of the earth wrapped around her, welcoming her back into its arms.

She got to the bottom of the stairs and was greeted by a long, dark, earthen hall. It was the last defense she had in case of an intruder.

At the end of the hall, she pressed her hand against the center of the wall and watched the door swing inward, ready to either defend or attack, depending on the next few seconds.

In the center of the large, brightly lit room, Bridget and Hazel faced each other. The lights were brighter than anything Morgana ever used, and the harshness of the glare illuminated every drop of sweat on the women and highlighted every irregularity of the uneven earthen floor. They were both stripped down to sports bras and spandex shorts, which was not a look most nuns adopted, at least as far as Morgana had observed.

They didn't grapple with each other, though. Instead, Bridget barked orders at Hazel, then attacked magically.

Morgana let her anger simmer on the back burner and watched the women. Hazel was desperately trying to follow Bridget's barked commands to ground herself and center her energy, but she was fumbling with her power and missing the mark more and more each time Bridget pushed her off-balance.

After a couple of minutes of observation, it was obvious Hazel was too exhausted to continue without making mistakes that could have dire consequences. Morgana stepped forward and held up a hand. "Stop."

Hazel slumped in relief, but Bridget didn't hear and attacked again. Her push, which was more than was needed to prove Hazel hadn't grounded herself before finding her center, crashed against the unprepared young witch. Hazel stumbled backwards and out of the protective circle Bridget had cast.

Hazel's head made contact with the drywall and snapped forward. She slipped to the ground with a scream and a curse.

"Stand down," Morgana commanded Bridget. She put the power of her will behind the directive.

Bridget tumbled to the ground. Seconds later, her eyes widened, and her mouth made an "o." "Hazel! Are you okay?" She tried to stand, but Morgana pushed the air against her, and Bridget stayed on the ground.

"I will check on her, but I'm sure she is fine. She is stunned, but it's nothing that a healing touch and a cup of tea won't heal." Morgana walked over to Hazel and crouched beside her. "May I feel your wound?"

Hazel didn't say anything but tipped her head to give Morgana access to where she'd cracked her head against the wall.

Morgana felt around gently, easing up further when Hazel hissed in pain. She spread her hand over the large goose egg forming at the base of Hazel's skull and concentrated. Healing was not her primary gift, but she had enough power and experience to make minor wounds heal faster.

After a couple minutes, Morgana felt her banked power waning and began to pull on the earth. This was her workshop, the place she created spells, and the earth offered her the power she needed.

Hazel's eyes brightened, and she moved her head back and forth. "Thank you. For a moment, all I could see was stars and cartoon birds."

"You will likely have a headache for the rest of the day," Morgana said. She stood and offered her hand to Hazel. The younger witch took it and let Morgana haul her to her feet.

"I am so sorry," Bridget said, tears in the corners of her eyes. "I didn't mean..."

"Of course you didn't," Hazel said. She walked forward and threw her arms around Bridget. "You've taught me so much today already! I almost had it that last time, right?"

Bridget smiled at her. "You did! Another day or two of practice, and you'll be able to ground yourself and find the center you need to cast shields to protect yourself."

Morgana pursed her lips and pushed her anger down—something she excelled at. What was done was done, and although there would be time to talk about boundaries and reparations later, now was not the time. Not when she had other questions to answer. She'd felt Hazel's power. It should've taken less than a couple hours to teach her to sink her roots and find her balance. She shook her head. Bridget was an excellent teacher, but she didn't have the same level of experience Morgana had; it made sense that she couldn't teach a person as well or as quickly.

"You must both be tired. It is time for a tea break." Morgana gestured towards the stairs and waited for the others to disappear through the trapdoor before looking around her refuge. Nothing had been moved. Her altar facing North was undisturbed, and the evidence showed that only the center circle had been used. She unfocused her eyes and reached out with her other senses and repeated the rotation, this time making sure she looked at the ceiling and floor, examining them on the magical and mundane planes at the same time.

Her nostrils flared as she considered how to address this violation. It was the best place in the house for the type of magical work Bridget and Hazel had been doing, but it was sacred. She may have shared her herbarium with Bridget and Hazel, but no one else, not even her brother, had ever been in the place she considered her temple.

Morgana took one last look around, then ascended the stairs. Neither of the other women were in the herbarium, so Morgana closed the trap door, then followed the sound of conversation into the kitchen.

"How did you find my—" she stopped herself from saying temple in the nick of time; there were some things she didn't want to share "—practice space. It was hidden, and no one has ever been there."

Bridget's eyes widened, and Hazel's shoulders curled in.

"It's my fault," Hazel whispered. Guilt suffused her expression, but her gaze darted to a place just above and to the right of

Morgana's face. "When you showed us your herb room, I could feel that there was empty space under the floor. Last night, after Bridget went to bed, I came back and did some exploring. When I moved the rug, I saw the seams of the trapdoor. I've read so many regency horror romances and knew immediately there would be a secret mechanism to open it."

Morgana closed her eyes. Just her luck to get a witch obsessed with oubliettes and secret passages. "Did it not occur to you that if it was hidden, it was for a reason? You could've stumbled into something terrible."

"Oh no," Hazel said quickly. "I could tell the magics that hid it and were used there were of the light. It looked like the best and safest place to have Bridget train me. Any accidents down there wouldn't affect anything else. And after what happened to the tea service on your counter..."

Morgana swallowed and maintained the pleasant expression she'd been holding. "What tea service?"

Hazel pointed at the counter and grimaced. "That one. I'll pay for it as soon as I make enough money."

Morgana took a deep breath and followed Hazel's finger. Hundreds, maybe thousands, of slivers of glass adorned an antique silver tray. Behind the now-empty tea tray was a second teapot illustrated with a delicately painted tree that altered with the four seasons as it encircled the teapot and twelve matching cups adorned with flowers representing the twelve months of the lunisolar calendar used during the early Qing Dynasty. She heaved a sigh of relief. The one that had shattered was her everyday service and not the one she'd owned since the mid-seventeenth century.

"How did that happen?" Morgana asked. She gritted her teeth and smiled. It could have been much worse, and she could magically repair it, but it was another blow on top of the earlier violation, and her control was wavering.

Hazel shrugged and kept her shoulders up by her ears. "I was having breakfast and felt something reach towards me. It felt kind of like what'd happened yesterday, and I panicked."

"It was me," Bridget confessed. "I was attempting to push her off-balance to see how much she'd kept of what she'd learned last night."

"Not much," Hazel said. "And that's when Bridget said she wished she had her magic workroom here, so we could practice without impacting the world around us, and I suggested we check out your basement. The dirt floor helped me find the earth, but I was wrong to suggest it. I'm sorry."

Morgana spread her forced smile wider. "No real harm has been done, and it was an excellent idea to use the warded workspace. I should have thought of it myself. I wish you had asked my permission before going into an obviously hidden room and hope that you will remember that although it can be easier to ask forgiveness than permission, violating a witch's work room can have consequences you will not be prepared to pay." Morgana could afford to be magnanimous for the time being. She would lock access to her basement. It had not occurred to her that it was necessary. The only ones in Oracle Bay with the power to access the room were Paska and Misty, and neither of them would dream of entering her space without permission. She pursed her lips and amended her thoughts. Misty would not, but Paska might if he thought he had a good reason.

Hazel and Bridget both hung their heads, although Morgana saw the mischief dancing in Bridget's eyes before she schooled her expression into contrition—likely something she'd had to do a lot in Catholic school as a child.

"I came home to check on you both to see how you were doing and if you needed anything from me before I go to work and continue my investigation."

"We're okay, but I'm exhausted," Hazel said. "I don't know how much more I can do this morning."

Bridget nodded. "She's worked very hard and made a lot of progress. It's no longer possible to knock her over with a feather-light thought. She's well-grounded, now."

"Can you maintain it even now when you're not touching the earth directly?" Morgana asked.

"Try me!" Hazel straightened up and looked at Morgana with a broad grin.

Morgana reached out with her mind and pushed gently. When Hazel didn't move, she pushed harder. It wasn't until she shoved hard that Hazel rocked. "Impressive," she said. "You have learned a lot in a very short period."

Hazel glowed under the compliment. "Thank you." She turned her gaze towards Bridget. "Bridget is a great teacher."

"She is at that. And now, you do need a break, although not too long of one. You might be unshakable, but you won't be able to hold your shields under a concerted attack if you don't have a place in yourself to tether to the ground. Why don't you spend a few hours with Donovan? He will keep you safe." Morgana hid the discomfort she felt at the idea of calling Donovan to ask for a favor.

"What about me?" Bridget asked. "And if we are safe here, shouldn't we just stay?"

"I would appreciate it if you would stay here. You're unlikely to be targeted; your power is realized and not potential. Perhaps you can do some research to see if any other similar crimes have happened elsewhere lately. It would be good to know if our murderer is still here or if she's moved on." Morgana picked up the silver tray and dumped the shattered glass into the waste bin. "I will text Donovan and ask him to collect you here, if you don't mind, Hazel."

"That's cool," Hazel said. "I like him. He used to live in Vegas, so we've talked a lot about all the cool places only locals know about. But are you sure I'll be safe? And that he'll be safe if he's with me?"

Morgana bit her lip. She should probably suggest that Donovan and Hazel hang out here, but the thought of having the too-tempting man she had to walk away from in her home was beyond what she was capable of after the violation she felt from the invasion of her work room.

"Please give me five minutes of privacy," Morgana said. "I need to speak with some other people to make the full plan for the day."

twenty-one

Morgana paused in her backyard sanctuary, taking a moment to refresh her spirit and let the last of her anger at Bridget and Hazel drain away. It would take longer for her anger with Paska to disappear. He, more than anyone else, had a way of getting under her skin that could outlast any other irritant she encountered, and the possibility that he might be correct only made things worse. However, the healing power of the space that had seldom hosted anyone but her started her on the path, if not to forgiveness, at least to acceptance.

Three spiral herb gardens formed the perimeter of her yard, and the various salvia bushes served as a privacy hedge and concealed the fence without blocking her view of the ocean.

In the center of her yard was a small pond. It was to this pond she went. There was recessed seating along the edge, and she dropped gracefully into one of the comfortably carved rock seats, took off her house shoes, and slipped her feet into the water. Then, she opened the messenger app on her phone and sent three quick texts.

While she waited for a reply, she leaned back and basked in the light of the sun. The days were almost at their longest, but the heat hadn't yet followed the sun to its zenith, and the breeze off the ocean was cool enough to make her shiver.

Her phone buzzed. Morgana sighed. There was never enough time and leisure to take full advantage of the sanctuary she'd created. It would be so lovely to lie in the soft grass, letting the cool water caress her feet, the sun warm her face, and the buzzing bees lull her into a meditative state. Unbidden, the image of Donovan beside her, cradling her head in his lap and stretching out his long, bare legs came to her.

Morgana opened her eyes and picked up her phone. She knew why her thoughts had wandered that way, but she needed to ensure they didn't stray again. It would be hard enough to stay away from him without daydreaming about what could never be.

While she'd gathered her thoughts, she'd received a second text. She opened the one from Russell first.

Russell: *I'm working today from 2-11. Hazel's welcome to hang out as long as she wants if you promise to cover the bill. I don't know how much good I'll be, though. I felt the veil slip before anyone else did, but I don't think I could've done anything but yell "duck!"* An emoji of a duck followed his text, and Morgana smiled.

She thought carefully about how to reply, and while she considered options, she read the next text that'd come in.

Ceri: *I am happy to lend you my "demon," although if you call him that and let him know you asked to borrow him, he may not be agreeable. He's brewing today, so Hazel would have to hang out there if she wanted to be safest. LMK.*

Morgana wrinkled her nose at the acronym. For the most part, the people she texted with were old enough that they preferred complete sentences and punctuation, although some were lax on capitalization.

Morgana replied: *LMK?*

Ceri's response was almost instantaneous. *Let me know. Sorry.*

Morgana sent a thumbs up emoji. She might prefer complete

sentences and proper grammar, but emojis were a fun addition to text communications.

She considered. She had two options, neither perfect. She could likely force Andy and Russell to leave their work and help Donovan protect Hazel, but that would bring attention to them and reveal that they were powerful enough to protect Hazel. Russell and Andy had closely guarded their abilities, and she would not force them to reveal themselves that way.

She couldn't make a final decision, though, until she heard from the third person she'd contacted. She opened the text thread she shared with Donovan and reread what she'd sent. *I would like to ask for a favor, although I know I do not deserve yours.*

Was it too vague? Should she have apologized for telling him they were through after a single blissful night?

Finally, the three dots that signified he was forming a reply appeared. She watched the dots for over a minute. With each second that passed, her agitation grew. What was taking him so long?

Finally, an answer appeared. *Ask.*

Morgana stared at the screen in consternation. That single word should not have taken so long to form.

Before she could type her reply, though, another message from Donovan appeared.

Sorry. I'm eating at my desk. Reviewing case files. Didn't mean to be terse.

Morgana felt lighter when she read those words. *I need to be at work. I would like Bridget to walk around town, trying to sense other potential victims. Can I ask you to keep Hazel company?*

Donovan replied immediately. *Sure. I'd be glad to. She's a good kid.*

She's twenty-five. Not a kid. Morgana hated the way people, particularly men, sometimes talked about women as if they were children rather than adults capable of their own agency.

She is, and I'm sorry. Anyone under 30 is a kid to me, but that's not a good excuse. I'll do better.

Morgana warmed a little bit. Men might almost universally be less laudable than women, but she did appreciate one who apologized when he recognized he was wrong.

Now she had to be careful. She hadn't told him the truth of what'd happened the evening before. Sending them to the Pour House to watch Andy in the brewery would elicit more questions than she was prepared to answer, particularly without the demon's agreement. But he knew Russell was a medium, if not a necromancer, and it would make sense that he could sense when the veil was disrupted by blood and death magic.

She didn't want to say any of those things over text, though. She was conformable enough with discussing the basics of what was happening and what their plans were, but she knew as well as, maybe better than, anyone how easy it was to access other people's communications, no matter how private they thought they were.

It would be good if you could pick her up at my home. There are things I need to tell you that I cannot say through this unsecured medium.

Donovan's reply took a minute longer this time. *You're worried about something.*

It wasn't a question, so Morgana did not feel the need to answer. *Can you pick her up here?*

A GIF of a white actor wearing a black mask, carrying a rapier, and bowing dramatically with the words "As You Wish" over the image was his only response. Something about the image unsettled her, but she couldn't put her finger on it. It was from a movie, one she'd seen. Drew hosted movie nights every once in a while, and although she pretended to be disinterested and to only attend unwillingly, she enjoyed them. It was a chance to drink wine and enjoy camaraderie among those she'd come to regard as friends. There was something about this phrase that meant more than mere acquiescence, but she could not remember right now.

She texted Ceri and Russell back and informed them that she would get back to them soon about the plans for the afternoon and received two thumbs up emojis in response.

Morgana went back into the house to wait for Donovan and

inform Bridget and Hazel that they should make themselves ready to leave the house, but that when Donovan arrived, she would need to speak with him privately.

Hazel grinned at her, and the smile seemed too knowing. Was everyone aware of what was transpiring? No, what had transpired in the past, between her and the witch hunter?

Morgana decided to ignore it and remind the women that from now on, the basement was off-limits and to reiterate that the back-yard was similarly private.

The other women disappeared upstairs, presumably to change and make themselves ready to leave.

Morgana took a deep breath. She could feel her thinking slow down and fall into the patterns of her youth. If she was not careful, she would slip into Brittonic, the language of what is now the United Kingdom before the Germanic invaders arrived to despoil the coun-tryside and the language.

The doorbell rang. Morgana glanced in the hallway mirror that she'd only recently rehung after Ceri's unfortunate descent into near madness brought on by too many scried visions. Her hair was a perfect brunette bob, and her makeup was as artful as befitted the costume she wore.

She hated it and wished that she could appear in front of Donovan the way she had last night, as her true self.

There was no help for it now, though. He knew the mask she wore now was not who she was, and she couldn't afford to show she cared about the way she looked to him.

Morgana opened the door, and her breath caught in her throat. Donovan towered over her, and power rolled off him in waves, heating her skin and inflaming her soul. He was wearing the same tight jeans that seemed sculpted to his muscular thighs, but instead of the t-shirts she'd seen him in thus far, he had on a chambray shirt rolled up to the elbows. He looked even more beautiful than he had last night when she looked down at him, his face framed by the white of the pillow and the spilled black tresses of her hair.

"Hi."

His lips quirked upwards in a smile, but the expression didn't reach his eyes. "Hi," he replied.

She stared at him a moment longer, before remembering that he didn't affect her in this way, and that she'd invited him here for a very different reason. She opened the door wider. "Please come in. After you remove your shoes, follow me to the garden. It is private, and we will be able to speak without interruption."

Donovan didn't say anything else until they reached Morgana's back yard. He stood for a moment and curled his toes in the lush, mossy grass.

Morgana watched the peace that infused her garden sanctuary fall over the man, then settled into her previous seat by the pond. "Please join me. These seats are more comfortable than they look, and it is a lovely day to have earth, water, and sky." The fire that still burned inside her added a fourth element, but she dared not speak that one aloud.

Donovan rolled up his jeans and did as she suggested. He wiggled in the stone chair until he was comfortable, then slid his feet into the water.

"This is a beautiful space," he said without looking at her.

"I know. It is one of two places that no one else but me uses." As soon as she said it, she realized her mistake.

Donovan turned to look at her, and the intensity in his gaze nearly melted the stone she sat on. "And yet, you invited me?"

"So we could speak without interruption," she said, too quickly.

This time, his smile reached his eyes, but he looked away before she could get lost in his gaze.

"What do you want to tell me that you couldn't say in front of anyone else?"

Morgana worried at her lower lip and tried to ignore the way Donovan watched the motion. "I am trying to decide what to tell you and how much without giving away anyone else's secrets."

Donovan leaned back, brushing against Morgana as he did so.

"That is fair, and since I know you don't trust me, it makes sense that the others in this town wouldn't either."

"How much power do you have, really?" Morgana asked. "And how does it work?"

A slow smile crept across Donovan's face. "Have we come to the exchanging of secrets portion of our relationship? Because those are big questions."

"We don't have a relationship," Morgana retorted, then inwardly grimaced.

"You tell me yours, and I'll tell you mine." Donovan pulled his feet out of the pond and walked across the grass, never taking his eyes off Morgana.

"I... I can't right now. And I'm not asking you for more than general information. I will rephrase. Can you sense the dark magic as it rears to attack? Are you in danger? And what can you do to protect Hazel?"

Donovan paced the length of the backyard, and Morgana watched him with not-quite detachment.

"I cannot sense it," Donovan finally admitted. "But I'm not in danger. My shields are good. It would take something more powerful than the blood witch to break through." The look Donovan leveled at Morgana heated the air between them. "You could penetrate them. But only a couple other people I've met."

"And can you protect Hazel?" Morgana pushed, ignoring the innuendo.

Donovan's shoulders slumped. "Not as well as I'd like. I thought it'd be easier to pinpoint the witch if I was ready for the attacks, but unless I'm ready for it, there's nothing to get a hold of to follow back."

Morgana grimaced. "It is the same for me."

"But somehow, she was protected yesterday." Donovan stopped pacing and dropped to sit beside Morgana again. "You don't have to tell me who did it if it would be betraying someone else, but it would be helpful to know how."

"Two of the people who were at the Pour House yesterday sensed the attack before it happened. One of them was able to sense the iciness of the grasping magic and place a ring of fire around Hazel, burning the connection. The other person who sensed it is Russell."

"The medium?" Donovan asked, staring at Morgana. He spoke again without giving Morgana a chance to answer. "It makes sense in a way. The blood witch is pulling life from one person through death magic. That would ride the veil between life and death, wouldn't it?"

Morgana sighed inwardly in relief. Donovan had come to the right conclusion, and Morgana didn't have to reveal that Russell was more than just a medium—he was a necromancer.

"My thought was if you and Hazel spend the afternoon at the Sleeping Inn, you could have drinks, and Russell could alert you of any magical attacks in time for you to pull Hazel into your shields and hopefully follow the power back to its source."

"That's not all, though, is it?" Donovan asked shrewdly.

Morgana shook her head. "It's not. There is something about Hazel's past that she won't talk about to me, and I was hoping you could tease it out of her. She likes you and trusts you more than me, and I have a feeling it will be important."

"Any hint as to what I'm digging for?" Donovan asked. "And just so you know, I'm not interrogating her and turning over all the information to you. That's not part of my job."

"I would not ask you to do that. But she cringed in the face of my perceived anger, almost like she was expecting a blow from me. There is something that happened that needs to be untangled. Sometimes knots like that go deeper than mind and soul. They twist up a person's power and make them easier to manipulate and less able to access their abilities. Helping unknot a source of pain and trauma might lead her to be better able to protect herself. There is power there, but only a trickle of it is getting out."

Donovan considered for a moment while Morgana tried very hard not to stare at the man beside her.

"I will see what I can find out, and if it doesn't feel like a violation of her trust, I will share it with you."

Morgana exhaled away some of her tension. "Thank you. I—"

Donovan turned towards Morgana, and their faces were mere inches apart. "I'm leaving now, Morgana. When you want to talk, you have my number. But until then, it's all business." Donovan climbed to his feet. "Don't wait too long. I like you, but I'm not willing to cool my heels forever waiting for you to trust me enough to tell me the secret that stands between us."

Morgana watched Donovan walk out of the garden, squashing down every emotion that threatened to rise. It didn't matter how much attraction crackled the air between them; walking away now was the only way to save her heart and her life.

twenty-two

Donovan and Hazel departed for the Sleeping Inn, and Bridget left to stroll Main Street with Ceri. They were going to have a cup of tea and look for potential witches who were unaware of their power—something more likely in Oracle Bay than anywhere else. Oracle Bay had a way of drawing in the powerful, and other than Misty, had pulled in everyone else in their psychic group.

Morgana was left alone in her house for the first time in over two weeks. She didn't have plans to stay there long, but for a few minutes, she took the chance to revel in the quiet and solitude. It's not that she didn't like other people. She just didn't want them in her space, touching her things, talking to her, or breathing too loudly.

The walk into town helped chase away the last of her disgruntlement at finding people in her workroom and went even further towards soothing away the hurt and anger that had overtaken her after her conversation with—no, chastisement from—her brother. Unfortunately, it also chased away all the reasons she needed to stay away from Donovan, replacing valid reasons with circular logic that she'd never let anyone else get away with.

Morgana was lost in a fantasy that involved silk scarves, expensive Champagne, and mundane life spans when she arrived at her shop. She unlocked the door, then locked it behind her. While the water boiled, she traded her sensible sneakers for even more sensible pumps, fluffed her bob, adjusted her pearls, and made sure her sweater was hanging correctly.

Once she had her tea service set out the way she liked, she unlocked the front door and flipped the sign to open. She'd barely sat down when the tinkling bell announced her first customer of the day.

"Violet," Morgana said. "Please sit, and I will brew the tea." She poured the boiling water into the teapot and placed it in the center of the tray on the table, then sat down.

"Please, concentrate on your question while the tea brews. After I fill your cup, tell me what answers you seek. As soon as you can tolerate the temperature, drink your tea, leaving the dregs behind for me to interpret."

Morgana didn't think Violet was the blood witch. Even knowing that with the amount of power stolen, Violet could hide it easily behind a façade of naïveté and the shield of the husband no one had done anything more than glance at; it didn't feel correct. But right now, she couldn't afford to take any chances. Fortunately, tasseography used only a small trickle of power, which was why she used that method of divination instead of real witchcraft, which would require her to open herself further and leave her vulnerable. Tasseography had more limits, but most querents didn't want to know anything more than the vague futures they received from the shapes formed in their tea leaves. If she revealed as much as she could find out about the path they were walking on, she'd send a lot of people running and screaming out of her shop, which would serve the effect of drying up her business completely.

Morgana cocked her head to one side. Maybe that was the

answer. Scare people so badly that she ruined her business. Of course, if she actually hated it, she could merely stop. It was difficult, though, to have power and not use it, which is one of the reasons so many powerful people found a way to use it, if only a little. She'd always found that low-level controlled use like this was enough to stem the desire to do great magics and controlling that part of oneself was what made long-lived witches with clear—for the most part—consciences.

Morgana filled one of the teacups and slid it in front of Violet, who'd been sitting silently with her eyes screwed up.

The teacup sliding across the table caused Violet's eyes to spring open, and in that moment, Morgana saw all the way into the young woman. She was no more a killer than Hazel was, but she was brimming with power. It was raw and untapped, but her well ran deep. She burned pure, bright light with nothing to tarnish her aura except fear. Swirling around her, though, was a black cloud heavy with malice and tinged with cyclonic green and blood red. It sent out probing tentacles into Violet's aura, and every time it brushed her energy, the malevolent cloud grew larger.

Violet blinked, and the vision was gone, but Morgana had seen enough to know that if she didn't do something, Violet would be the next victim of the blood witch. The only question now was what to do. For the moment, she was protected, but the minute Violet left Morgana's shop, she'd be vulnerable.

Violet was speaking, and Morgana had to bring her mind back to the present.

"I am so sorry. Can you start over?" Morgana thought quickly, trying to come up with a reasonable excuse why she'd not been paying attention. "Sometimes, the visions come unbidden before the tea is even consumed, and I saw something now that I would like to share with you when we're finished with your reading, if that would be okay."

Violet's eyes widened even further, and Morgana was careful not to look too deeply.

"Yes. Please. I want to know everything." The eagerness in her voice made her sound even younger than the twenty-five years old that she appeared.

Twenty-five? Morgana made a note to double check the ages of the more recent victims. Hazel was twenty-five, but the women in Vancouver had been older.

She shook herself again before she could get distracted. "And your question now?" Morgana prompted.

"Right." Violet took a deep breath. "It's the dreams. They aren't stopping. Tom—that's my husband—says it's this town that's doing it to me, but it started before we got here."

"Tell me about the dream again," Morgana said. "And if it's cool enough, start drinking your tea."

Violet picked up her cup and brought it to her lips, then winced and set it back down. "It's changed a bit now, but I'm being chased down a dark corridor, and the further I go, the darker it gets. All I can see is blood dripping down the walls. And then, I burst through a beaded curtain, and the beads fall off the curtain, and they just keep coming until I'm buried in them. They fill my mouth and ears and lungs, and I suffocate on them."

Violet spoke more and more quickly, and her words slid into run-on sentences, then run-on words. Her hands were shaking when she picked up her teacup, and she nearly spilled the hot liquid onto her lap. She took a deep breath and closed her eyes. Her hands steadied, and she took a drink of the tea.

When she opened her eyes, the calm had returned.

Morgana was impressed. Few people could move from terror to calm that quickly. Violet might not know the power threatening to break free inside her, but she was definitely tapping it, and probably had been for years, to self-soothe.

"I know this may be difficult to think about, but can you describe what the beads look like?" Morgana slid her hand into the pocket of her white capris and closed her fingers around the bead she'd found in the Pour House after Hazel's attack.

Violet nodded, took another drink of her tea, then opened her purse. She pulled out a quilted silk coin purse, unzipped it, and let a single bead fall onto the table. "I found this in my jacket pocket this morning. It's identical to the ones in my dream. What does it mean?"

Morgana reached out towards the bead. "May I?"

Violet smiled tremulously. "Yeah. Sure." She took another drink of tea, then drained the cup, set it on the saucer, and pushed it towards Morgana.

Morgana rolled the bead around in her hand. She didn't want to compare it to the one in her pocket, not in front of Violet, but if it wasn't an exact match, it was close enough that it wouldn't make a difference. She inverted the cup over the saucer, and after a minute, she rotated it three times, and turned it upright. She set it on the tray in front of her, handle pointing south, and looked into the cup.

Morgana didn't need tasseography to tell the future. Her vison moments ago told her everything she knew, but the leaves were an excellent channel for her abilities. And regardless of what *knowing* she tapped into, there were things that were generally true.

Perhaps she would see a different future for Violet here. Patterns near the rim indicated the querents present, those in the middle, the immediate future, and patterns on the bottom of the cup were the long-term future.

Violet's cup didn't have any tea leaves on the bottom of the cup. Around the rim were wavy lines that broke up towards the handle and took on the form of clouds. In the middle, but closer to the rim than the bottom, was a heart that blurred into an hourglass figure.

There are always multiple meanings to every symbol, whether it was in the tea leaves, tarot cards, or runes. But the hourglass had few interpretations other than imminent danger. This newlywed, who'd been plagued by nightmares since her honeymoon, was going to die if Morgana couldn't prevent it.

"I'm sorry," Morgana said slowly, trying to figure out how to convey what she'd seen, both in the leaves and in the young woman's aura. "Your dreams are more than just dreams—they are portents. You are being targeted." She took a deep breath. Now came the part that might make Violet run screaming out of her shop and straight into danger. "When I looked at you after you'd concentrated on what you wanted to see in the leaves, your soul was laid bare to me."

"Are you... Are you hitting on me?" Violet's lips drew back to show her gritted teeth, as if the very idea was repellant.

"No. Absolutely not." Morgana did not roll her eyes, yet one more marker of her excellent control. "But what I saw is a wellspring of power. It's been lying dormant in you your entire life, but that is the reason you've been targeted."

Violet laughed. "Power? What are you talking about? It's fun to pretend to believe in magic and psychics while I'm in Oracle Bay, but there's no need to get ridiculous."

"And yet, you've visited every oracle in town who would see you, and you've returned to me with horrible nightmares of darkness and blood and death. Why will you believe enough to seek our guidance but not enough to believe the power lies within you, too?"

Violet stood, dug in her pockets, and pulled out a crumpled wad of twenties, dropped them on the table, then picked up the crystal bead. "Thank you."

"Wait," Morgana said. "I haven't told you how to protect yourself."

Violet laughed bitterly. "I'm planning on energy drinks and insomnia until I get far, far away from here." She took a breath and calm visibly descended over her. "The ordinary girl waking up with magical powers is all well and good in a fairytale, but I haven't believed in magic since I was a girl."

"That's tragic." Even if a person didn't have power, they had access to the everyday magic that was life and death, earth and sky, and spirit and soul. There were wonders everywhere if one knew how to see them. The magic in a misty forest at dawn was the equal of the spark that allowed Morgana to see the future.

"Not tragic. Realistic," Violet corrected firmly.

"Your ability to calm yourself is impressive," Morgana said. She needed to keep Violet in her shop and talking until she could figure out how to protect her, no matter how unwilling she was to be protected. "I'll bet that's always been the case. Did your mother ever tell you what a quiet, calm baby you were?"

Violet shoulders rose towards her shoulders, and she squeezed her eyes closed. "My mother was murdered when I was sixteen," she said. Then she turned and walked towards the door.

"Wait!" Morgana said. "I'm sorry; I didn't know. Please don't leave." She stood and walked towards Violet. "At least take this amulet before you leave." Morgana dipped her hand into her pocket, pushed the bead aside, and held out a black tourmaline necklace while she pulled her shields from the building in preparation for throwing them over Violet. Something was wrong, though, and they didn't come when she called. A wave of dizziness swept over Morgana, and she swayed on her feet.

Violet turned and looked at Morgana over her shoulder. "I'll be back before I leave town. Promise."

The young woman opened the door and stepped across the threshold onto the sidewalk. Her body stiffened, then jerked as if she was a marionette on a string. She screamed.

Morgana rushed forward, throwing a shield of fire around Violet. Either she was too slow or the power was too fast and targeted, but her shield compressed on itself and disappeared with an audible pop.

Violet opened her mouth, and her scream reverberated on the magical plane, then she collapsed to the ground and was still.

Morgana knew without looking what she'd find.

What skin of Violet's was visible was covered in runes and mystical symbols, and in the hollow of her throat were the Ogham runes Quert, Straif, and Gort. The marks looked freshly carved into her skin, but there was no blood oozing from her wounds that would show it'd happened at the moment of her death.

Morgana looked down at the young woman, a sick feeling rising in her chest. All the work she'd done the last few months to lure out the killer and protect the innocent had resulted in nothing more than having to watch the latest victim of the blood witch die in front of her.

Without taking her eyes off the body—off Violet, she reminded herself—she pulled her phone from her pocket.

"Call Donovan," she said.

The phone rang several times, then went to voicemail.

She tried again, then again. Finally, she sent a text. *Blood witch murder on Main Street. Violet. Get Hazel to my house and call me.*

Sirens sounded in the distance and Morgana braced herself to deal with the generally incompetent Oracle Bay police for whom Donovan hadn't yet hired replacements. But the police car sped right on by without slowing down, followed almost immediately by an ambulance. Morgana stared after it. Just before it disappeared from sight, it turned off Main Street into the Sleeping Inn parking lot.

Morgana glanced between Violet's body and the Sleeping Inn, barely visible in the distance. Fear rose so fast she nearly choked on it. Movement caught her eye. Leslie, the new proprietor of Title Wave, had walked out of the bookstore they were preparing to reopen to see what the commotion was.

"Leslie!" Morgana shouted. "Stay with her!"

Leslie looked down at the body lying on the ground. "Is she okay?"

"She's dead," Morgana said, already taking off down the street. "I'll call 911 on my way." She didn't wait for Leslie's answer before breaking into a run.

The thought that she wouldn't get to make that choice spurred her faster. When she stumbled in the heels, she hissed a command at them, and they turned into black running shoes between one step and the next. The next step replaced her khaki capris with black running tights and her sweater set with a tank top.

She picked up the pace, pushing herself with all the magic at her disposal, and skidded into the parking lot in a cloud of dust, nearly running into Russell.

He shook his head. "I'm so sorry, Morgana. I failed."

Morgana choked back a wave of nausea. Her legs wobbled, then gave out. Hopelessness washed over her, and for the first time in longer than she could remember, she burst into tears.

twenty-three

A gentle hand on Morgana's back brought her back to herself enough for the humiliation of crying in public to seep in.

"I'm sorry, I'm so sorry," Donovan said. "I didn't know."

Morgana raised her tear-streaked face and met Donovan's eyes. "You're okay," she gasped. "I thought... When you didn't answer the phone, and the cops, and Russell..."

Donovan sank into the dirt next to Morgana. "I'm okay. Hazel's okay." He pulled his phone out of his pocket and swore. "I must have had it on silent, and then I was needed in my official capacity until the ambulance arrived. I'll need to go back in and ensure the scene is being secured."

Morgana took a deep breath. "What happened?"

Donovan's face crumpled. "There was a server, Joanna. She was refilling Hazel's and my sodas when Russell ran over, yelling at me to shield. I dove across the table and pulled Hazel into my arms and dropped my shields on her."

The sick feeling Morgana had been feeling intensified. "I didn't even think about Joanna. Of course she'd be vulnerable. How could I have failed so completely?"

Donovan pulled Morgana closer. "You haven't. I knew who she was and her role in Ceri's attempted murder. I made the unfounded assumption that her power wouldn't be enough to be tempting or unpracticed enough to leave her unprotected."

Morgana shook her head and buried her face in Donovan's shoulder. It felt good to not have to be the strong one for once. "None of us did. I knew she was a witch, but out of respect for Ceri, we didn't press her into joining us. Ceri would've gotten over it eventually and been able to move on with good grace and even honest friendliness, but she wasn't there yet. I thought we'd have time."

"Stop blaming yourself," Donovan said. "Every one of us knew the victim profile, and no one suggested her as a potential victim. Hell, I didn't look into her, and even Bridget didn't mark her as someone with enough power to be a target. This isn't on you. You don't have to carry the weight of all the blame for this."

Morgana raised her face from Donovan's shoulder and shook her head. "This was my job, my mark. And these are my people. Joanna and Violet. It never occurred to me that the witch could take out both in the same day—at practically the same time."

Donovan stiffened, then reared back. "Violet? The woman the oracles fingered as a suspect?"

Morgana nodded. "She came to see me again. When she opened her eyes, I saw all the way into her soul. She was brimming with power, raw, untapped power. I tried to get her to stay, to warn her, but she didn't believe me. The minute she walked out of my shop and away from the protection of my shields, she was struck down. That's why I was calling you."

Donovan reached over and stroked one thumb along Morgana's jaw. "Why are you here?"

Morgana inhaled deeply and let the calm mask she wore settle back over her. "I saw the police and ambulance come here instead of where I was, and when you didn't answer, I feared for Hazel."

Donovan caught Morgana's eyes. "Only her?"

Morgana looked at Donovan and took a deep breath. "I've known Russell almost as long as I've lived in Oracle Bay, and I'd charged him with using his powers to keep Hazel safe. When I saw the emergency vehicles and didn't hear from you, I worried that he'd put himself in harm's way at my request and hadn't survived."

The corners of Donovan's lips quirked up. "I'm glad you weren't worried about me."

Morgana moved out from underneath the shelter of Donovan's arm and smiled at him. "You told me you were unassailable. Who am I to doubt your confidence?"

Donovan's arm tightened around Morgana, then dropped to her side. "I wish you'd let go of your need for control. I can take care of you."

Morgana stiffened. "I don't need you to take care of me. I have managed to survive for over sixteen hundred years on my own, and a child such as yourself could not possibly have a positive effect on the length of my existence."

Donovan sighed. "Of course not. My sixty years of life can't possibly compare, and it was silly of me to think you'd ever need someone to help you carry the burden."

Morgana bit her lip to keep herself from telling Donovan how much he was needed, how he could hold Morgana and shield her from the rest of the world while Morgana kept them shielded from the magic. If she let herself speak aloud what she was feeling, it would make it true. She'd become practiced in many things in her lifetime, but one of the things she'd perfected was lying to herself.

"Where is Hazel now?" Morgana asked. She was surprised at herself for not asking earlier. But when she thought about it, she realized she'd assumed that Donovan wouldn't be here comforting her if he hadn't already seen to Hazel's safety.

"Bridget showed up right before you did. She took her back to your house." Donovan moved his arm as if to put it around Morgana again, then dropped it to his side.

Morgana breathed a sigh of relief. "I'm glad Bridget showed up to take her home. Her shields aren't as good as mine, but they are at least the equal of yours. Did you see anyone that looked suspicious?"

Donovan shook her head. "Violet's husband was having a drink at the bar, but there was no one else I recognized. When I questioned Russell, he said the same."

She paused for a moment, then looked at Donovan. "Someone is going to have to tell Violet's husband she's dead before he stumbles on the scene.

"Everyone who was in the bar when Joanna died is being held there while we question them. When I go back in, I'll talk to him first, then let him know. Did you see anyone on the street when she died?"

Morgana thought it over. "The only person I saw was Leslie. They're new to town and own the local bookshop, but they were not in Ireland during any of the murders there, nor were they in Vancouver for those murders."

"You had them checked out?" Donovan asked.

Morgana nodded. "I had everyone in Oracle Bay checked out. We are a town of magic users, after all. I looked at everyone from Leslie to Antonia, the elderly woman who owns the tea shop, to Brandy, the manager of the Pour House. The only people I didn't alibi were the seasonal residents and tourists." She shot a sharp glance towards Donovan. "I might be upset now, but I am a professional. You're the one who pointed out I have worked for The Silver Eye for over seventy years. Until this case, no one has ever called into question my qualifications."

"I am not questioning your qualifications, nor your commitment to solving this case. I am just asking if you are okay. This is a lot closer to home than a case is supposed to be. If you want to step back, it's understandable. You won't even have to explain yourself. Just say it's a conflict of interest now that it's affected someone you know personally." Donovan's eyes caught Morgana's gaze, but instead of the accusations Morgana expected to see, there was nothing but compassion. Well, compassion and something else that Morgana couldn't quite put a finger on, which heated her skin.

She shook herself. Attraction was unwelcome at all times, but especially now. Two women had died. Two women who Morgana was responsible for, two women she'd failed.

"I need to go," Morgana said.

"I'll walk back to your shop with you," Donovan said.

"That's unnecessary," Morgana replied stiffly.

Donovan rose to his feet effortlessly, a feat that shouldn't be possible for a man on the other side of sixty. He held his hand out to Morgana, who took it grudgingly and let the much, much younger man pull her to her feet.

"It is, actually. I've spoken with the officers on the scene here, but I'm still the police chief in this town, and if there was a second death in front of your shop, I need to have a presence." Donovan crooked his elbow and held it out to Morgana.

Morgana ignored the elbow and looked down at herself. She was still wearing the black outfit she'd put on while running here. She looked around, but no one was looking at them. "I need to change," she hissed to Donovan.

He let her gaze slide up and down Morgana's body. "Never change, gorgeous."

"This isn't the right look," Morgana said.

Donovan shook her head. "I don't know if it matters anymore. You're not bait. The blood witch is working in Oracle Bay. There is no guarantee they know who and what you are, but if they've done any research at all, they know. You're not bait anymore."

Morgana pursed her lips. Donovan was right, but she'd been playing this role in an effort to draw out the murderer for so long that it was weird to think of letting it go. "I'll send a message to ensure it's okay, but I suspect you are correct. I cannot wait to get rid of this hair."

"You will always be beautiful, no matter what look you're sporting, but that long, black hair is something special." Donovan's lids dropped halfway, and he smirked.

Morgana ignored him. "I'm going to change. I want to hold this persona until it's clear I don't need to. Do you see anyone looking?"

Donovan's head turned as he scanned the area. "If you're fast, no one will notice."

Morgana closed her eyes and let the power wash over her. Seconds later, her black sneakers were beige low-heeled pumps, her tank top was a sweater set, and the running tights were once again khaki capris. "Good?" she asked.

"Not as good as the real you, but you're hitting the cosplay you've been aiming for." Donovan held out his elbow again.

This time, Morgana took the proffered arm. "I'm glad you know who I am." She'd meant it lightly, but after the words came out, she realized that even though her secrets went back centuries, this man knew more about her than she did about him. She felt unsteady about the way the power disparity tipped away from her for the first time in ages.

"Do I, though?" Donovan asked. "I don't think anyone ever will."

twenty-four

Morgana walked into her house. It'd been three hours since Violet had died in front of her shop and ten minutes since Donovan had handed her off to Drew so the crystal ball reader could drive her home.

"Thank you for driving me home," Morgana said. "I'd love to offer you a drink and invite you to stay, but—"

"But it doesn't matter what you say," Drew retorted. "You are one of the four scariest people I've ever met, and for that reason alone, I'd usually do what you told me to. But two of the other three have all commanded me to stay until they arrive."

Morgana racked her brains trying to figure out who besides Paska would be considered terrifying.

Drew saved her the trouble. "We have a fallen angel in our midst. He might be my best friend's boyfriend, but he scares me on so many levels."

Morgana shook her head. "So, Andy and Ceri are two of the three?"

"Nope. Just Andy. I've known Ceri for a hundred and more years. She's powerful, but she doesn't scare me. Andy and Paska are two of the three, and the ones who told me to stay until one of them arrived.”

“Who’s the third person who frightens you?” Morgana asked.

Drew grinned. “My grandmother was scarier than all of you put together, but since she passed a couple hundred years ago, we’re probably safe from her.”

Morgana laughed. “We may need to check with Russell before declaring ourselves safe. You must have wonderful stories about your grandmother. I’ve never heard any of them.”

“You’ve never been interested in any of our lives,” Drew said.

The statement hurt, but there was no way to counter it.

“You are correct,” she said. “That is a failing I intend to rectify. How can I protect you all if I don’t know who and what I’m protecting?”

Drew tilted his head and looked at her. “It’s not your job to protect us. All we ask is for you to tell us what threats are out there. You did that. It wasn’t your fault that none of us spent enough time with Joanna to think of her as a target. And it’s not your fault that Violet chose you to visit today. If she’d chosen any of the rest of us, we would’ve watched her die, too.”

Morgana’s lips creased into a thin line, and she didn’t reply.

Drew seemed to take her silence as objection.

“You could not have stopped what happened. We all screwed up. You aren’t the one who kept her out of our circle.” Drew directed a half smile her way. “It’s my fault more than anyone’s. I knew she needed us, but Ceri wasn’t ready, so I didn’t push the issue.”

“It does not behoove us to play a game to determine who is to blame. It was my responsibility to keep the seers in this town safe, and I failed. I not only failed, but I did not recognize the women who were in danger until it was too late. Now, I believe you were just leaving. Is that correct?” Morgana liked Drew, but she didn’t know him well enough to confide in him or discuss her feelings.

“We’re friendly, but not friends,” Drew said, echoing her

thoughts. "But I have lived for a very long time and recognize unreasonable guilt. Let it go, Morgana."

Drew's words pricked at the secret defenses Morgana kept in the darkness of her soul, and she dragged out the name he was born with to throw at him like a barb. "You cannot tell me what to let go of and what to feel guilty about, Solomon. You are a child."

Drew nodded as if that was nothing more than he expected. "I'm going to stay and keep you safe until either Paska or Andy arrive. You are capable of keeping yourself safe, more than I am, but I have instructions, and I'm not going to fight Paska and Andy, no matter how much you try to run me off."

Morgana knew a losing battle when she was in one, and it was never a good idea to keep fighting where there was no hope. That made one look ridiculous, and Morgana never was ridiculous. She didn't have to be gracious in defeat, though.

"Fine. Come in. Bridget and Hazel are inside. In the meantime, you may make yourself a cup of tea if you want. I am going to be in my garden, and you are not welcome out there. It is a private place."

Drew sighed noisily. "Since we both know I'm not your protection detail, that's fine. But if you turn into a bat and fly away, I'm going to be in real trouble."

"A bat?" Morgana's voice rose an octave, and she'd have to rein it in if she didn't want to veer into a screech.

"You have powers I don't understand. You might be able to turn into a bat or ride around on a broomstick. I'm just asking you to stay put until someone else gets here. Please."

"Fine." Morgana took off her shoes and grabbed her garden shoes from the shoe rack, then headed outside to let the water and earth start the process of healing her soul for the second time that day.

twenty-five

Morgana was still in the garden when Paska arrived. Her shoulders relaxed in his presence. He might be a pain in the ass, but he would never let her carry this burden alone, not if there was anything he could do to help her bear it.

When she turned, he held up a hand before she could say anything. "It's not your fault."

"I wish people would stop saying that to me." Morgana was petulant, but at least she didn't have to pretend to be put together for Paska. He'd seen her in every mood imaginable over their long lives together. They'd gone their separate ways from time to time when they grew tired of being together, but they always found their way back to each other.

Part of it was the curse. It bound their souls together as surely as their lives. Part of it was the long habit of knowing each other better than anyone else ever could.

And part of it was the almost incomprehensible tie of family. They were lucky in that. So many people weren't close to their families for a variety of reasons. Ceri's family, other than her nan, had rejected her when she started seeing the future. Drew's—other than his grandmother—had threatened his life when they found out he was gay. Andy's mother had cast him into hell when he rebelled, although Morgana wasn't sure it counted as "estranged" when your mother was also a god.

But she and Paska, for all their differences and squabbles over the centuries, had remained close.

"Are you listening to me?" Paska sounded peevish.

"Not more than necessary. Did you speak to Bridget and Hazel? How are they?" Morgana didn't want to dwell on her guilt more than she had to, and right now, there were bigger concerns.

"Bridget was a bit hysterical at first, but she's fine now that she knows Hazel is okay. Hazel is panicked and likely to flee. Donovan is with her now, and that behemoth of a man has a comforting effect on the girl." Paska sank into the soft grass and folded his legs in front of him. "It's too bad the beast will kill us. He's not a bad person other than that."

"Don't call him the beast," Morgana said. "It's rude and untrue."

Paska smiled slightly. "Rude maybe. I'll grant you that. But untrue? Have you asked him to show you his true form yet?"

"When would I have done that? Why? I already told him last night was a one-night stand. The conversation you and I had this morning further cemented that decision." Morgana smiled tightly at Paska.

"He was here with you earlier. You don't allow anyone in your garden, yet you invited him." Paska gave Morgana a hard, knowing look.

Morgana huffed out a long breath. "We needed somewhere to talk privately, and that's a difficult place to find when one has house-guests who have little compunction about violating personal space."

"Surely your bedroom has remained inviolate."

"You think inviting Donovan into my bedroom would be better than hosting him in my private garden? You have a greater opinion of my self-control than is warranted." Morgana tried to infuse her voice with light-hearted teasing to belay the hurt that welled up when she thought about the impossibility of ever having Donovan in her bedroom.

"Your self-control has never been the problem. There have been many times in the past where letting go of the tight rein you keep on yourself would've been better than the rigidity of control you take comfort in. If you'd tumbled this man when you first met, the brief infatuation likely would've grown cold. But you let yourself long privately while keeping your legs together publicly, and now you yearn for him," Paska said.

"I don't yearn," Morgana snapped. "Passing lust and yearning are different."

"If I thought it nothing more than passing lust, I would not have warned you to end things. As it is, you've almost gone too far. If you fall in love with him, that's what will activate the curse, not consummation."

Morgana shook her head. "It has to be more than love. It has to be the connection of body and soul wrapped in love. Love without physical connection would not cause our lives to end, nor will sex without love."

Paska considered for a moment, his head cocked to one side. "You may be right. I've fallen in love a dozen times over the centuries, but never approached the people I loved, so the bonds had no time to strengthen. You could tie your heart to someone strongly enough that the physicality would not be necessary, but sex will strengthen it faster."

"It has to be requited. There is no reason to believe feelings, should I develop them, would be returned." Morgana tried to carry the lie in her voice and imbue it with truth, but from the look of deep compassion and sadness on Paska's face, he heard the desire she felt but didn't want to admit.

"I've seen the way Donovan looks at you. He's as close to falling in love as you are. As soon as this case is over, walk away from him and never see him again. If he chooses to stay in Oracle Bay to continue to serve as the police chief, you will need to leave," Paska said.

Morgana's shoulders slumped. Paska was right. He often was, which was an infuriating habit he'd developed over their centuries together. He seldom hesitated to say "I told you so" when they disagreed, and he was proven right again.

"I will come with you," Paska said. "You don't have to be alone."

"No. You'll have to stay. They need someone to keep them safe, and you are the best one to do that." Morgana felt emotion rise and her eyes prickled with it.

"Andy is as capable as either of us, maybe more so. He is a creature of near infinite power, and I suspect what little he gave up when he chose to stay on earth rather than taking up residence in either heaven or hell will return within in the year." Paska's eyes went distant as they did when the visions came unbidden, something that seldom happened after sixteen hundred years of learning to control what and when the knowing came.

"You have seen this? You know what happens on the planes of the Christian heaven and hell?" Morgana leaned forward, intrigued despite herself. She and Paska had lived in the period just after the Roman withdrawal from Britain and the rise of Christianity, but they had never proscribed to the new gods, instead choosing to maintain their casual connection to the gods of their people and their birth.

"There is a powerful wave coming, one that was started by the prematurely planned apocalypse the Christian god and devil pushed the world into last December. They will see the results of the ripples they started in motion within a year." Paska blinked and returned to the present. "I do not think it will affect us overmuch."

"But will it make Andy powerful enough to take on the role I've tried to play?"

Paska nodded after a moment. "In combination with Misty—should she choose to harness the power available to her instead of letting it flow around her as if she is a small rock in a large river—they would be able to keep the town and all its residents safe. We would not be needed. And I would never let you go out on your own, especially when you'd be leaving with a broken heart."

Morgana was saved from the false protestation that her heart was in no more danger of being broken than Andy was in danger of perishing in fire by footsteps padding softly across the lush grass in her garden. She didn't have to turn to know it was Donovan.

"What do you want?" Paska asked harshly. "And how dare you violate Morgana's private space without an express invitation?"

"I wanted to update you on Hazel's condition and let you know I'm leaving," Donovan said. "And I was under the impression that I had a standing invitation to join Morgana in her garden."

The look Paska shot towards Morgana made her wince, but he didn't say anything.

She took a moment to school her face into an expression of polite indifference before turning around. "How is Hazel?"

"Asleep for now. Ceri and Andy showed up, and Drew went home. Andy will stay as long as you need him to, although he said he hoped it wouldn't be too long. I don't think he's comfortable here," Donovan said.

"What did he say?" Morgana asked.

"Are you sure you want to know?" Donovan answered with a grin.

"Please tell me, so I have a chance to think of a suitable response."

"You asked for it. He said, 'Tell the witch she needs to get her shit together and get back in here so she can do the job she said she was going to do. I don't want to spend any more time here than I have to in case I get the urge to ride a broom.'" Donovan's grin widened even further, and laughter danced in his eyes.

Morgana almost retorted with her standard response, calling him a demon, when she remembered Donovan wasn't privy to Andy's origin story. "I will come back inside in a moment to relieve him of this unwanted task."

Donovan nodded. "I'll get out of your space now."

"Wait!" Morgana said, then bit the inside of her lip when she saw the hard glance Paska was fixing her with. "Did Hazel share what she was hesitant to talk about with me?"

Donovan nodded again. "I don't know how much it matters, but her mother was murdered when she was sixteen. She gave me permission to tell you, so I'm not breaking her confidence."

Morgana stood in one swift movement. She reached into her pocket and pulled out the bead she'd found. "Violet's mother was also murdered when she was sixteen. And she found a bead after having a recurring nightmare about beads and murder. I found this bead, which was identical to the one Violet showed me, in the Pour House and wondered if it had been on Hazel's person."

Donovan pursed his lips. "That could be the link we're looking for. I'll need to look into Joanna's background and ask the CSI team to keep an eye out for a small quartz crystal bead."

"I'll put a call into..." Morgana broke off what she was about to stay and glanced at Paska. "If we're done here, you can go."

Paska rolled his eyes. "If it makes you feel better to talk about your clandestine work without me present in order to preserve the veil of secrecy you believe I couldn't penetrate, that's okay. But remember what I said. Keep it short." He walked out of the backyard without a second glance.

"What's he talking about?" Donovan asked. "Does he know what you do?"

"Probably. There are few secrets he cannot see. He's more powerful than the rest of us put together, although he often prefers to keep the illusion that he's my equal instead of my superior." Morgana tapped her lips, trying to remember what she'd been going to say. "Oh! I'll call in about the Vancouver murders and see if there are similar links in their backgrounds and if any beads were found in their possession. Those women were older than the current group."

"Do you think it is a different perpetrator, after all?" Donovan asked.

Morgana shook her head. "No. The method and the markings are the same. It is possible that the blood witch, if she'd marked the victims long before they were taken, needed to achieve a certain level of power before she could begin, and started with the oldest potential witches before moving on to the younger ones."

"There's also the fact that a woman of forty who hasn't woken her potential is an easier mark than a younger woman. We saw what happened when she tried to take Hazel yesterday. It woke something in her."

"She'd already been exposed to magic, too. Soon, she won't be as vulnerable," Morgana said, considering. "In fact, she is the only one I know of who's been practicing at all before she was targeted. I wonder what the difference is?"

"May I join you?" Bridget called from the doorway.

"We were about to come in," Morgana answered smoothly. There'd already been too many people in her garden today, and she wasn't sure she could handle another, no matter how long she and Bridget had known each other.

Bridget laughed. "Let me make you a cup of tea, then. Hazel is asleep. I don't know what Andy did to her, but she dropped off immediately."

This time, Bridget's expression looked more covetous than angry.

Morgana couldn't blame her. Andy was an attractive man, and a lifetime of celibacy was enough to make anyone lustful in the face of such beauty.

"It's amazing what fear, exhaustion, and a warm blanket can do for someone," Andy said from where he sat on the couch with Ceri perched on his lap.

"If you don't need us anymore, we are leaving. Immediately," Ceri said with an uncharacteristic glare at Bridget.

"We'll be okay," Morgana said. "Nothing can get through my shields, not even a homicidal maniac."

"Maniac seems a bit strong," Bridget said, looking offended. "There is no need to conflate the desire for power with mental illness."

"A bit strong?" Donovan said. "This person has killed and drained of power and blood close to twenty women that we know of. Perhaps maniac is the wrong term, though. I don't want to use ableist language. If that's what you meant, then thank you for the correction."

"Of course that's what I meant," Bridget said.

Ceri huffed. "Goodbye." She slid off Andy's lap, then held a hand to him to haul him to his feet.

Andy nodded once at Morgana. "Call me if you need me, witch."

"Thank you for the offer." She left the "demon" unspoken, but she could tell by the quirk of his lips he heard it, nonetheless.

Donovan looked at Bridget, then Morgana. "Bridget, I need to interview you about what happened today and find out if you sensed the power in Joanna and Violet, and if there's anyone else you identified. We can do that here, or if you'd prefer privacy, we can head to the station."

Brigit's eyes widened. "Are you arresting me?"

Donovan laughed. "No. If I was arresting you, you'd know." He pulled a set of handcuffs out of his pocket, and Morgana sensed the magic pulsing from them the minute they appeared. How Donovan had kept the power suppressed until they were visible was a mystery Morgana was interested in solving.

Bridget eyed the cuffs warily. "I didn't know those were there."

"You wouldn't expect me to go on a witch hunt without the tools needed to subdue someone much more powerful than me, would you? And you know who I work for. It shouldn't surprise you that I've been given a pair of magical cloaking restraints." Donovan stowed the handcuffs back in his pocket, and the power emanating from them winked out.

Bridget cast a quick glance at Morgana, then back to Donovan. "Let's go to the station. I'm sure Morgana would like some privacy in her house, and with Hazel asleep, this is the best chance."

"Thank you," Morgana said. "That is a gift beyond measure right now."

Bridget smiled. "I'll call before returning home. Donovan, I'll be outside; take your time." She picked up a small purse from the side table by the doorway and disappeared outside.

Donovan looked down at Morgana. "I will let you know what she says, and anything I find out about the other victims and their similarities to Violet, Joanna, or Hazel."

"I'll do the same." Morgana licked her lips nervously and shivered when Donovan followed the motion. She wanted nothing so much as to kiss him, but she couldn't. She shouldn't.

"Goodbye, Donovan," she said instead. "Please don't come here again. We should meet at the station for all further conversations."

"As you wish," Donovan said. "I'll call you."

Morgana watched Donovan walk out of her house, and this time, it felt final.

twenty-six

The house shuddered, waking Morgana with a jolt. She sat up from her position on the sofa and looked around wildly. A flash of light followed almost immediately by a crash of thunder pulled her to her feet and over to the window.

The sky was covered with a black, roiling mass of clouds. The lightning was nearly constant and judging by the nearly imperceptible time between the bolts and the thunder, the storm was right on top of Oracle Bay.

Morgana shook her head, trying to clear the sleep from her mind. She hadn't meant to fall asleep, but between the stress of the day and her lack of sleep last night, it wasn't surprising that she'd given into the exhaustion as soon as she had a moment of quiet.

Another crash of thunder rattled the windows, nearly masking the footsteps on the stairs.

"Morgana? What's going on?" Hazel sounded even more muddled than Morgana felt.

"Sudden storm," Morgana said shortly. "I should've known this would happen. The amount of magic it took to steal the power of two people almost simultaneously would have a cost, and since I can't imagine the witch cares about masking her black magic by using any of the power she banked or stole, this storm is likely the effect of what she pulled from the earth and sky.

"I didn't know you could do that," Hazel said with wide eyes.

"It is something that should never be done. Disrupting the earth's natural systems to preserve your own power is a terrible way to practice magic. If you can't afford to pay the cost of magic yourself, it is not an act you should be doing." Morgana paused, wondering if she should say more. "What do you know of where your power comes from and the price that is paid for wielding it?"

Hazel didn't answer for a moment, something Morgana appreciated. Considering an answer carefully rather than blurting the first thing that came to mind was a sign of the control Hazel was still grappling with.

"Well, I'm a witch, right?"

Morgana nodded.

"So, my power comes from the earth and the elements. My strength is with air, right? That's how I can make people see something else."

"Correct. You are full of your power, and you draw that from the earth and the elements, but mostly from the air. That makes it easy for you—you can never be cut off from your element the way those of us with a different affinity can be. Most witches have a personal store of magic that varies in capacity and amount depending on several factors, including how powerful that particular witch is. There is also the ability to train oneself to carry more power, but that takes years. It is possible to pull energy from the elements, but it is not something that should be done lightly. You must know everything about the earth, water, and weather in your vicinity."

"Because if I pull too hard, I can..." Hazel's face crinkled up as she thought. "I can create wind. And maybe that's what I want to do, but if I do it in the wrong place or the wrong way, I can stir up something dangerous."

"Yes, and with the amount of power you have, you could accidentally create a tornado," Morgana said.

"How far? I mean, how far do I need to look to make sure I'm not messing things up?" Hazel asked.

"It depends on many variables, not least of which is how much you'll need to borrow. That is why I caution witches to never do great works by themselves. It is better to enlist others so you can draw on their power instead of the earth's. If you disrupt the ground, and you're near a fault about to slip, you can cause a catastrophic earthquake. Weather is especially sensitive to the pull of magic from the air, and that is often the most obvious symptom that magic has been misused."

"But aren't there weather witches?" Hazel asked.

"Yes, but they work with existing weather patterns, nudging what's there into what they need. They encourage rain in drought, push unpleasant weather along to the next place, or hold things steady when needed. It requires superb control, if little power, and requires knowing what the climate is and should be, knowing that if a rainstorm is moved further east that it won't have even more devastating effects where it is sent. A witch with little power but great control, knowledge, and training can often do more effective magic than one with great power but none of the others." Morgana hesitated only a moment before adding, "You are a witch with immense power, but no knowledge and no training. The control you have is more instinct than anything else, and you are one misstep away from catastrophe. In addition to the possibility that you can disrupt the natural world by taking too much too quickly from the surrounding elements, you can also destroy yourself if you pull in more power than you can synthesize easily."

Hazel's face crumpled, and for a moment, Morgana thought she'd gone too far.

Then the younger woman's shoulders straightened, and a look of fierce determination hardened her features. "I don't want to be helpless, and I don't want to be afraid of my power anymore."

Morgana tipped her head and regarded Hazel. "Have you been afraid?"

Hazel nodded emphatically. "Just before my mother died, before she was murdered, she told me what I was. I didn't believe her at first, of course. It sounded like a fairytale. You know the kind—the ordinary girl wakes up with magical powers, a fairy godmother, and a kiss at midnight. Then, she proved it to me. Nothing major—just a few things that were beyond a birthday party magician's abilities. She promised me training, said I was going to be a force to be reckoned with. Then, a week later, she was dead." Hazel's voice flattened out as she talked about her mother's murder.

"I am very sorry," Morgana said. It was the kind of sentiment you were supposed to offer when hearing another person talk about their tragedies.

"It was a long time ago." Hazel brushed away Morgana's concern, then made a sound that was half choking and half laughing. The noise devolved into a sob. Hazel wrapped her arms around herself and shook with great wracking cries.

Morgana stood by, not sure what to do. Should she pat the girl on the head? She had a vague notion that offering a "There, there" to the younger woman might help, but before she could bring herself to act so inanely, Hazel's sudden storm passed.

"Sorry," Hazel said stiffly.

The younger woman's emotional discomfort did what her sobs hadn't. "There is no need to apologize. Loss is painful, and there is no time limit on grief. I lost the most important person of my life years and years ago, longer than you've been alive, and there are days when I am overcome." Her confession tightened her chest in a way that she seldom experienced anymore, for while she'd spoken truly about the eternal length of grief, time did draw out the space between spiraling guilt and despair and the softness of memory.

"Who did you lose?" Hazel asked, then immediately added, "That was rude. You don't have to tell me anything. I shouldn't have asked."

"It's okay," Morgana said, and she meant it sincerely. "My daughter died when she was not even as old as you. She was so beautiful—it was her image you pulled from my mind when you tried to influence me to feel kindly to you when we first met."

Hazel shrugged. "I never see what others see. I pull a memory of a loved one someone has a lot of compassion for, but not the image. I think it's so I can affect a lot of people at once without having to target anyone specific. I don't use it much—it seems like lying—but I was pretty scared and stressed out and thought that any advantage would help."

"It might have helped if you'd been able to keep the illusion up, but since you couldn't, it revealed that you'd used witchcraft to manipulate, and that invariably angers people." Morgana tipped her head to one side and considered the woman in front of her. Creating a glamour didn't require a great deal of power, but creating a half-dozen individual glamours at the same time was something Morgana didn't think she could do without a great deal of research and preparation. Yet Hazel had done in instinctively. "How long have you been able to glamour like this?"

"Glamour?" Hazel tipped her head to one side in a near-perfect imitation of Morgana.

Morgana waved her hand in a small circle in front of her face. "Create the illusion that you're someone else."

"Oh, as long as I can remember," Hazel said, then added with a small giggle, "It used to drive my teachers crazy. My mother could always see through it, though, and she was almost never amused."

The mischievous fondness in Hazel's voice made Morgana very much wish she'd had the opportunity to meet Hazel's mother. "And how long have you been able to glamour yourself to look different depending on who is looking at you?" Morgana had a theory but didn't want to lead Hazel to a conclusion that didn't exist.

Hazel tapped her index finger against her nose, then said doubtfully, "I think since I was a junior in high school. I didn't mean to the first time, but I was in trouble at school—I was in trouble a lot that year—and was called into the principal's office to be dressed down for…" She hesitated, turned a little pink, then continued, "…a number of minor infractions. There were so many adults there, and they were all so big and angry and menacing. I remember wishing they could see that I wasn't a bad person. My chest got really tight, then I felt like the wind had been knocked out of me, and I almost collapsed. The PE teacher leaped forward and grabbed me to keep me from falling. Then, they had a quick whispered conversation and let me go with a warning. As I was backing out of the office half-convinced it was a joke, I heard the vice principal say I reminded her of her daughter Ann, and the guidance counselor said that was funny, because I looked a lot like her little sister, and she'd never noticed before. After that, I tried to do it a couple times on purpose, but it never really worked unless I was stressed or scared or angry. And it always made me fall asleep after. Like turkey dinners or really good sex."

"Have you done it since coming to Oracle Bay?" Morgana asked.

Hazel's eyes shifted briefly to the left before coming back to meet Morgana's. "No?"

"Don't lie to me. It doesn't matter what you think I want to hear. The only thing I'm interested in is the truth." Morgana let her voice turn hard. She liked Hazel and didn't believe she could've killed anyone, but she wasn't about to leave that stone unturned and live to regret it.

Hazel sighed. "Once, and I didn't really mean to. I was tired and stressed, and I messed up."

"Tell me about it," Morgana commanded.

"I'm not sure it was really that important," Hazel hedged.

"Please," Morgana said more gently.

Hazel took a deep breath and looked down at her hands. "Fine. It was my first day at work at the Pour House. Bridget was there babysitting me… Or whatever you want to call it. A tall white man with super red hair came into the bar, ordered a drink from Zeke, and then stared at me. It freaked me out. Not just that he was staring, but that no one seemed to notice. And he was wearing a long coat, which seemed weird since it was pretty warm that day. I got really stressed out. I don't know why. It felt…almost familiar. Like I'd been in this situation before." She grimaced. "I shrieked. A little. Not really a scream. But then everyone looked at me, and it just…happened. I pushed out of me, and everyone softened a little, smiled, and went back to what they were doing. It was like nothing had happened at all."

"Everyone?" Morgana asked, wondering if Violet's husband was still a suspect, even though it was his wife who'd been killed. She'd looked into him at the same time she'd dug into Violet's background but hadn't found anything more about him than she had about Violet. He had an Associate's degree in hospitality management from Central Oregon Community College and managed the Shelburne Hotel… Morgana went cold. The Shelburne Hotel was where she and Donovan had discussed the murders… Was that what drew his attention to Oracle Bay? There were too many coincidences for him to be innocent now. "Was Andy there?"

Hazel shook her head. "No. Brandy was there, but she looked dazed, like my glamour had worked on her. The only people who weren't were Bridget and the strange man." She shivered. "I really didn't like him."

"What about Ezekiel?" Morgana pressed.

"Zeke? The prophet?"

Morgana nodded but said nothing else, just waited.

Hazel chewed at her lower lip. "I didn't notice him. Or notice if he was affected. Should I have?"

"Not necessarily. I was merely curious. What happened next with Bridget and the strange man? Did you speak to him?" Morgana tried to keep her tone light, or as light as she was able, while replaying the last few days to determine if Tom had been seen anywhere else without Violet.

"No. When the glamour dissolved, I was exhausted. I took a break, and when I came back to the floor, he was gone. I asked

Bridget about him, but she said she hadn't really noticed anything odd about him. She didn't mention the glamour at all, either, and I was too embarrassed to bring it up."

Morgana smiled. She was there to comfort the young woman, not scare her further, after all. "I'm sure Bridget had the right of the story, which is why she didn't mention it to anyone else. As for her not mentioning the glamour—she likely could see your embarrassment and didn't want to make it worse. No one was harmed, so there is no reason to carry any guilt with you. Control will come with practice."

"You said I was a ticking time bomb. I think you're right." Guilt clouded Hazel's eyes. She briefly met Morgana's gaze, then looked down again.

"You are powerful and untrained. Not a ticking time bomb. Be careful with what you do, but never hesitate to defend yourself or others if you need to. You have good instincts and a good heart." Morgana hoped she was right. She was seldom wrong, but when she was, it was usually about something catastrophic, or so Paska liked to claim.

"Thank you. I think I'll go to bed now." Hazel stood. Her eyelids were already drooping.

Morgana watched her go upstairs, then headed to the kitchen to make another pot of tea. She reached into her pocket and pulled out the quartz bead. She set it on the table while waiting for her tea to steep. There was something here. Something about this bead, the strange man, and murdered mothers that were all tied together, and she couldn't connect the dots.

If she had someone to talk it out with, maybe she could see the connection, but she didn't. She worked alone—she'd always worked alone. That didn't negate the need to tell someone what she'd discovered about Tom. She pulled out her phone, thought for a moment with her finger hovering over the keypad, then typed rapidly. *I think Tom is guilty. He's been in too many places to be coincidence. Maybe not working alone.*

A moment later, Donovan's answer came back. *I talked to him earlier, and he was a wreck. I'll bring him in for another round of questioning. Thanks for the tip. I'll let you know.*

Donovan would be an excellent partner in more than just solving this string of murders. If only...

Morgana stood, dumped the tea out without drinking any, grabbed her jacket, and went to her garden sanctuary. If she couldn't have a partner, even for a brief time, she'd have to make do with talking to herself. After all, she'd spent this long needing no one else; there was no reason to long for what she'd never had.

twenty-seven

The sky was turning peachy grey with the imminent sunrise before Morgana rose from her cross-legged position on the ground. She interlaced her fingers and stretched her arms over her head, then folded forward at the waist, twisting until she felt it in her low back and hamstrings. She returned to a neutral position and dropped her arms to her side with a growl of frustration that undid everything her meditation had done to relax her.

Something didn't feel right. She was safe here—not only couldn't anything get through the shields she kept over her house, her garden was sacrosanct. Just like her basement workroom, the garden was protected. Even if a threat managed to get into her house, no one with ill intent towards her could violate those two spaces. But even if she and Hazel were safe, no one else was. The killer was still at large, and she hadn't figured out why she hadn't been able to shield Violet. If she couldn't do a simple protection spell, she was as useless as anyone else at protecting the vulnerable.

No. She could not dwell on what she was unable to do. It was important to look to what she could do. She should add the extra layer of shields to the rest of her house—particularly her bedroom—but shields took a lot of energy to create and maintain. Unlike the general shields protecting her house from magical attack, those specifically meant to recognize intent had to be tied to her and not the land she'd claimed as hers, which meant a trickle of energy was constantly being drained out of her and into them.

The backdoor opened quietly, then swung closed with a light bang.

Morgana took a deep breath and felt the familiar comfort of her layers of protection settle over her like a lightweight cloak. Only then did she turn around to see who had violated her sanctuary.

Bridget stood on the grass just outside the back door. Her hands were clasped in front of her with her rosary dangling from her hands, the quartz and marble beads catching the first rays of morning.

Morgana's eyes widened slightly before she could school her expression. Her first thought was to chide herself for not seeing the truth. She reached down to pull energy from her earth and fill her coffers to overflowing.

Nothing happened.

A wrinkle appeared between Morgana's brows, and she opened her conduit even further. This was her space, her land. She was tied to it and it to her, and there should be an immediate flow of power with minimal effort.

Beads of sweat formed on her forehead, and finally she stopped her ineffectual draw.

Bridget laughed, hugging herself. "Do you know how hard it is to steal power while staying positive? Getting past whatever spells you have protecting this space was difficult. Well done." Bridget golf clapped, the beads of her rosary swinging gently back and forth with the motion.

"What do you want?" Morgana asked, her voice smooth. The how was less important now. She'd figure it out later and fix whatever chinks in her armor Bridget had found. She dropped her channel to the earth and reached out to her shields. She let go of the one in the workroom, reabsorbing the power into herself. She didn't need the protection there now, and although it'd be difficult to rebuild when it was over, better to rebuild than to get herself killed. Once she'd pulled that back into herself, she opened the smallest of siphons to the rest of the shields she'd placed on her house, on her business, and then on the homes and businesses of the people she'd come to care for. Hopefully, if she kept it small, Bridget wouldn't sense it. It'd take a lot longer to replenish herself enough to have a chance against the blood witch standing in front of her, but the egomaniacal did like to talk about themselves.

Bridget laughed, and the cheerful expression she usually wore disappeared. "Power. Obviously."

Morgana shook her head. "That's not a real answer, Bridget, and you know it. You had power. What do you want with this much power, and what do you want from me?"

"What's mine. Do you know how hard it is to feel all the power around me all the time, and not even be able to see it without help? There are so many people walking who don't what they carry. Even when the truth-compelling gift came to me, it was weak. I deserve so much more." Bridget clasped her hands in front of her and widened her eyes, looking earnest.

A wave of pity overtook Morgana, and for a second, she sympathized with Bridget. It would be difficult to know what was out there and not be able to touch it. Reality whiplashed back. Wanting more and killing to get it were two very different things. She was being manipulated. Morgana's anger singed the cord holding her temper in check. She hadn't lost her temper in decades, and she would not now. She never lost control completely, but anger could cause even her to make a mistake. When she took this power-mad witch out, she wanted to be deliberate in how she did it.

"Don't you want to know how I got past your shields to steal your power?" Bridget asked.

"I'll figure it out eventually," Morgana said with a careless shrug. "No matter how much you stole from my connections to the earth and from the innocents you've been murdering, you'll never be more powerful than me." She wasn't sure any of that was true. She was more powerful than Bridget, but with the blood witch's influx of power, complete dearth of morals, lack of desire to keep the balance, and the madness glinting in her eyes, she might be able to overcome Morgana. There was no way Morgana could let that fear overcome her confidence. She didn't want to give Bridget any openings.

Confidence, false or not, wouldn't keep her safe. She needed help, if only to keep Bridget from escaping.

Morgana reached for the part of her that was buried too deep for anyone to sense and tugged. She didn't have the gift of telepathy, and that was unreliable anyway, but the connection between her and her brother was strong and unbreakable. He'd feel her need, feel the urgency, and he would come to her aid.

While she vibrated the connection between her and Paska like a violin string, she watched Bridget. The witch had lapsed into silence and was staring at the fountain behind Morgana.

She let go of the connection she shared with Paska and mentally tripped over another. There shouldn't be anything there. She could form strong mental connections with others, but since she'd lost her daughter and her daughter's father, since she and Paska had been cursed, she'd steered clear of bonding with anyone else.

Worry and desire flooded through the bond she didn't recognize, and she gasped, covering her shock and surprise at finding Donovan at the other end. She didn't love him, didn't even care enough to be tied to him. But she couldn't deny the bond forming them.

Paska was right. It was almost too late. If she couldn't walk away from him when this was all over, her feelings for Donovan Davies would kill her and her brother.

"Do you keep fish?" Bridget asked. "It looks like there might be fish in there. The big orange and black ones. Something with teeth." She shuddered and made the sign of the cross.

"Koi?" Morgana asked in the same calm, friendly voice she'd been using. "I travel enough that caring for a pet isn't something that would make sense for me, although koi aren't pets, are they?" She wasn't answering the question until she found out why Bridget was asking.

"Not even if it was a familiar?" Bridget's smile stretched out, and the madness that Morgana had glimpsed in the other woman's eyes slid over her face.

"Not even then," Morgana said. "I've never had a familiar, never wanted to use an animal as a storage vessel for my magic when my internal stores are nearly limitless. Do you have a familiar?"

Bridget nodded enthusiastically. "I do, but no mere animal. Oh no, I've bound the spirit of an animal in human form. It makes everything a lot easier for me, although I can't let him know I've done it, and human familiars don't last as long as animals. I think the conflict between free will and being bound to service breaks them faster."

Dread grew in Morgana's stomach, and she found the cord between her and Donovan again. Paska had called him "the beast." She hadn't asked Donovan about it; he was nothing more than a one-night stand, a colleague. She didn't need to know what he was. That was a privilege reserved for friends and lovers.

Regret and guilt flooded the connection, and she knew the truth. Donovan had betrayed her. The curse was activated.

There was only one thing she could do to protect her town, to protect her friends, and to make sure Bridget and Donovan couldn't hurt anyone else. Take them out with everything she had left. It would drain her past recovery, and it might not even be enough, but she had an ace in her back pocket—her brother. Of course, she wouldn't draw on Paska unless she had no other choice. No sense in both of them dying with their connection to the goddess severed, drifting eternally untethered instead of finding their way to rest and rebirth. If she could, she'd leave him the choice to stay for another life and another chance.

"That's why you're coming after me now, isn't it?" Morgana

asked. She didn't try to keep the sadness from her voice. "Donovan told you how close I was getting to connecting the dots."

Bridget nodded. "Not willingly. I had to drag it out of him. I think he's starting to remember what he's doing for me when we're not together. I wasn't sure what you'd do if you realized it was me. I was preparing for the eventuality—that's why I had to claim the power of those two unrealized witches." She clucked her tongue reprovingly. "That amount of power is wasted on those who don't know what to do with it. I can use it."

"What are you going to do with it?" Morgana asked. "More murders?"

"It's not murder. It's reclaiming what should be mine." Bridget's smile returned to the cheerful placidity she usually showed the world. "And once I have what I deserve, I can do whatever I want. Have whoever I want. I won't be the quiet little nun in the back of the room or the timid little witch at the back of the coven. I will be somebody people look at, bow to, fear the way they do you."

"All this so you can set yourself up as a pale imitation of me?"

"No! I'll be better than you. Greater than you. You don't know how much you could do with your power. You don't deserve it any more than the rest of them! That's why they had to die!" Bridget shrieked.

Morgana had faced down a lot of people during her long life, including a lot of magically inclined folks whose misuse of power had upset the balance in their minds, but she'd never looked in the eyes of someone who was so far removed from reality as to claim with sincerity that leaving a trail of bodies drained of power wasn't murder. She had to keep her talking to give herself a chance of finding the weakness she knew had to exist. No one was infallible.

"Why is Hazel still alive?" Morgana asked. "I thought she was a target, but you could've taken her at any time, couldn't you have? We trusted you, and you've been alone with her countless times."

Bridget clasped her hands in front of her mouth. "Haven't you guessed? Haven't you seen?"

"I haven't. Why don't you tell me?"

"I wanted her at first, but then Donovan told me what she was. She's a lodestone. She attracts magic and power to her like a porch light draws moths, and the power instinctively trusts her. She's so pure of heart, it's sickening. But she has her uses. I just wish I'd discovered her earlier. And this town... The combination of the town's pull on the magical and her magnetism is remarkable." Bridget closed her eyes and raised her shoulders up, and delight settled on her face.

Bridget continued monologuing, her eyes closed in near ecstasy. "Fortunately, I won't have to give either up. I reported my rosary missing a couple days ago. The bar owner doesn't like me, but he'll remember me talking about it. And that old magician—I can't tell how he's managed to muster enough power to live more than a century—he heard me, too. When they find Hazel and me unconscious in your living room with the dark magic symbols drawn on our bodies and you dead with the rosary in your hands as well as files on everyone I've drawn power from, it will be obvious that you're the murderer. Hazel and I will be regarded as victims in need of sympathy. We'll be asked to stay, to heal. I'll have to be more circumspect for a while, but it will be worth it."

"How is it you claim to be innocent of murder, but have no hesitation in using the word 'murderer' when you discuss framing me?" Morgana knew the answer already. Bridget was too full of power that wasn't hers and that she didn't have space for, and it was driving her mad.

Bridget flicked her fingers in dismissal. "What I know to be the truth and what others perceive as truth do not need to align. All that is needed is the belief that you are the dangerous one. Donovan will back me up—he'll have no choice. I don't think I'll be able to keep him much longer, though; his mind is starting to break free. He's already starting to remember the tasks I've set for him. A familiar with free will is no use to me. I'll take care of him after he vouches for your guilt. It'll be a mercy, then. He won't have to wonder if he's losing his mind," Bridget said conversationally.

"Why do you believe the people in this town will believe I'm the homicidal maniac, even with your planted evidence?" Morgana poked the witch in front of her with the words Bridget had objected to the day before. Angering her might not be the best idea, but Morgana could feel the power growing around Bridget and knew that if she didn't distract her, the battle would start before Morgana was ready. And angry people were more prone to mistakes.

Bridget laughed, a note of hysteria sending her laughter into a pitch that made Morgana wince. "My ability to demand truth, to drive my will into a person and force them to tell the truth, has another facet that I only discovered when I grew more powerful. I can push any thought or belief into those with less power than me— or even you, if you're not paying attention."

Several pieces clicked into place. "That's what you did to Miranda."

"If I hadn't been so foolish as to invite you to the Beltane circle, Miranda would've kept believing Hazel was guilty, and the rest of the coven wouldn't have argued."

"Why did you invite me?" Morgana asked.

"The athame. I needed it if I was going to go further. I should have known better." She shook her head, but there was a glint of amusement in her eyes.

"Why Rowan?" Morgana asked. "She didn't have any power."

"Who told you that?" Bridget asked, a sly smile creeping across her face.

Morgana didn't answer. She didn't need to.

"I've stayed so many steps ahead of you because I am so much cleverer. Between my gift and because you've held yourself so apart from them, the rest of your stupid friends will believe you're guilty. You have secrets that will come out when you're dead, and it will make the people you consider friends doubt the face you've always put forward. If you are capable of lying about your job hunting down rogue magic users, about where you draw your power, about the covens you've founded, and how long ago you were born, why wouldn't you be the kind of witch who'd do anything to find enough power to keep living forever?"

Morgana didn't want to believe her friends would believe her to be a blood witch, but she had held herself apart from them. She shook her head. No. Bridget was pushing her will on her again, and all of Morgana's energy was going into replenishing her magical stores, not serving as mental shields. She had to be stronger than this if she was going to delay Bridget long enough to survive. She moved on to another line of questioning, hoping the opportunity to talk about how clever she was would be the motivation Bridget needed to let go of her anger, at least for a few minutes, and spin out more time. "You haven't told me what your plans are for the power you're claiming from the women who don't know how to use it. That and how you're finding so many with the same stories are what I'm really curious about."

Bridget tapped one finger against her mouth. "I guess it doesn't matter how much you know. It's not like we'll be interrupted. Hazel will remain asleep until I need her to wake to play her part, and no one else will be here this early, not when they know we're all safe in your house. And I very much want you to know why you lost to me so that you go to your death with the knowledge that you will never be as good as me."

Morgana quelled the urge to roll her eyes. She might be dead soon, probably would be if she was right about the curse that had been laid on her and Paska over sixteen hundred years ago finally coming home to roost because she'd started to fall for Donovan Davies, but there was no need to hasten things and every reason to keep this witch talking while Morgana recharged her magical batteries and waited for Paska to arrive.

A raptor flew into the garden and landed on the bough of an apple tree, then dropped a mouse on the branch.

"Is that a hawk?" Bridget asked, staring at the bird as he ripped apart the rodent in front of him while staring directly at the people in the garden.

A smile ghosted over Morgana's lips. "A falcon," she replied. "We have five kinds of falcons around here. Kestrels, Gyrfalcons, Prairie Falcons, Peregrine Falcons, and Merlins."

twenty-eight

Bridget looked more fascinated than worried by the bird of prey that was ripping a mouse to shreds without looking at it. "I didn't know they were tame."

"Tame?" Morgana snorted. "He's not tame. He's wild and free, and no one would even dare try."

"But he's here in your backyard." Bridget didn't look at Morgana, instead continuing to stare at the bird.

Morgana wondered if the witch could tell there was something a little different about this raptor, or if she'd just never seen one up close. "A lot of hawks and falcons hunt people's backyards, especially with people having spread over their natural hunting territory. There are a lot of rodents and small birds to choose from."

Bridget finally turned back towards Morgana after one last, long look at the Merlin.

Now that he'd appeared, Morgana breathed a little easier. "You were going to tell me how you're finding the women and what you were going to do with all that power," she reminded Bridget.

Bridget pursed her lips. "I was, but I don't really feel like it anymore. I'm bored, and the longer I linger, the more likely it is that someone will call you to check up on Hazel."

"I rarely get phone calls," Morgana said honestly. "It's all texting with this younger generation, and I frequently go hours, even days, without responding. No one will look for me."

"Still, it's not good to delay too much, even if it is enjoyable watching you sit there, weak, knowing you're not only going to give me all your power, but be remembered as a blood witch."

Morgana felt a frisson of energy like a lightning-laced gust of wind whip through the yard, stinging her cheek and almost knocking her back into the pond.

"How did you do that?" Morgana asked. She could feel the shield against ill intent still surrounding her outdoor sanctuary, and fear bubbled up inside. There was a lot of power behind that punch, which meant Bridget was overflowing with so much power she either wasn't worried about wasting any, or she couldn't control what she had. It was just like Morgana had warned Hazel—too much power when there was no place to store it was dangerous.

"Are you afraid, yet?" Bridget asked. "You should be."

Another blast of wind gusted out, although this one fizzled out before reaching her.

"What did you do?" Bridget asked.

Morgana opened herself up as far as she could, knowing it would leave her vulnerable, and yanked. Shields all over town snapped, collapsed, and rushed back to her. And since the garden shield was barely effective anymore, she pulled that back into herself, too.

She wasn't at capacity—she seldom bothered anymore. It was uncomfortable to walk around full of power. It was almost like static electricity, giving her little shocks all the time and shocking others if she wasn't careful. But now, she regretted her decision to continue to channel everything into the shields to protect her friends and keep nothing extra for herself. Her complacency would cost her everything.

For the first time in longer than she could remember, fear froze her. Morgana was the most powerful witch alive and had been for centuries. No one but Paska could ever have challenged her and won. And now, she was staring down death at the hands of a witch who shouldn't be able to light a candle without help, much less throw around so much raw magic that Morgana's hopes of a quick and easy victory died almost as quickly as the other victims of Bridget's madness. Her breathing shallowed, and her chest ached as panic rolled over her. The power she drained from her shields barely buoyed her, but she couldn't let Bridget see her fear.

"That won't help you," Bridget said conversationally. Then, she threw her rosary at Morgana.

Morgana caught it instinctively, then dropped it just as quickly when she felt the barbs of magic grab her soul. It was too late. The quartz beads that were set between the Connemara marble beads dropped off the chain and swirled around her in a vortex, then flew at her, hitting her skin and embedding themselves in her with several little pops.

Pain flared immediately, stealing her breath and making her light-headed with terror. Morgana screamed and crashed to her knees as they burrowed their way in, burning the channels into her soul faster than her magic could heal them.

After what felt like hours of agony, she was able to block the pain from her mind. Morgana looked down at her skin, knowing what she'd see. Each bead that had entered her had created a symbol carved out of her skin.

"I don't feel the ones along my collarbone," Morgana croaked. Her throat was raw, and her words were barely intelligible.

"Oh, I like to add those myself at the end, if I can," Bridget said. "It completes the transfer, and if I'm touching your body while the last of your power comes to me, it feels complete. However, if I can't do it personally, I do have a way to finish it without me there."

"The crystals," Morgana gasped. She could feel the symbols deepen as they burrowed further into her body, touching her power and consuming her soul.

Bridget nodded enthusiastically. "Exactly. That's why I make sure to slip a quartz bead into all the pockets of those I've selected to share their power with me. It was just my luck that you picked one up. Even if I hadn't brought you to your knees in the place you felt most safe, I would've been able to destroy you at any time."

Morgana took a deep breath, trying to think through the pain that wanted to break through her mental barriers. She tipped her head back to feel the warmth of the morning sun. The Merlin was still sitting on the branch, although he was no longer bothering with his prey.

Why was he just watching? What was he waiting for?

The front door slammed. Bridget's head swiveled around, and her hold on the words of power in Morgana's body wavered enough for Morgana to slam a shield between them and the soul they were slowly shredding. The blood witch shot a look back at Morgana and pointed a finger. "Stay," she commanded before entering the house.

Morgana felt the net of the command settle over her, and with it, the haze of Bridget's command. It stole her fear almost as much as it took her will. She was going to die, but she could not find the panic that had mobilized her before.

The falcon flew down from the tree and landed in front of her. He tilted his head to one side the way only raptors can. A brush of power against her brain broke through the haze, pulling back her clarity and reigniting her amygdala. She breathed deeply, then screamed from the pain that caused. Her vision greyed for a moment. She held still and took slow, shallow breaths until her connection to consciousness strengthened. Then she opened her eyes.

Morgana couldn't read expressions on a bird's face, but she knew him well enough to know what he was asking.

"No, I am not okay, and yes, I would love some help," she said through gritted teeth. She wasn't sure if birds could show amusement, but the half-open beak certainly felt like mockery to her.

The Merlin hopped a couple times; falcons were nowhere near as graceful on land as they were on the sky, and if Morgana hadn't been in soul-searing agony, she might have laughed at her brother. He held out his wings and beat them up, back, down a few times. A light breeze stirred up behind him as the bird started growing.

Once he was the size of a bobcat, the air around him shimmered. He stood in front of her, naked as the day he was born. His skin was covered in blue tattoos; only his face, neck, hands, and forearms were bare.

He looked down at himself. "Knew I forgot something," he muttered. He waved a hand negligently, and blue jeans, a long-sleeved, ribbed Henley, and sturdy boots appeared.

"You look like you're about to go for a hike," Morgana rasped.

He looked at her, then strode over and held out a hand.

She hesitated, then placed her hand in his and allowed him to pull her gently to her feet and into his arms.

"Is it the end, then?" he asked.

Morgana hissed in pain, then tried to smile up at her brother. "I think it might be. I'm sorry, brother." Her voice broke, but before she could apologize again, the love between them that went back centuries poured out of him and into her, strengthening her further and washing away some of the guilt.

He tipped his head down and rested his forehead on hers. "Do you love him?"

Morgana slowly shook her head. "Not quite. I think I could have. Or maybe I did. Everything is tangled and confused. You were right. The beast will end us. He's Bridget's familiar, and the way she was able to violate my sanctuary. He's been working for her this whole time." The betrayal she'd compartmentalized earlier welled up. She'd trusted him with her body, if not her heart. How had she read him so wrongly?

Paska froze. "Did you say she made a human imbued with an animal spirit into a familiar?" The shock in his voice reverberated through Morgana's body.

"That's what she told me," Morgana said. Another wave of agony washed through her, and she nearly collapsed.

"Hold on a bit longer, little sister," Paska said. "You will not lose your soul and go untethered into the darkness. We will walk through the veil together or not at all."

"I wish not at all was an option," she said.

"Me, too."

Morgana breathed slowly. Paska's strength flowed through their link, giving her enough strength to block the pain again and weave more powerful nets to keep the words of power from sinking their hooks in further. Although they wouldn't hold against another attack if she couldn't find her own absent power. Power borrowed from another wouldn't work as well, even if that other was someone as close to her as her brother.

"Maybe she's gone?" Morgana whispered to Paska.

He looked at her with the same "Are you a complete idiot?" glance she'd seen hundreds of times in her life. It was so familiar, she almost smiled.

The backdoor opened with a bang, and Bridget stomped through it, Donovan right behind her.

"What are you doing here?" Bridget yelled at Paska. "How did you get here?"

Paska turned away from Morgana but slid an arm around her waist to keep her upright.

Morgana didn't listen to Paska's answer. Her attention was on Donovan. He looked different, less imposing, for all he towered over Bridget. He hung his head and didn't look around. Morgana didn't see a collar and leash, but there was one there, regardless.

Grief washed through her. If she was going to die, it would've been better to die in his arms.

His head jerked up, and he stared at her. His eyes flashed greenish-gold, and a surge of possessiveness rocked Morgana.

Paska tightened the arm he had around her to keep her on her feet.

"Get your hands off her!" Bridget shrieked. "You can't save her, anyway."

Paska let his arm slide away from Morgana. She stumbled forward and barely kept herself from hitting the ground. He held up his hands and took a step away from her. "I was just stopping by and thought I heard some weird noises coming from the backyard, so I popped in to see."

Bridget paced the length of the back patio without ever stepping foot into the yard.

That was interesting. She hadn't noticed the barrier was gone instead of merely weakened. Somehow, Morgana had to be able to use that to her advantage.

Bridget stopped walking and pointed at Morgana. "Why are you still standing? You should be bleeding on the ground by now."

"I am bleeding plenty," Morgana said. "My clothes are soaked in blood."

"No, no, no." Bridget was practically vibrating, but she still didn't step forward. "You should be on the ground, begging me for mercy."

"Would it help if I did?" Morgana asked.

"I need you to be too weak to hold on to the stupid shield you have over the backyard!" She was shrieking again, and Morgana winced.

Something about this magical blood loss was heightening her other senses and making everything louder and brighter.

Morgana glanced at Paska. He was a couple feet away from her, slightly hunched and exuding penitent fear hard enough that it was almost palpable. If it wasn't for the slight quirk of his lips, it might almost be believable.

"Can I go?" he asked meekly.

"Yes. Get out of here," Bridget snapped. "No, wait. You can't go yet. Donovan, grab the stupid psychic and put him in the room with Hazel. I'll alter both of their memories when I'm done with this."

Donovan didn't say anything. He stepped off the patio and paused, surprise dashing across his face.

Morgana suppressed a groan. Donovan could tell the shield was gone. Any hope of keeping Bridget occupied long enough for Paska to execute whatever stupid plan he had brewing in his head was shot.

Donovan shot a surreptitious glance at Morgana, nodded quickly, then grabbed Paska's forearm. "Come with me. If you won't walk under your own power, I will knock you out and carry you inside."

Paska surprised Morgana by shrugging. "A nap and a memory wipe are better than dead. You'll get no fight from me." He linked his arm through Donovan's and walked inside with him.

Morgana gritted her teeth as much in frustration as in pain. She trusted her brother implicitly. He wouldn't let her die like this, and he wouldn't let her die alone. She rarely wished for telepathy—the few people she knew who'd been cursed with it had gone mad when they hadn't been able to shut out the voices in their heads—but it would be nice to be able to ask Paska what the hell he was doing and when he was planning on rescuing her already.

A wave of comfort overlaid with amusement pulsed down their shared link.

He was going to do something showy and impressive, making the last stand Morgana could not.

twenty-nine

The adrenaline of panic was the only thing fueling Morgana, and soon even that wouldn't be enough to survive. She was keeping the pain at bay, but she couldn't negate the effects of blood loss at the same time, and things were starting to warp and blur together.

Morgana shook her head in an effort to stay awake until Paska neutralized Donovan and returned to save her. She barked out a short laugh that was more hysteria than anything. She hadn't wanted or needed saving since she was a child, and now that was the only way to survive.

Her pulse quickened and lost its steady rhythm, and her breath shallowed until she was gasping for air and grasping for anything she could do to hold on just a little longer.

Morgana pulled at the earth over and over, but there was nothing there to answer her. Nothing to grab onto.

Her eyes drooped closed. She'd set herself on this path when she let Donovan into her heart, and he invited her into his bed, but she'd never imagined things would end in such an ignominious way. Defeated at the hands of a witch who should never have been her equal. But now, she was so tired. She stopped trying to find power in the earth. There was nothing left, and she was having trouble remembering why it mattered. She was so tired.

Unconscious gnawed at the edges of her mind, and she reached for it. Anything to stop the pain, hopelessness, and defeat.

Just before she gave up completely, something stronger crept by the promise of death. There was something still here, something more than the protection she'd woven and broken, the protection that Donovan hadn't told Bridget about.

Something about the water?

Morgana squeezed her eyes closed and tried to grasp onto the thought that was as slippery as a salmon in a waterfall.

Her eyes flew open. Fish. Bridget hated fish. She hadn't been able to even look in the pond in case it had fish. That meant there was still one conduit of elemental energy open. She stumbled backwards, only half faking weakness.

"Finally," Bridget said. "A couple more minutes, and you'll be too weak to stop me anymore."

"I haven't been doing a great job of stopping you so far," Morgana said, gasping as a wave of pain broke through the barriers in her mind.

"Some of this is made possible by using the power I stole from your sanctuary to fuel the spells I've sent back at you. I whisper to the beads, you know, tell them how much they're helping make this world a better place. Taking power from where it lies stagnant and unused and giving it to someone who can love and care for it." Bridget smiled. At least Morgana thought she had. The world was definitely taking on a grayish cast.

Just a few feet more. She could hear the water gurgling through the fountain pump and could feel the moisture in the air increase as she got closer.

Another foot.

She collapsed as her mental barrier fell, and the pain she'd been keeping back overwhelmed her. The only line of defense she still had was the paper-thin wall between the words of power and her soul.

She scooted back another few inches. Sweat broke out on her face, and the world spun.

"You can't escape that way," Bridget called. "A couple more minutes, and you'll be mine."

Morgana slid a couple more inches, then paused to breathe before she could lose the battle with unconsciousness. She should be panicking. Anyone would be in this situation. But she couldn't feel anything other than the sheer desperation to reach the water.

Her hand hit stone, then slid across it, tearing the skin, and dipped into the pond.

For a moment, nothing happened, and the panic Morgana thought she couldn't feel bubbled up.

Then the water curled around her arm, encasing her in the cool liquidity of the element that she loved best. She breathed, letting her eyes flutter closed. She might not have much time, but the water would begin her healing, and maybe that would be enough to tip the scales.

"Are you awake?" Bridget called.

Morgana raised the arm not in the pond, flipped up her index and middle finger, and shook it towards Bridget.

An exclamation of shock sounded from the porch. "Why I... I never would've guessed you to be so crude."

"After all this, that is what you worry about?" Donovan's voice rumbled across the yard, and even knowing what she knew about his complicity in the murders, his tether to the blood witch, his use of her and the reason she and her brother were going to die, part of her soul woke up and hoped.

She let her arm fall and used the motion to push herself closer to the pond. She rolled over and curled into a fetal position, then she rolled over and fell into the water with a splash.

"What is she doing? Stop her! I don't want to get fish on me when I end her, and if she drowns before I complete the spell, the transfer won't be permanent!"

"What do you want me to do?" Donovan asked, his voice quiet and reasonable. He sounded more sure of himself, stronger than he had when he'd escorted Paska inside.

"Get over there and lift her out of the water." Bridget sounded shaky.

"As you say," Donovan answered.

Morgana didn't bother watching him stride towards her. Instead, she opened her senses to the water and let it encase her, flow into her, and heal the pieces of her soul that had been damaged.

Arms slipped around her and raised her head out of the water. "I've got you, sweetheart," he murmured.

"Don't call me that," Morgana said. She let the water play over her body, then wrapped it around his. She meant her power to frighten him, but her intent hadn't been clear enough, and it pulled him closer until he was pressed against her and unable to move away.

"You're okay?" he whispered urgently.

"Do you care?" She couldn't feel the pulse of the tides and the sea, not yet, but the water was anchoring her body and soul to the world, and the dreamy wonderment that overtook her when she opened herself so fully to the earth and her elements took advantage of her psychical weakness to wash away everything but awareness of the goddess.

"Of course I care, you stupid woman," Donovan said.

His vehemence brought Morgana back to herself a little. "You tricked me. You used me and lied to me. You were a spy, and you're a murderer. You are her creature."

Donovan blanched and rocked backwards. "No. I didn't, no I'm not. I didn't kill anyone, and I never spied on you." He scrubbed a hand across his face. "There are too many memories breaking free. Paska wasn't gentle when he broke whatever it was Bridget did to me. It's all jumbled up, but I know I didn't kill anyone."

"Why was I in your bed, Donovan? Because you wanted me, or because she wanted you to seduce me?" She didn't have enough energy to make her words sound anything but tired.

"I have never wanted anyone the way I wanted you when I laid eyes on you in the Portland airport. I wasn't supposed to sleep with you. Just befriend you, get you to trust me. Not to be vulnerable." Truth threaded through his words.

"Why are you telling me this now?"

"I can't get her out of the water, Bridget!" Donovan yelled, sounding a little panicky. "I think there are fish starting to eat her. They have teeth!"

"Stop them! Kill them! You have to get her out of there!" Bridget's voice was shrill, and her words were clipped with fear.

"That should give us another couple minutes. Will you be strong enough to stand soon?" Donovan helped her sit, so she was immersed from the neck down, but kept his body between her and Bridget.

"Why are you doing this? How can you do this?"

"Paska might not be the powerhouse you are, but he has some very specific skills." Donovan grinned down at her, and she shook her head.

"I don't understand what you're talking about." Her strength was returning, and her magical reserves were refilling. The power she'd pulled from the shields had been enough to keep her alive, to keep the power words from digging any further into her soul, and to keep the pain at bay long enough to figure this out, but there hadn't been enough to do anything else.

"He found the tie between me and Bridget and snapped it while muttering about abominations. I'm not sure if he meant me or the witch." A smile ghosted over his face. He lurched forward and convulsed a couple times, then yelled, "I think they're piranhas! I killed one, but there are a dozen more."

"If you can do something, you'd better do it soon," Donovan whispered. "I don't know how long her fear of fish will keep her away from you, especially if she thinks you'll die before she gets here."

"Where's Paska now?" Morgana asked. "He's supposed to be here saving the girl."

"He's trying to break the spell that's holding Hazel in stasis and outsourced the rescue to you," Donovan said. "I'm your plucky side-kick, and your plucky sidekick says you need to figure out what you're going to do and how."

"Almost there," Morgana said. She held her breath and slipped under the surface. She needed more, but she couldn't take without asking, not even to save her own life. She reached out to the water and made her request. There was little hesitance from the element she'd loved and cared for over the centuries.

The sky darkened, and a breeze picked up. She smiled. Paska was getting in on the action, even if he wasn't here rescuing her right now.

She rose out of the pond. She could feel the power words pulsing under her skin, but it was no longer painful, only an uncomfortable annoyance. "Help me stand?"

"As you wish," he said.

Donovan rose to his full height and scooped her into his arms. "I've got her," he yelled. "Should I bring her to you?"

"No!" Morgana hissed.

"No!" Bridget yelled.

"Set me down in the circle of moss halfway between here and the patio, then get inside. Something's coming, and unless you want to be swept up in it, you'll need to get out of the way." Her vision was clearing rapidly, and the waves of dizziness disappeared.

Donovan carried her forward. With every footstep, the air became heavier, and a fog started rolling in. Thunder rumbled and the breeze off the ocean carried the scent of saltwater and rain. He set her down in the mossy circle and stepped away. "Don't die," he said, then turned and walked into the house.

She did like a man who knew how to let someone fight the

battles they were best equipped for. Morgana took a breath, inhaling the moisture of the fog and the oncoming storm and letting the elements who'd answered her call lend her their strength.

"What are you doing?" Bridget asked.

"Preparing," Morgana answered.

Bridget pulled a long knife with a sharp, wavy blade out of the purse on the ground beside her. "It won't help. No one is ever prepared for death, and your soul isn't going to find an afterlife. Why don't you just lay back and let me work."

"No." The rain started slowly, mixing mist and fog into clouds and encasing Morgana in soggy cotton.

Bridget stepped out onto the lawn and stood, unmoving, as if she was waiting for a lightning bolt to strike her for breaking Morgana's boundaries.

Lightning flashed overhead, although nowhere near Bridget, and thunder rumbled almost immediately after. The windows rattled in their frames, and Morgana half-grinned. Paska always was a bit of a showman.

"I hate rain," Bridget muttered. "If this town wasn't a magical magnet, I wouldn't even consider staying."

An enormous wave splashed over the seawall on the other side of Morgana's back fence and sea spray misted through the garden. Bridget screamed and jumped back.

Another wave crested the garden wall, then the ocean quieted again.

Bridget took a cautious step forward, then stopped again. When another bolt of lightning didn't follow her movement, she took another step.

Morgana pulled in the saltwater spray, swirled it into the mist and fog, and waited for the downpour to fuel her spell.

"Here, here, here," the mist seemed to whisper as it whirled around her.

The sky broke open.

Rain lashed Morgana, blurring her vision.

Bridget took another step.

Morgana pulled the rain in, washing away the last vestiges of the net Bridget had thrown over her earlier. It would take more than a summer storm to finish the healing, but it was enough for now.

She rose to her feet and held up her arms.

Bridget gasped. "You can't be standing."

"Okay," Morgana agreed. "I'm not standing."

"You are damaged, nearly broken. It doesn't matter that a freak storm is enough power to get you to your feet. I have so much more than you, and a lot is yours, which makes it an even better weapon to use against you. You aren't defended against your own magic. You won't survive this." Bridget was a little less confident than she'd been a few moments before.

Morgana raised her arms above her head; the cocoon of mist, fog, and sea foam encased her in a protective shell. Seconds later, the wind howled through the backyard. She pulled it into the downpour and flicked her wrist.

Motions weren't necessary—it took will and imagination—but in her weakened state, it helped.

The wind spun around her, spinning the water she'd harnessed.

A waterspout rose in the backyard.

"This isn't possible," Bridget gasped.

Morgana smiled, and she could feel the coldness in it. "You have murdered innocents, practiced blood magic, stolen power, attempted to kill me and frame me for your crimes, and you have forced a familiar bond with a human. I have every right to judge you and carry out your sentence."

"I'm the maiden in your grove and have never been a power. If you kill me now, no one will believe you," Bridget said, bravado in her voice as she took another step forward and raised her knife. The waterspout pushed her backwards.

"Enough will. There are witnesses to your crime. Paska, Hazel, and Donovan know who you are and what you've done." Morgana dropped her arms to her sides, and the waterspout slowed, although it continued to spin lazily around her, waiting for her next command.

"I don't need to touch you to finish this!" Bridget yelled. She reached into her pocket and flung the contents towards Morgana.

The three stones turned into obsidian darts.

The waterspout slid between Bridget's darts—imbued with power from Morgana's sanctuary—and pulled them into its vortex.

The projectiles spun with the waterspout three times, six, nine times, while Morgana unraveled the dark magic they were imbued with. When the blood-created magic had been stripped from the arrows and dissolved into water and scattered by air, they shot out of the water and back towards their wielder.

Bridget didn't have a chance to duck or throw up a shield against physical attack.

The darts pierced the skin just below her collarbone, and she collapsed backwards without a sound.

Bridget hadn't moved even an inch in over ten minutes. Morgana released the waterspout. The wind that had fueled it whipped around the garden a couple times, encased Morgana in what felt like a hug, then disappeared.

Without removing the armor of mist, fog, and sea foam, Morgana walked across the lawn. Her knees wobbled, and she nearly stumbled. Only stubbornness and the determination that Bridget would not see her weakness kept her on her feet.

Bridget was prone, but conscious. The madness that had snuck out a few times during their standoff had charged to the forefront of her eyes, and if looks could kill—and they could, if the witch was powerful enough—Morgana would be dead.

"So, you'll steal my power now?" Bridget spat.

Morgana shook her head. She stayed more than an arm's length away from her former friend. "I have no need of your power, nor of anyone else's. I have enough of my own."

"It's easy for you to say. You have so much you don't know what it's like to watch people have more than they need and to not even know what they have." Spittle flew from her mouth. Blood spread across the top of her white blouse, saturating it. It wouldn't kill her —Morgana had stripped the dark magic but wrapped the darts in binding spells that would hold until they were removed, or the distance became too great to keep them in place—but the wounds would hurt and keep her immobile.

"I was blessed with great power and a greater capacity to store magic than most people," Morgana agreed. "I have never taken that gift for granted, nor have I ever used what I have to cut down the innocent."

"You've killed with your magic." Bridget's eyes were wild, and a dark glow formed around her body. "And the wind wasn't yours; you stole that and try to call me evil?"

Morgana breathed slowly and evenly, trying not to wonder if Bridget's madness would be enough to break the spells Morgana had cast while weak. "I have used my magic to kill," she agreed. "More than once. But I have never used my magic that way unless the person I was targeting had already raped, killed, or tortured."

Footsteps from the patio caused Bridget's eyes to dart in that direction.

"The wind was mine, and it was lent, not stolen. She might not execute you for your crimes; but I have no compunctions about doing that in her stead. But I won't use magic." Paska walked across the grass to Bridget, then bent and picked up the obsidian knife she'd dropped. "This feels like a fitting tool to carry out your sentence."

"Stop!" Donovan's voice echoed through the dissipating rain.

Paska paused with his knife a couple inches above Bridget's chest. "You dare step between me and justice?"

"Please, wait," Donovan said. "She deserves death for her crimes, but I would rather her sentence be carried out in front of the council after her crimes have been made clear."

The icy anger in Paska's voice was enough to make anyone quail. "You dare make a request of me? The walking curse who broke my sister's heart? Because of you, she will die." He lowered the knife and glared at Donovan.

Donovan was by Morgana's side in a flash. "I thought she'd be okay? Is she not?"

"This won't kill me," Morgana said, indicating her body. "The words saturated with blood magic are still embedded in my body, and it will take much time and power to dissolve them without destroying myself, but they aren't what will end my life."

"Then what?" Donovan's voice was nearly hysterical.

"You," Paska said. "We don't know how, but you are the one who captured Morgana's interest, if not yet her heart. If you look within yourself, you'll see the ties that bind you together. Within a year, she will be dead because of you. Her death will flood the cord between her and I, and I will follow her into the afterlife before I can even take my revenge."

"I have your heart?" Donovan looked at Morgana. Water streaked down his face, and she couldn't tell if it was leftover rain dripping from his hair or tears.

"That's not what I said, and you're missing the point," Paska said.

"And that could kill you? I could kill you?" A note of hysteria threaded its way through Donovan's voice.

Morgana shrugged, and the motion made her gasp. She had little time left before she'd need to find a place to heal and replenish her garden. "I don't know how it will happen; neither of us do. If we were to continue down the path we're on and let our feelings for each other deepen, either you'll kill me or something you set in motion will. I thought it'd be Bridget. Her binding of you was what allowed her to drain my power reserves and nearly killed me."

Donovan swallowed. "I'm falling in love with you. I know it's too soon, too fast. I know you can't ever trust me again because of who I am, what I did, but I need you to know that you were loved."

The word "were" stuck in Morgana's brain.

Donovan stepped to Paska. "There are reinforcements from the Scales just outside of town waiting to take Bridget into custody and transport her to a holding cell to await sentencing and execution. They should have already been here, but…"

"But you told them to stay away at her behest?" Morgana asked dully. She knew he wasn't a willing accomplice, but it didn't take away the sting of knowing his tie to Bridget nearly killed them all. "Did you ever question Tom again?"

He shook his head. "I didn't have time, and Bridget told me not to."

"That's curious," Paska said. "One would think she'd want another suspect to divert attention."

Donovan shrugged helplessly. "I don't know. She never told me what she was thinking, only what to do. Once the reinforcements from the Scales are here, I'll surrender to you. You can kill me so that I don't have a chance to harm her."

Paska laughed, and it was an ugly sound. "Look inside, really look at the bindings between you. Do you honestly believe that your death would keep her safe? There is every chance that the shock of it would have the same effect. I will not hasten our end, not even for the satisfaction of killing you." He dropped to his knees beside Bridget, raised his hand high over his head, and brought the knife down in one quick, slashing movement.

The knife vibrated in the ground next to Bridget's face.

Paska stood, brushed off his knees, and looked at Donovan. "Make your call, but I want you to leave with them. I don't want you anywhere near Morgana. If I see you again, I'll take my chances and kill you myself." He looked down at Bridget and spat out a single word.

Bridget went rigid. Her eyes were wide, and her mouth pressed closed.

Paska looked at Morgana. "Let go of whatever you're using to hold her. She won't move on her own now, although if the moggie has any binding restraints cuffs on him, this would be an excellent time to use them." He turned and walked towards the back wall, growing smaller with every step. When he was a little smaller than a bobcat, the air shimmered and he turned into a raptor and flew away.

"A Merlin?" Donovan asked quietly.

Morgana nodded, then reached out and took his hand.

"I'm sorry. For everything. But mostly that we didn't have a real chance to enjoy whatever this is between us."

"Me, too," Morgana said softly. "But it was never going to be that way."

"Leave with me. I can protect you, and we can stay together until the end," Donovan pleaded.

Morgana was already shaking her head before he stopped talking. "No. You have to leave. Maybe I'll be able to cheat the curse or find a way around it, but not with you here. Paska says the end will come through you, and if you're not here, maybe it won't come." She wouldn't beat it, of course. Not if Paska thought it was inevitable. But she would not admit to it until she had to.

Donovan didn't say anything. He looked down at Bridget, then dropped Morgana's hand.

It was cold without his touch, and she shivered.

Donovan pulled silver and iron cuffs with leather straps wrapped around them out of his pocket. "These are laced with black tourmaline and are like the ones we used on Miranda. They'll nullify her magic." He cuffed Bridget, then removed a handful of long zip ties from the same pocket and began wrapping the witch with them, pulling them tight.

"Magic zip ties?" Morgana asked.

"Ordinary zip ties, just extra insurance that she won't take off running. I'll call in our backup, then take her to the jail. They'll be here in a couple hours, tops, and I'll leave with them when they go." He stood and looked at Morgana across Bridget's prone form. "Should I—?"

"No. No more time together. No more goodbyes. I can't..." Her voice cracked. She swallowed. "Do you know how to release the power she stole? I could really use that back."

"I do, but I don't have the tools with me. When we get her back to London, we'll have the mages release all the power. It'll flow back to you instantly, and the other stolen powers will find their next hosts in the bloodline. It might be a good idea to round up everyone you can find, because that kind of influx will be shocking." He reached out to her, but she took a step back.

"Text me before the magic is released, so we have some warning." Morgana held her voice steady. "I have to take the obsidian out of her now so I can have that back. Will you hold me while I do, make sure I don't fall?"

Donovan stepped over Bridget and pulled Morgana into his arms. "I will hold you for as long as you'll let me."

Morgana looked up at him and smiled sadly, then reached up and cupped her hand on his face. She stood on tiptoe and brushed a kiss across his lips. "Goodbye, Donovan Davies."

She looked back down at Bridget, gathered all the energy she had left, and pulled. The stones flew back into her hand with a sickening pop as they left Bridget's chest. Relief surged through her for just a moment, followed by grief and guilt. So many mistakes made. So many dead because of her ego. Morgana had just enough energy left to send the obsidian darts back into the earth where the magic they carried would flow back into the ground and begin the healing process before the world spun around her and went grey.

Just before she sipped into unawareness, a voice floated across the space between consciousness and unconsciousness. "I love you, Morgana Bellflower. Goodbye."

epilogue

Morgana stared into the red wine and swirled her glass absently. She'd spent three days and nights in her sanctuary healing from the damage that'd been done to her body, soul, and gardens, and another three weeks resting and meditating and wrapping the blood-fueled power words Bridget had flung at her in as many individual packets as she could to keep them from burrowing further. Her power wasn't anywhere near replenished, and it wouldn't be until Bridget was stripped of what she'd stolen—after the Source made a thorough study of her, of course—but Morgana was strong enough again to leave the house and meet her friends for drinks at the Pour House.

Most of her friends had gone home already, but Andy, Ceri, and Misty sat across from her, and Paska was at her side. No one else knew exactly what'd happened, and the secrets she and Paska held were still safe.

Paska had woken Hazel in time for her to see the final showdown between Bridget and Morgana and located most of the likely recipients of the magic that'd been stolen. Not many had believed that they were about to get a heavy dose of magic in one, giant shot, but more than Morgana would've guessed were making their way to Oracle Bay, and the rest had Paska's contact information and would call when it happened.

Hazel was staying in Oracle Bay permanently and had kept her job at the Pour House.

As soon as she could, Morgana was going to weave more protections, replacing those in her house, workroom, and garden, then slowly rebuild the ones she'd yanked back into herself from the homes and business of her friends. And she would spend extra time building layers of shields around Hazel and teaching her to augment them with her own power.

Hazel was going to live with her until she'd learned enough about her own magic and control—and had earned enough money to move out on her own.

It was strange, having another person in the house all the time, but not unpleasant. It felt much like the time before the curse when she shared a home with Elaine. There was an easy companionship that went beyond the teacher/pupil relationship Morgana had expected to fall into place.

"Penny for your thoughts, witch," Andy said, his voice holding none of the mockery that usually accompanied it when he spoke to her.

"My thoughts are worth significantly more than that, demon," she replied. "I'm not sure you could afford them."

"We might have to break the rule we've set into place to not look into each other's futures," Ceri said, folding her hands in front of her. "This shouldn't have happened."

Morgana considered, then shook her head. "I don't want anyone peeking into my mind and life, no matter how much warning I might get about the next threat. I know how my life will end, even if I don't know when, and that's enough."

Ceri's lips tightened into a thin line, and Morgana remembered that she wasn't the only one who'd nearly died in Oracle Bay.

"You had warning. Even if you didn't know exactly what was

happening, you knew, and you did nothing about it until it was almost too late. There is nothing we can do with the knowledge that would change what's going to happen." Morgana tried to gentle her voice, but from the glare Andy shot her, she hadn't done enough.

"I don't believe in immutable fate," Ceri said.

Paska reached across the table and took Ceri's hands, ignoring the scowl Andy turned on him. "Neither do I, lass. Neither do any of us. But the choices we make trying to avoid the warnings we've seen might lead us down the wrong path into something even worse. You know this. We all know this."

Misty leaned forward and pulled her beer closer to her. "I've seen it, you know. The threads of our lives and futures. There are so many potential paths, and the threads crisscross through our lives, or souls, and all the possibilities. Knowing what lies along one thread fixes our sights on that end and can blind us to all the other futures." She ducked her head for a moment, then looked directly at Morgana. "I can't unsee the threads anymore. Whatever happened to Oracle Bay last spring"—she darted a look at Ceri before turning back to Morgana—"whether it was the scrying we did as a group to find a way to...help...or something about opening a portal to the end of the universe, I don't know. But it woke something, and now I can see everyone and everything. I can see how people are connected and where they might go next, the decisions they'll have in front of them, and what each decision will mean. I can see how Ceri and Andy are bound together in love, and I can see how Ceri is connected to Drew through years of history and friendship that has tied them closer together than most siblings."

Morgana nodded in understanding. Misty knew she and Paska were connected and that it wasn't a romantic relationship, but rather familial. She might not know if they were siblings in fact or just in heart, but she knew they were more closely connected than they'd ever let on.

"I can help you dampen the sight," Paska offered. "Seeing too much with no way to shut it off is not good for your long-term stability."

Relief flooded Misty's eyes. "Can you? That would be really cool. I don't need to see who's connecting to who and how. The number of secret relationships in this town—not all infidelities, but a number that no one would thank me for revealing—is almost alarming."

"Meet me at the lighthouse tomorrow morning at dawn and we will start this work," Paska commanded.

"The lighthouse?" Misty asked.

Paska shrugged. "It is the physical heart of Oracle Bay, just as you are the metaphysical heart. It casts light in the darkness, and your sight pierces the veil. It is symmetry, and I like symmetry."

Morgana smiled. Now that the curse had woken, and they were going to die anyway, Paska no longer felt he had to keep himself aloof from friendships. It was good for him to surround himself with people he loved for as long as he could.

Morgana's cellphone beeped to announce a text message, and she pulled it out of her pocket. She had a text from Donovan, and she tensed. Soon her power would be released back to her, and then she would see if she could save her soul, even if she couldn't save her life.

She tapped on the message app. There was only one sentence.

Bridget escaped.

READ ON FOR A PREVIEW OF ELEMENTS OF SURPRISE - THE CONCLUSION TO Morgana's story - or go ahead and one-click it now!

want more amy cissell?

And why wouldn't you?

Love it, hate it, somewhere in between? Please leave a review for Belle of the Ball at Goodreads, Bookbub, or your favorite online retailer.

Links to all retails sites are at:
https://books2read.com/TempestInATeapot

Reviews are always appreciated & allow me to keep writing what you love!

Sign up for Cissell's Epistles at https://amycissell.com for new release updates, exclusive content, and a bevy of book recommendations! (You'll also get to choose a free book as a thank you for hanging out!)

Come hang out in my Facebook Reader Group - the Amyzonians can always use another shenaniganator. (It's a word. Promise.)

https://www.facebook.com/groups/amycissellauthor/

Join my patreon - https://www.patreon.com/ACissellWrites - for early access to books, free copies of my digital books, free paperbacks, and access to my entire back catalog!

* * * * ★ ★ ★ ★ * * *

elements of suprise

ORACLE BAY BOOK 7

Morgana stared into the red wine and swirled her glass absently. She wasn't quite relaxed, but she was closer than she'd been in over a year. The last few months had been terrible mentally, physically, and magically. She wasn't even going to think about the emotional wounds left by walking away from the first man she'd loved since her first lifetime.

The three days and nights in her sanctuary healed much of the damage that'd been done to her body and the garden that housed her magical repository, and three weeks resting and meditating started the journey towards healing her mind and soul, although that was another wound that would leave a jagged scar.

She'd been too late save Violet and Joanna and the twenty-two women that'd been victims of the power-mad witch, and those deaths would always hang on the guilt scales in her mind. But they'd stopped the dark witch, Bridget had been remanded into custody, and no one else would die by her hand.

Morgana's power wasn't anywhere near replenished, and it wouldn't be until Bridget was forced to release what she'd stolen—something that should happen any day now—but Morgana was finally strong enough again to leave the house and meet the other psychics for drinks at the Pour House without worrying about looking psychically weak or emotionally compromised.

It was nice to be in company with the people she considered friends. Most had gone home, but Andy, Ceri, and Misty sat across from her, and Paska was at her side.

Morgana would never admit it, but she considered Andy to be almost as close a friend as she'd ever had. Part of it was the deep understanding of power he shared with her, as well as the weight of ages that weighed on a person's mind. Her experience was minuscule compared to a nearly ageless, immortal fallen angel who'd recently risen from hell to take his place among mortals.

As if he sensed her thoughts, he turned towards her with silver eyebrows raised quizzically above his stormy grey eyes.

Morgana sighed deeply, shook her head, and mouthed, "Demon."

Andy pulled a pen from his shirt pocket, scribbled something on a bar napkin, then folded it and pushed it over to her. *See something you like, witch? You'll have to fight Ceri for me.*

Morgana rolled her eyes, and Andy laughed. For a moment, the world felt in balance.

There were still secrets, of course. No one in Oracle Bay knew the truth about her connection to Paska, other than they'd known each other for a very long time and were older than they looked. Morgana looked like she was in her late thirties, and now that she'd been able to drop her suburban housewife disguise, she was back to her long black hair and the pale skin that perfectly matched her Morticia Addams goth vibe. Today she was in leather pants, a tight wrap-around sweater, and lace-up leather boots—all black, of course.

Paska appeared to be in his early forties. He kept the build he'd had for more than a thousand years, toned without being muscle-bound, and had light brown skin, salt and pepper hair, and eyes so dark there was no definition between the pupil and iris.

They looked nothing alike. They had once, but sixteen hundred years leaves marks on a person, even if they're not immediately apparent. But now, no one would ever guess they were related, much less siblings. And it needed to stay that way, although the reasons for that seemed less and less clear the closer she grew to this small community of psychics in Oracle Bay.

There was one secret she held, however, that could not be shared. The words of power fueled by blood magic and thrown at her by Bridget had not been destroyed. Morgana had crafted spells to contain them and keep them from burrowing further into her and shredding her soul, but they were still there. She was safe for now, but all it would take would be another unexpected power drain or magical attack, and her internal shields would fail.

By then, however, it might not matter anymore. The curse that'd been activated when she fell in love with Donovan Davies would likely kill her before Bridget's black magic did.

Morgana sighed quietly. The tension she'd thought drained from her body returned. She had so little life left, and after centuries, it should be enough. But it wasn't. She didn't want to die, and she didn't want to live out her last months trying to keep from losing her soul to the darkness and her heart to despair.

"Penny for your thoughts, witch," Andy said, his voice holding none of the mockery that usually accompanied it when he spoke to her.

"My thoughts are worth significantly more than that, demon," she replied. "I'm not sure you could afford them."

Morgana's cellphone beeped to announce a text message, and she pulled it out of her pocket. She had a text from Donovan, and she tensed. Soon her power would be released back to her, and then she would see if she could save her soul, even if she couldn't save her life.

She tapped on the message app. There was only one sentence.

Bridget has escaped.

Morgana looked up from her phone.

Paska went from his public persona of an indolent, perpetually tipsy man to alert. For a moment, power thrummed through him, and the table vibrated. "What is it? What's happened?" He grabbed Morgana's cell phone, cursed loudly and creatively, then shoved Morgana's phone back to her.

She took a second to reply to Donovan. *When? Do you know where she's going? Are you safe?*

Andy leaned forward. "I'm sure Paska will share with us eventually, but I've heard him swear before, and it will be awhile before he runs out of anatomically impossible, illegal, and highly unethical suggestions. What's going on?"

Morgana licked her lips and willed her heart to resume its normal pace. "I just received a text from Donovan. Bridget escaped the Scales." She held up her hand to forestall any questions. "I know nothing else. That was all the text said. As soon as I learn more, I'll be sure to share it with you."

"Will she come back here?" Misty asked. "If so, we need to be better prepared than we were last time."

"At least we'll know who it is," Ceri said. Her pale complexion could give Morgana's a run for her money, but where Morgana was dark-haired and eyed, Ceri was fair. She had strawberry blonde hair that gently curled around her slightly pointed ears, clear, blue eyes, and a smattering of freckles across her elfin nose. She was the picture of summer innocence, and looked nothing like a powerful seer who held the key to infinity in her mind.

"That will help," Misty agreed. "We need to find out when this happened, see if there's a trail, and bring in everyone we can to defend Oracle Bay. I know it's not guaranteed that she'll return here —it would be monumentally stupid to do so since this is where she was defeated, *and* we'll obviously be expecting her—but I think the stolen power is rapidly destroying her mind."

Paska's curses had wound down. "You're not wrong about that. She was never meant to hold that much power—few people could, and even those with the ability and capacity would be hard-pressed to stay sane."

"You probably know that better than any of us," Morgana said sweetly. It was an old joke between them, although lately, Morgana had wondered if there was more truth than jest in it.

"Indeed I would," Paska said. A dark thread was laced through his words, but the smile he turned on the rest of the table was cheerful. "We are the five most powerful beings in this town, and now we know the full breadth of the evil that rides that witch's soul. There is little doubt that she will be unable to gain a toehold in this town again if we can work together to keep it safe."

Ceri worried at her lower lip and stared at the beer in the glass in front of her without taking a drink. "I cannot tap most of the power I hold, so I'm not sure I deserve a seat at this table."

"Nonsense," Paska said. "Unless we're in danger of imminent

apocalypse, I don't want you to reach for the power that's hidden in your mind. It protects itself from people like Bridget, and it will protect you in case your angel isn't there to do it himself."

Andy growled lightly, and a tendril of smoke floated above him.

"No insult meant, Andras," Paska said. "But even you must admit that you cannot keep her glued to your side every minute of every day."

"Mostly because I'd kill you if you tried," Ceri muttered. "You might be a powerful immortal demon, but I have the key to everything in here—" she tapped her temple "—and I'm pretty sure that includes several ways to imprison and murder one's fallen angel boyfriend."

Andy smiled at her and wrapped an arm around her, pulling her close.

A pang of jealousy shot through Morgana, and she squashed it down immediately. She was not jealous of what they had. She'd always known that wasn't in the cards for her, and she wasn't about to get angry about it now, no matter how much the events of the past few weeks had driven home how truly alone she was.

Morgana's phone beeped again, and silence dropped over the table as they waited for her to read the message.

I'm ok. 7 dead. 10 more injured. 3-4 hrs. ago. No idea where she's going. Don't assume you're safe. I'll be there as soon as I get out of the hospital.

"Let me see," Paska demanded, holding out his hand.

"No!" Morgana clenched the phone to her chest and took a deep breath, then read the message.

"Where are they? Where'd she escape from?" Misty asked.

"London."

Misty was on her phone, pulling up a flight app. "The earliest she could be here is..." There was a long pause while Misty sorted various flights, made mental adjustments for time changes, and added in driving time. "Four hours ago was five o'clock here, so one tomorrow morning in the UK." Misty looked up, her green eyes wide with fear.

"She could be on a flight by noon, in Seattle by three, and here by six tomorrow night."

"Okay," Morgana said more decisively than she felt. "We have twenty-one hours to prepare. That's better than none. At least there were survivors—" *at least Donovan survived* "—who could warn us. Let's come up with a plan tonight, then call everyone in tomorrow morning to go over it."

"I don't think we should have that conversation here," Ceri said with an apologetic look at Andy. "I know this bar is secure, but it's still a public house. I don't want to risk anyone overhearing us."

Paska nodded. "That is an excellent point. We will gather at my home."

Morgana wasn't the only one staring at Paska in shock. In all the years they'd lived in Oracle Bay, he'd never invited anyone into his home except her.

"Um, okay, that sounds perfect," Misty said. "Let's get some sleep tonight, and start fresh with the group thing at Paska's in the morning."

It was a sign of the tension he was holding that Paska did not make an off-color joke at Misty's suggestion.

"I'll let Hazel and Brandy know they're closing tonight and meet you there," Andy said. He stood, dropped a kiss on Ceri's upturned lips, and strode out of the alcove.

Morgana let the others file out ahead of her, then turned her phone back over and quickly typed. *Glad you're okay. Please be careful. See you soon.*

One-click Elements of Surprise - the conclusion to Morgana's story - now!

raising a demon

MIDLIFE MAGIC IN EDEN VALLEY #1

Raising a Demon is the first book in Midlife Magic in Eden Valley, a magical new paranormal women's fiction series. Eden Valley & Oracle Bay are in the same universe, and there are some crossover characters and cameos!

Being a single mother has its challenges, but Evie never imagined that "the talk" would involve Ouija boards and pentagrams.

Evelyn Addams is forty-three and fabulous. She has a great kid, fantastic friends, and doesn't need a man to complete her. But when she catches ten-year-old Lily summoning a demon to ask for birthday wishes—and the demon who turns up is Evie's summer fling from eleven years ago—her comfortable life is shattered.

Reuniting with an old flame is tricky enough but finding out he grows horns and a tail makes a romantic reconnection downright complicated. And when Lily is kidnapped by her newfound grandfather, the last shred of her old life is destroyed, and everything goes to hell.

Will Evie and her friends rescue Lily from hell before the lights go out and the lost souls come out to play? And can she ignore past and Luc's family complications to take a second chance on love and learn how to raise a demon's daughter? Get your copy of Raising a Demon today!

http://www.books2read.com/raisingademon

acknowledgments

First and foremost - thank you, thank you, thank you to my newest patrons! Samantha H and Robin S - y'all are the bees' knees. I appreciate your support and hope you love this book!

All my love to the Amyzonians—my Facebook reader group—you guys are fantastic. Thanks for liking and sharing my posts, reading and reviewing, staying engaged with me, and voting on all my weird polls.

Thank you to my editor Suzanne Lahna. Working with you was such an amazing experience. Thanks for caring about Morgana's story and working so hard to make it better.

Christopher—my line editor, proofreader, business partner, fellow author, and probably even more importantly, husband—thanks for listening to my traditional 66% of the way through "this is the worst book ever, I'm quitting" angst and never once mocking me more than just a little.

There is no way to talk about the people who support and lift me up without mentioning Liana. My best girl, favorite kid, most challenging person I know, and greatest love. Maybe someday I'll let you read more than the dedication and acknowledgments. Love you to the moon and the stars and back.

There are so many other people who help me along the way, and I want to give them all a shoutout! Elizabeth Hunter & Cat Tan - our group chat is one of the highlights of my life. Samesies for Carrie B, Steph M, and Amelia P. Best coven ever, right? this wouldn't be complete without my local friends who drink wine with me and occasionally whine with me. Sam H (holla, 2 mentions, one acknowledgements section, Shea M (fellow author extraordinaire and future Portugal commune co-founder), and Alisha P.

amy cissell ~ i spell trouble

Amy can be found on most social media channels @acissellwrites. Come visit her website at amycissell.com for blogs & books! (autographed copies, if you want!)

Amy Cissell is a USA Today Bestselling Author of urban fantasy and paranormal romance novels. She lives in Portland, OR with her husband, her haunted house-obsessed daughter, their three cats, and the murder of crows she's conspiring to turn into her vengeful army.

When she's not working or writing, she's sleeping because that's all she has time to do! There are few things Amy loves more than a well-timed pun, a good book, a glass of wine, and time at the Oregon Coast.

Although she reads anything and everything, her first love is fantasy. Eleven-year-old Amy discovered fantasy when she 'borrowed' her father's copy of The Hobbit and an enduring love affair (mostly with dragons) was born.

facebook.com/acissellwrites

instagram.com/acissellwrites

bookbub.com/authors/amy-cissell

goodreads.com/acissellwrites

tiktok.com/@acissellwrites

patreon.com/ACissellWrites

also by amy cissell

Paranormal Romance

Psychics of Oracle Bay

Not in the Cards (October 2018)

First Hand Knowledge (November 2018)

Wing and a Prayer (January 2019)

Belle of the Ball (December 2019)

Hell and High Water (June 2022)

Tempest in a Teapot (April 2023)

Elements of Surprise (April 2023)

Dead Giveaway (2024)

Bad to the Bones

Shoot for the Stars

Fun and Prophet

Box Sets (ebook only)

Seeing is Believing in Oracle Bay (Books 1-4)

Paranormal Women's Fiction

Midlife Magic in Eden Valley

(complete series)

Raising a Demon (June 2021)

Devil and the Deep, Blue Lake (September 2021)

Valley of Angels (November 2021)

Guardian of Eden (February 2022)

Eden Valley World Novellas

Match Made in Hell (June 2021)

Hell's Bells (December 2021)

Fall From Grace (January 2022)

Devil May Care (February 2022)

Box Sets (ebook only)

Welcome to Eden Valley (Novellas 1-4)

Vamps in the Vineyard

Here to Slay (September 2022)

Vamps in the Vineyard Novellas

(newsletter subscribers only)

Stakes and Stems (September 2023)

Slay Bells Ring (January 2023)

Contemporary/Urban Fantasy

An Eleanor Morgan Fantasy Adventure

(complete series)

The Cardinal Gate (February 2017)

The Waning Moon (June 2017)

The Ruby Blade (October 2017)

The Broken World (March 2018)

The Lost Child (June 2019)

The Iron River (May 2020)

The Dark Throne (February 2021)

Box Sets (ebook only)

Eleanor Morgan Books 1-4

Eleanor Morgan Books 5-7

* * * ★ ★ ★ ★ ★ ★ ★ * * *

Ghosts of Valhalla

As Yet Untitled (late 2023)

* * * ★ ★ ★ ★ ★ ★ ★ * * *

www.ingramcontent.com/pod-product-compliance
Lightning Source LLC
Chambersburg PA
CBHW060911210726
48293CB00006B/2060